FLOR DE MUERTOS BOOK 2

VIOLENT ATTRACTION

JOCELYNE SOTO

Copyright © 2021 by Jocelyne Soto, Mystic Luna Publishing LLC

All rights reserved.

Photography by Oleg Gekman

Cover design by Book and Moods PR.

Copy Edits by My Brother's Editor.

This is a work of fiction. Names, characters, places, and incidents either are the product of the author's imagination or are used fictitiously. Any resemblance to actual persons, living or dead, events, or locales is entirely coincidental.

All rights reserved. No part of this book may be reproduced or used in any manner without written permission of the copyright owner except for the use of quotations in a book review. For more information, address: info@jocelynesoto.com.

Paperback ISBN : 978-1-956430-01-1

She was a cartel princess.
I was a soldier. A helping hand. A life that didn't matter.
None of that stopped me from falling in love with her the first time I laid eyes on her.
This cartel princess was everything to me.
And I was able to show her, but only in secret.
After years of hiding I had finally found the courage to tell her father, but he announced he'd arranged a marriage for her. One that will bound families.
One that is all about power and money.
The man that she is set to marry is a dangerous man. He doesn't love her. He only wants her for the money and power that she comes with.
I need to try my hardest to stop this arrangement.
No matter how much blood I shed.
Isabella Morales is mine.

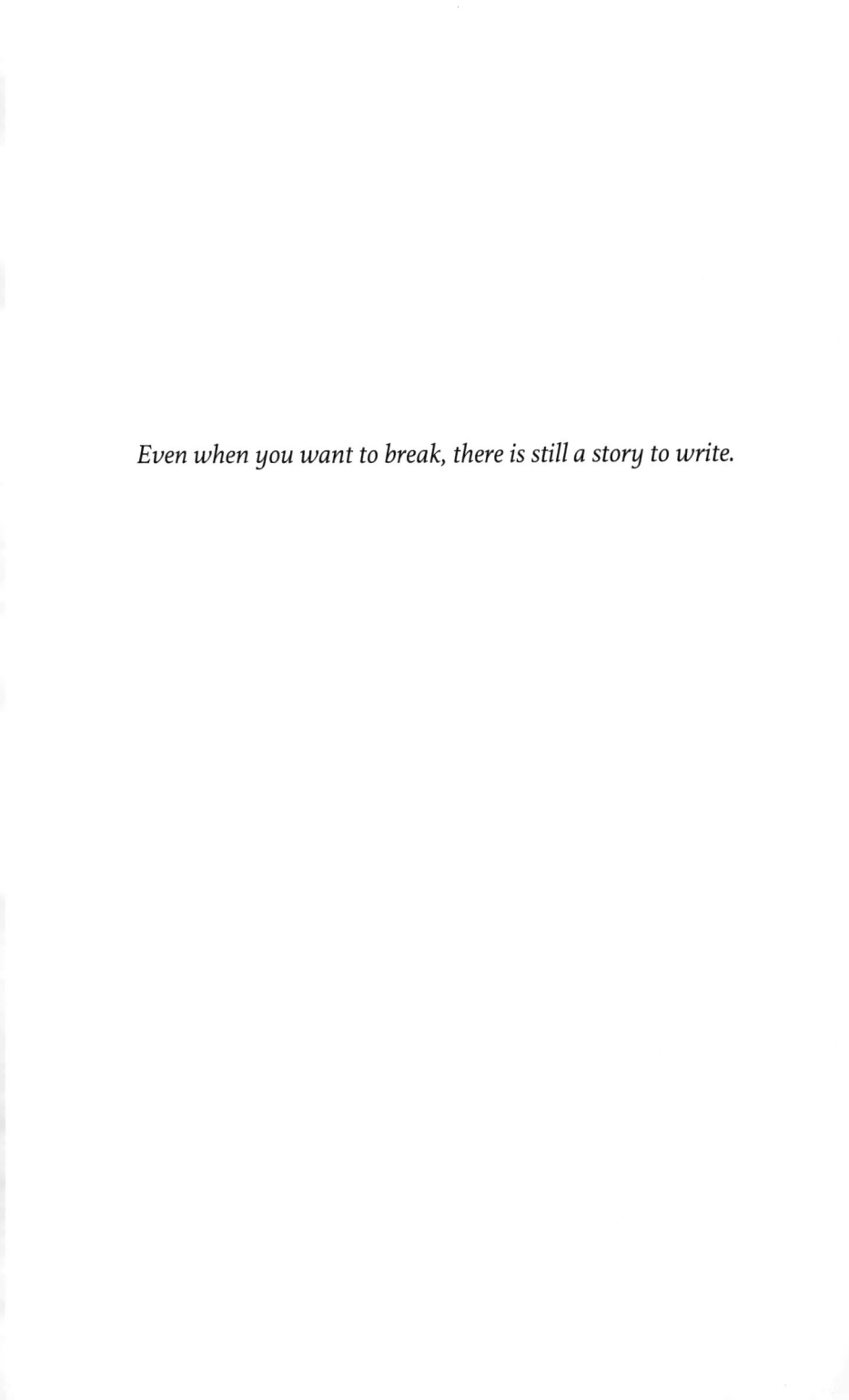

Even when you want to break, there is still a story to write.

CONTENTS

Prologue	1
Chapter 1	3
Chapter 2	10
Chapter 3	18
Chapter 4	24
Chapter 5	32
Chapter 6	43
Chapter 7	45
Chapter 8	55
Chapter 9	65
Chapter 10	78
Chapter 11	86
Chapter 12	97
Chapter 13	109
Chapter 14	123
Chapter 15	134
Chapter 16	143
Chapter 17	152
Chapter 18	167
Chapter 19	179
Chapter 20	189
Chapter 21	202
Chapter 22	209
Chapter 23	219
Chapter 24	229
Chapter 25	239
Chapter 26	251
Chapter 27	259
Chapter 28	269
Chapter 29	277

Chapter 30	284
Chapter 31	293
Chapter 32	302
Chapter 33	312
Chapter 34	322
Epilogue	333
Extended Epilogue	343
Playlist	349
Acknowledgments	351
Books by Jocelyne Soto	355
About the Author	357
Join My Reader Group	359
Newsletter	361

bella (Spanish pronunciation) - /beh-yah/ - pretty or beautiful

PROLOGUE

SANTOS

She's the most beautiful girl I have ever laid eyes on.

Dark hair that went down the length of her back. Skin that looked soft to the touch, with an olive tint to it. Eyes that looked as if they belonged to a princess and not to the girl that I have known most of my life.

She was the daughter of Ronaldo Morales, the head of the Muertos Cartel.

She was, in fact a princess.

A cartel princess, but still royalty, nonetheless.

One I wanted to talk to, get to know, to spend time with. Someone that I would never be able to get close enough to. A girl that I would never be able to call mine.

She was untouchable, nothing more than a dream.

Even if and when I was able to hold the dream in my hands, it would have felt like I would wake up any second and lose it all.

And that's what happened.

I had the dream in the palm of my hand, and for a few

glorious moments, the dream was mine. Holding it as tight as I could.

The girl that I saw as royalty was mine.

Until the dream was ripped away from me and forever taken.

Because in the end, she was a princess to the cartel that needed a prince, not a soldier.

No matter how much I loved her, she would never belong to me.

Isabella Morales would never belong to me, Santiago Reyes.

Not even in death.

1

ISABELLA

Present Day

I look at myself in the mirror and the reflection staring back at me makes me want to vomit.

Not a feeling that a bride should be having as she looks at herself wearing her wedding dress. Especially not on her wedding day.

The dress in itself is beautiful, so is the makeup and the jewelry and how my hair is styled.

If circumstances were different, I would be looking at myself and crying happy tears, not ones of despair.

Despair because I'm about to walk down the aisle and marry a man that my father is forcing me to. Despair because once I walk down that aisle and say my vows, the person I am will be gone.

I can't seem to make the tears stop.

I'm losing so much in such a short amount of time and it's all my father's fault.

If it wasn't for his thirst for more dominance and money, I wouldn't be forced into this situation.

If it wasn't you, then it would have been Camila.

God.

I can't even begin to think what I would've done if it was my little sister in this situation and not me. It makes me want to throw up even more just thinking about it.

Almost a year ago, my father called me into his office and introduced me to the man that would be my future husband.

I had no say in the matter.

It didn't matter that I didn't know the man, or that I was in love with another. I was going to marry Emilio Castro whether I wanted to or not.

Throughout my life, I have heard my father talk about finding me a good husband, but I always thought that he was just being a father. That's what dads did, right? They joked about finding the perfect husband for their daughters because they couldn't fathom their little girls marrying someone that they didn't approve of. Right? That's something that normal dads did?

Never did I think that my father was talking in the literal sense. Never did I think that he would force me to marry the son of another cartel drug lord so that he can gain power.

Because that's what this is. A power move.

One that makes Ronaldo Morales more powerful than ever.

Just thinking about it has more tears forming in my eyes again.

God, I wish that my mother was here. I wish she was here to help calm me, like only she knew how. I wish she was here to tell my father that I wasn't going to marry Emilio. That she would make him understand that the man he wants me to marry is evil in every sense of the word.

Of course, my father would know a thing or two about that, since he is the evilest of them all.

I just wish that my mom was here to hold me and to tell me that everything will be okay.

But she's not, of course, because being my father's wife killed her and now my siblings and I have to go through life without her.

"Okay, Isabella. You need to calm down. You need to calm down because in a few minutes all eyes will be on you and you have to pretend like this is the happiest day of your life."

I shake my hands, trying to calm myself down as best as I can.

I don't want to do this.

I don't want to leave this room and become the wife of Emilio Castro, I just don't.

But I have to.

In a matter of minutes, I will become Isabella Castro, a doting wife that is happy and in love with her husband.

I will give up everything that I worked so hard for, only to become the perfect housewife.

God, help me.

I close my eyes and I take deep breath after deep

breath, trying to get every single emotion running through my body in check.

I can do this.

I can do *this*.

There is a knock on the door. My eyes spring open. It's time. As the knock sounds through the room, the church bells are ringing, signaling that it's almost time for the bride to come out.

I can't fucking do this.

"Come in," I announce to whoever is on the other side of the door.

The door opens, but I don't turn to see who walks in. I keep my eyes on the mirror in front of me, just waiting for the material to catch spontaneously on fire so I won't have to leave.

"Are you ready?" Camila's voice comes up behind me. There is a sadness to it and I try to remember to keep the tears in.

My little sister is just as pissed about this as I am.

With one final look at the material covering my body, I turn to my sister and give her a sad smile.

"I'm ready," my voice shakes and a second doesn't even go by before Camila's arms are around me.

"I'm sorry." Her hold grows tighter and I breathe in the familiarity of her perfume.

"I know."

Everyone is sorry.

No matter how hard everyone tried, we are still here. The wedding day is still here and I still have to get married.

We pull apart and we both wipe away the tears that seemed to have escaped.

"Let's get this over with," I tell her with a curt nod and square my shoulders.

The faster that I'm out there, the closer I will be to living this new life of mine. The quicker that life will pass by.

I grab the skirt of my dress and walk out of the bridal suite. Standing right outside of the room are my brother, Leonardo, and his wife Serena, who gives me a sad smile before coming to me and giving me a hug.

"You look beautiful." I know she is telling me the truth but at the moment, I hate the words.

"Thank you," I hug my sister-in-law and give my brother a smile over her shoulder.

After a few moments with my siblings, we finally start making our way to the front of the church.

It's time.

It's time and nothing is going to stop this wedding.

As I make my way over to where me and my father need to be before the music starts, I get the sensation that I'm being watched.

I look up until I meet a pair of light-brown eyes staring back at me. Light-brown eyes that I have spent countless hours and nights thinking, dreaming about and looking into.

Light-brown eyes that are my favorite shade of brown and can tell me countless stories.

Light-brown eyes that belong to the one man that will forever hold my heart in his hands.

He's here.

I can't believe he's here. I told him not to come. If he was here, there would be a possibility of me not going through with the wedding. Not only that but I have this irrational fear that if Emilio saw that he was here, things would get ugly.

As Santiago gives me a small smile, I forget everything bad that is about to happen and just concentrate on the happiness that that smile brings me.

That smile is only meant for me.

I don't smile back.

"Are you ready, Isabella?" My father's voice comes up next to me, taking my gaze off Santiago Reyes.

I look at my father and he looks unbothered, as if he wasn't about to walk his daughter down the aisle.

I give him a nod. "I'm ready."

Without a word, he nods and walks over to our designated spot, dragging me along with him and we take our place next to each other.

The church bells continue to ring and soon the sound of the orchestra starts to fill the church.

Then the doors open.

First, Leo and Serena walk out arm and arm, then they are followed by Camila with Emilio's friend.

All that is left is me and my father.

"This will be a good life for you," my father says seconds before it's our turn to walk.

I don't say anything. I just keep my vision straight.

Out of all the lives I envisioned for myself, this wasn't one of them. This type of life will never be good for me.

The march starts, and soon we're walking.

Everything about this church is beautiful and like my dress, under different circumstances, I would be admiring it but not today. Not when the only thing that I can concentrate on is the menacing smile that Emilio is currently sporting at the front the chapel.

A smile that will haunt me for the rest of my life.

The music stops when my father and I approach the altar and as my hand is about to be placed in Emilio's, a shot rings out.

One shot.

Just one single shot that is so silent that the people around it would have been able to hear.

But yet, it was enough.

There is chaos. There are screams.

And all I can concentrate on is the splatter of red that is currently covering my hand.

Is it mine?

Someone else's?

I don't know but all I can seem to ask myself is, has there ever been a moment in my life where blood and pain weren't the focus?

2

ISABELLA

Twelve Years Old

"Isabella, *hija, ven por favor*," I hear my mom call me from somewhere in the house. At the sound of her voice, I put down my pencil and go looking for her.

When *Mamá* calls, you answer, no matter what you're doing.

I walk through the house to find her. The house itself is big, so big that when we first moved in here I would get lost. There are so many rooms that you would think it was a castle or something. But even with living in a big house, it's not a lot of work to find my mom.

She's in the sewing room that my dad made for her, looking down at some pictures.

"*¿Si Mamá?*" I enter the room and as I walk closer to the table, I get a good look at the pictures she is looking at. They are of beautiful summer dresses. A smile takes over my face when I realize what she is doing.

We are going to start a new project.

"*Mi niña bonita*, I need you to pick a dress pattern that you like. I want to make some for you and your sister since you're going to be out of school soon. You need something to wear besides your school uniform."

I hate my school uniform. Sometimes I wish that we could go to a regular school like the kids on TV get to do, and be able to wear anything we want.

I give my mom a bright smile before picking up one of the pictures. "Can I help you make them?"

My mom gives me the most beautiful smile that I have ever seen. I hope that when I'm older, I look just like her and can have that pretty of a smile.

"Of course, *mi niña*. Let's pick out the ones that you like and then I will go to the fabric store sometime this week, so that we can get started."

For the next hour or so, my mom and I pick out dress after dress to make for me and Camila. I pick out all the ones with the flowers for my sister and I take all the ones with the solid colors.

"Can I go get the fabric with you?" I like picking out fabric, it's one of my favorite things to do besides actually using the sewing machine.

"*Sabes qué,* I was going to go when I took you three to school tomorrow, but I think we can convince your *papí* to let us go right now. What do you think?" I'm already nodding before she can even finish the sentence.

"Yes."

My mom's smile grows even more as she swipes at a piece of hair that fell out of my ponytail.

"Let me go talk to him. Go play and I will come find you." She places a kiss on my hair before she walks out of the room.

I watch her walk away, before I turn back to the table to continue looking at the pictures of the dresses. I'm so happy to be starting this project with my mom and to be going to the fabric store. The dresses are going to be so pretty.

Finally deciding to do what my mom told me to do, I leave the pictures on the table and head back to my room. Might as well get ready to head to out.

It's while I'm fixing my ponytail that I hear my older brother's voice.

"We can play until dinner." He's talking to someone, and being the nosy person that I am, I look through the doorway to see who.

He's talking to his friend Santiago. He and Leo have been friends practically all their lives, and since they're the same age, go to school together and with Santiago living here on the property, they spend all their time together.

"What are you guys doing?" I open the door once my hair is in its place.

The two boys stop and look over to me. Leo gives me an annoyed sigh while Santiago gives me a small smile.

"We are going to throw the ball around for a little bit." Leo sounds just as annoyed as he looks. "Where are you going?" he asks, looking me up and down, probably noticing that I changed into a dress to go to the store with mom.

I smile. "Mom and I are going to the fabric store to get

some stuff for a new project. If we come back before dinner, can I throw the ball around with you guys?"

Just because I like making dresses doesn't mean that I don't like throwing a football or baseball around. I can be a total tomboy sometimes.

Santiago nods. "Yeah, we will be out in the grass. Come out and find us."

Even with the frustrated grunt that my brother releases, the smile on Santiago's face doesn't disappear. Sometimes I like Santiago better than my brother, he's even a better listener than Leo is.

"Isabella!" my mom yells out and I turn to see that she is coming down the hall.

She has a smile on her face and when she sees the boys standing with me, it grows.

"*Niños*, what are you up to?"

"We were about to go play outside," Leo tells her. Even at fourteen-years-old my brother is still a total mama's boy.

"Just don't get into too much trouble, okay? I'm going to go to the store, but I will be back in a little bit."

Both boys nod. "We will, *Mamá*." Leo says before they turn and continue on their way. I watch the boys leave the hallway until I can no longer see them.

"You can stay and play with them, Bella." My mom's voice is soft and encouraging.

I shake my head. "But I'm heading to the store with you."

She bends her knees and gets at eye level with me. "You don't have to. If you want to stay and play, you can. I can pick out the fabric and as soon as I get back, we will get started. You go play."

I think about the offer. We have all summer, so I can go to the fabric store when we go on a different day. I don't have to go today, and I can play with Leo and Santiago for a little bit.

"Are you sure?"

"Of course, *mija*. Go play. I will make sure to get some beautiful fabric for you." I hug my mom and after a quick outfit change, I make my way out to the courtyard to join the boys.

Leo grunts at my appearance and isn't happy that I'm there for a good five minutes but he gets over it.

We spend hours out in the courtyard, and I don't pay attention how long we were outside for until I notice how low the sun is in the sky.

Huh. My mom didn't come to get me when she got home from the store.

"I'm going to find Mom," I say to the boys before abandoning the game and running inside.

I check the kitchen first but she's not there.

I then head to the sewing room.

Maybe she started without me, not wanting to take me away from the game.

I walk into the sewing room but find it just as I left it earlier today, and still no sign of my mom.

Maybe she's with Camila. I head to my sister's room but it's empty. Then I remember that Camila was with Mrs. Reyes while me and mom were talking about the dresses.

Is she not back yet?

She left a good four hours ago, it doesn't take that long to pick out fabric.

Deciding to look for her in different parts of the house, I head over to my dad's office. Maybe she is in there talking to him or something.

I hear voices the closer and closer I get to my father's office doors. That's not out of the ordinary, he always has people around, but these voices sound sad and angry, like something is definitely wrong.

"No! You don't get to come in here and tell me that my wife is fucking dead and not tell me who did it!"

A gasp leaves my mouth and I feel this pain inside of me that I can't explain.

That was my father's voice.

It was my father's voice saying how his wife was dead.

His wife.

My mother.

She's dead.

I must have walked into the office at some point, because there are eyes of about fifteen men staring at me.

The only eyes I want to see are the ones that matter the most.

"She's dead?" I don't know how I was able to get the words out because it feels like my throat is on fire and everything is going to burst.

My father just looks at me, not saying a word. He just stands there and looks at me from behind his desk. His face is red and his eyes are filled with anger, but he doesn't look sad.

"Is my mother dead?!" I ask more forcefully. Just

because I'm twelve doesn't mean that I can't put together what is going on.

Finally, after what feels like the longest moments of my life, my father nods. "Yes, Isabella. She's dead."

Something in me snaps. It's like whatever line was holding me together just ripped apart and broke something inside of me.

I can't move. I can't even go running to my father so that he can console me about this. I'm just rooted in place, watching everything around me move.

That's how I am when Leo comes in and my father tells him what happened to our mother. That's how I am when Leo blames him for her death. That's how I am when Leo has to go get Camila and tell her that our mother is not coming back. And that's how I am for the days that come. Rooted in place, not wanting to leave the comfort of my own room.

She's gone.

She's dead.

She went to the fabric store because I wanted to go and now she's dead.

I could have been with her while it happened. I could have been there to hold her hand in her final moments. I could have been the one to take whatever killed her. I should have gone with her to get the fabric and then maybe I would still have my mother here with me. Maybe if I had gone with her, my father wouldn't be looking at me like I was to blame.

Maybe I am to blame.

"Isabella?" I hear my name, and turning, I see Santiago

standing a few feet away. Hands in his pockets, his head slightly down, looking at me with concern. "Are you okay?"

Am I?

My mother is dead and there is nothing that I can do to change that.

I shake my head.

When it comes to Santiago, I have always been truthful, no point in not being so now.

Santiago comes over to where I'm sitting on my bed and hesitates for a second before he sits next to me and wraps an arm around my shoulders.

The only other person that has done this in the last few days has been Leo, and when he does it, it doesn't feel like enough.

I don't know if it's the added affection but whatever it is, it makes me burst into tears.

Wrapping my arms around Santiago, I burrow into him and cry the pain of losing my mother away.

"It's okay, Isabella. It will be okay. I will always be here for you."

I continue to cry.

I really hope that he is telling the truth.

3

SANTOS

Fourteen Years Old

I've never experienced anyone close to me dying. My parents have talked to me about it and how unpredictable it can be, but I have never experienced it firsthand.

Not until Rosa Maria Morales.

She was like a second mother to me and when I heard that she died, no that she was killed, I felt something in me break.

Whatever it was broke even more when I saw how much her death affected the Morales kids. Leo blamed his father, Camila was too young to grasp what was going on, but it was Isabella who was the one that broke me the most.

She was supposed to go with her mother that day, but instead she stayed behind to play catch with Leo and me. I didn't have to ask her to know that she blamed herself for her mother no longer being here. You can see it in her eyes and how detached she is with everything.

Isabella may only be twelve but she feels strongly, and the death of her mother shattered her.

And for some reason, I feel compelled to help her through the pain.

Don't ask me why, I just do.

That's why I'm currently standing outside her bedroom door with a bag. A bag that I hope will bring her some sort of happiness and not sadness.

Hope. I have to hope that's her reaction.

I take a deep breath and knock on the giant wooden door in front of me.

She's twelve. Why are you nervous?

Because I don't want to make the situation worse than what it already is.

A few seconds after my knock, the door opens just slightly. Enough for Isabella to see who it is through the small crack.

The eye that I can see is red and her face looks pale, like she hasn't seen the sunlight in a while.

"Santiago?" Her voice comes out low but it's enough for me to hear the surprise in it.

I never actively seek her out. The one other time that I did was a few days ago when I walked by and saw her crying all by herself.

"Hi." I give her a little wave.

"What do you want?" Maybe she thinks Leo or my mom sent me to check on her, because me being here is really out of character.

"I brought you something," I hold up the bag that's in my hand.

She looks from the bag to me, her eyebrows bunching up in confusion.

"What is it?"

"Um…" How do I tell her? "Can I come in and show you? I don't think you will want to open it out here."

She is a little hesitant but soon the door opens wide enough for me to walk in.

I close the door behind me and place the bag on her bed, waving for her to open it.

Again she's hesitant, like she thinks the bag holds something that will explode, but after a few seconds, she walks over and opens the bag carefully.

I stand back as she opens the bag. When I hear a gasp, I don't know if I should be happy or afraid of her reaction.

"Where did you get this?" Isabella turns to me and I see fresh tears running down her face.

I swallow the lump that is forming in my throat.

How do I tell her that it was my father that found her mother's body in the parking lot of the fabric store? That it was him that got the call from her security team that she was gunned down and was the first person on the scene?

How do I make the words come out that my father found the bag of fabric that was purchased by Rosa to bring back to her daughter? The same bag I was holding on to until I found the right time to give to Isabella.

"Um…" Think, Santiago. Think. "My dad found it, and I kept it to give it to you. I can take it back, that way it doesn't make you sadder than what you already are."

Of course, it's going to make her sad. I just gave her a bag full of fabric that her mom purchased for one of their projects.

Isabella looks at me with wide eyes and when I see the tears escaping her eyes faster than they were a second ago, I start to panic.

Way to go Santiago, you made the girl a blubbering mess.

I'm about to excuse myself, so that she can cry in peace, when she throws herself at me. Her arms go around my waist and she hugs me tightly, like she's grasping for a life vest.

For a second I have no idea what to do, like I've never hugged a person before. Eventually my brain and body finally communicate, and I wrap my arms around Isabella's small frame.

"I didn't want to make you cry," I say to her, my arms holding her just a little tighter.

"They are happy tears, not sad ones," Isabella pulls herself away from my arms and goes back to the bag of fabric sitting on her bed.

"Happy?" I watch as she picks up a bundle of floral fabric.

She nods. "I thought that I lost this piece of my mom forever, and then you brought me a small part of her back."

"You were going to give up something that you loved because she died?"

As long as I have known Isabella, she has always liked to make things with a sewing machine. It's something that she is really good at. Her giving that up would feel wrong.

She nods again, keeping her eyes on the fabric. I think she isn't going to say anything else until she finally breaks the silence.

"Doing something I love isn't worth it if I can't share it with her."

There's sadness in her voice and for some reason, I want it to go away. No one should sound so sad.

"Share it with me."

Did those words just leave my mouth?

"What?"

"Share what you love with me."

The more I say the words the more I realize just how crazy I sound. Isabella and I aren't close. There is no reason for her to share anything with me. She probably thinks I'm taking pity on her or something just because she's Leo's sister.

"Why would I share this with you?"

Good question. I have no idea, so I just make something up.

"Because I don't like seeing you sad and you giving up something you love will make you lose your smile. Share it with me and remember your mom with every project that you do."

I want to see her happy. I want to see her smile again and to see her out in the world doing things like playing catch with Leo and me.

Isabella just stands there looking at me, not saying anything. I take that as my cue to leave.

Giving her a small smile, I turn toward the door. The door is open and my foot is over the threshold when I hear my name said in a small whisper.

I turn, seeing Isabella holding on to a piece of fabric tightly in her hand.

"Thank you for giving me the fabric. Thank you for caring."

"I will always care about you, Bella."

I may be only fourteen, but I know that Isabella deserves someone who cares.

Hopefully, I can be that person, if she lets me.

4

ISABELLA

Sixteen Years Old

I WILL ALWAYS CARE about you, Bella.

A set of words that have been stuck in my head since I heard them four years ago.

You would think that a twelve-year-old girl would forget something that her brother's friend said to her, but no. They have been swimming in my head and are something that I hold near and dear to my heart.

Not only do I hold the words close to me, in recent years I have found myself holding the boy that voiced them close too.

It started off as just a small crush and then it transformed into more.

It was like a swarm of butterflies that showed up every time that he was around. Every time that he said my name or said even a word to me, the swarm would attack inside of my belly.

Being around him made me happy and nervous all at the same time.

Every time I shared one of my projects with him and I got a bright smile, the things I was feeling for him started to feel more and more different.

That's when I realized that the crush that was once there was something different.

I had feelings for a boy that had been there for me and had become a pivotal part of my life.

Feelings that torture me every single day.

Feelings that for the life of me, I can't voice.

Why can't I voice how I feel about this individual?

Well, because Santiago Reyes, or Santos as everyone else in the world calls him, is off-limits. Not because he has a girlfriend or anything but because he's my brother's best friend and my father has this lovely rule about boys.

No muchachos, Isabella. No muchachos hasta qué yo te diga.

Translation, no boys until he tells me otherwise.

And I'm sure anyone that my brother is friends with is high on the no-boys-allowed list. Even if he is the one person that has been there for me constantly since the death of my mother.

That isn't something my father cares about.

It was my mother's death actually, that told me exactly what my father cares about, and it's not how his daughter feels. Or how his kids feel about anything for that matter.

Power and money are the two most important things to Ronaldo Morales, not what his kids might be going through or feeling.

I've actually learned a lot about my father these last few years that makes me question a number of things about him.

I asked him about it once a few months ago, and all he said was that I shouldn't worry about anything. As long as I had food on the table, a roof over my head and didn't want for anything, then I shouldn't go looking for answers.

That answer piqued my curiosity even more.

Wait, how did I get into this whole tangent about my father and all his mysteriousness?

Oh right, his no-boys rule.

I understand the no-boys rule when it comes to some of the douchebags that are at this hoity-toity school, but Santiago Reyes should not be put in that same category.

That man should be in a category of his own.

And I say man because there is nothing boyish about this high school senior.

Everything that I have ever dreamed up in a guy, is all wrapped up nice and tight within him. He is what girls would call a wet dream, with light-brown hair, eyes that have a goldish tint in them and everything opposite of your everyday Hispanic man.

You wouldn't even know he was Mexican unless he told you. His mother is Canadian and his father is Mexican and somehow, someway, they met and created this fine specimen. A specimen that has spent his life in Mexico and Texas.

A true and fine specimen.

If only he saw me the same way I saw him.

One could hope, right?

"You're staring, *bella*." His voice breaks the trance that I was in while he puts his things away in his locker.

Did I mention that I spend any chance I can with him while we are at school? I'm like a clingy girlfriend without the girlfriend title.

And...

He calls me *bella*.

Not Bella, like that girl from those *Twilight* vampire books or like the model, but *bella*, with a y sound. Essentially, he calls me beautiful, okay? The Spanish language is all over the place when it comes to translating things in English.

He started calling me *bella*, sometime around my fifteenth birthday and every time I hear it, the swarm of butterflies come out in full swing.

"I wasn't staring. I was simply wondering how someone like you can be in high school." I flutter my eyelashes at him and gift him with my sweetest smile that only he gets to see.

There are many sides of me that only a certain few are allowed to see and Santiago is one of those people.

"Someone like me?" He turns his torso slightly to face me, with an eyebrow raised.

C'mon, he can't be this clueless.

"No eighteen-year-old has the right to look the way you do." I throw in a wink to tell him exactly what I mean.

"And how do I look?" Santiago closes his locker and turns to face me, arms crossed and body mere inches from mine.

The school-issued shirt forms along the lines of his

biceps, really making them pop out. Do all boys outside of this douchy school look like this or is it just him?

"Full of muscles and yummy that it makes me want to lick you all over." Bold? Yes. A necessary statement to say while we are in school? Not really, but I did. I need to get my point across. It's not like any of my attempts to show that I have feelings for this man have gone unnoticed.

"Isabella." He growls out my name, like he's mad or something and I absolutely love it.

"What? It's the truth and if you were a lesser man, you would have taken me up on my offer already."

For the past year and a half, I've been making my feelings for him known. Not only to him but also to my brother. They both need to know how I feel and what better way to do that than to show them every chance I get. By me showing Leo, I'm telling him that I don't care that he feels a certain type of way about me being with his friend if it ever happens.

I've done a lot of things since my feelings for Santiago went from a crush to actual feelings. I started doing my makeup differently, dressing even more differently whenever I'm outside of my school uniform. I have tried everything that teenage movies tell you to do to get a guy's attention. Nothing has worked so far.

A big part of me thinks that I will only ever be looked at as Leo's little sister and that is it.

I just wish that he would be straight up and say it if that were the case. Maybe then I would stop my advances.

Sometimes though, Santiago's actions take me off

guard. The smirk he is currently giving me right now is definitely one of those times.

I get too lost in the way his eyes are looking at me that I don't notice that he places a hand on my hip and turns me so that my back is against the lockers. Santiago looks down at me as he places his hands on either side of my face.

What is he doing?

"If I was a lesser man." He leans in, his mouth so close to my ear. I can't breathe with how close he is. "I would finally give in to your advances and would hike up this little skirt of yours and find out what kind of panties you are wearing. All for the whole school to see. For them to know that you were mine, just by that small action."

It's when his teeth meet my earlobe that I think that I'm in a whole other dimension.

Holy. Shit.

What is happening?

Better yet, what has gotten into him? With all my advances, Santiago has not acted this way toward me. Why else would I think that he only saw me as his friend's sister?

Did something change between my advances yesterday and the ones from a few minutes ago? Not that I'm complaining but it doesn't stop me from being curious. Neither do his words.

"Am I? Am I yours?"

Please tell me that I am. Please tell me that I'm yours.

"One day you will be." It's not a question, it's a promise.

Fuck. Fuck.

What is seriously happening? Did Santiago Reyes really just say that one day I will be *his*?

Am I dreaming?

I keep my eyes on his and I try to search for anything that will tell me that he's trying to pull my leg and is messing with me. That he's just lying to placate a teenage girl.

But I don't see anything but sincerity in his eyes.

He's telling me the truth.

Santiago Reyes wants me to be his one day.

"Why one day? Why not right now?"

Why are you telling me this now?

I also want to ask how long he has felt this way, but I keep that question in. I guess I'm blind if I didn't see that he might have felt the same way I did. Or he is more skilled at hiding what he was feeling than I am. I'm going for the latter.

He chuckles against my ear, before placing a kiss on my cheek and pulling away fully.

"Because if I were to make you mine at this moment, I would be dead before the day's end. Dead or your father will castrate me. I won't make you mine until you are older, and I can go to your father and ask him for permission."

To some girls those words would cause them to roll their eyes. For me, it warms my heart that he cares about me so much that he is willing to go to my father and ask him permission. It's traditional and never did I think I would be all for it.

And he is right, I'm sixteen. Santiago is eighteen. If my father had seen what he just did right now and how he had my earlobe between his teeth, my father wouldn't have hesitated in doing anything drastic. Death is the most logical possibility.

Even if a part of me is saying that my father won't care.

I look at the boy in front of me. He's not the same boy he was when he was consoling me about my mother's death and telling me to share my clothing designs with him. This boy is different but still the same in some way.

As I continue to look at him, to find any indication that he's pulling a prank on me, I realize something. In only a few minutes everything between us has changed. I don't really know how to comprehend the truth that he just told me, but I do know one thing.

If I have to wait for him, I will.

No matter how many months or years that may be. That is one thing that I'm certain about.

"Okay, I will hold you to that promise." I give him a smile that is small and timid and nothing like the smiles I'm used to plastering on my face.

One day I will belong to Santiago Reyes, and I will be counting the days until that day arrives.

5

SANTOS

Eighteen Years Old

IN A MATTER OF MINUTES, I let my guard down. Maybe it was the way she was smiling at me or fluttering her eyelashes, but something made me throw the words that I've been holding in for months, out.

Yes, months.

I'm not stupid, I knew from an early age that Isabella Morales was going to be beautiful girl and eventually a gorgeous woman. Not only that she was going to be beautiful, but special in her own way. I just didn't think that when that time came it would hit me like a ton of bricks.

I didn't think that I would notice her beauty the way I did or that it would affect me so much.

But it did.

Even at sixteen, she's the most beautiful girl I have ever laid eyes on, but I didn't voice it.

I kept the thoughts of how beautiful this girl was to

myself. That didn't stop me from silently suffering every single time she was near me, because I noticed everything she was doing to get my attention. I noticed the way she would dress differently, how her makeup changed and how her school-issued skirt was always rolled up just an inch higher when I was around.

Everything about Isabella Morales, I've noticed.

And if she were older, then I would be doing everything in my power to make her mine, but she's not.

Hopefully I can keep my word and make her mine one day.

Because one day is better than never.

"You're fucking staring."

Leo's voice is loud in my ear, and that still doesn't have me taking my eyes off Isabella, his sister.

The two of us are currently in the school courtyard eating our lunch, all the while Isabella is about fifty feet away, sitting with her friends.

She looks beautiful today. Her dark hair is pulled back in a braid, with a few pieces of hair falling around her face. She looks innocent and everything that a guy dreams of.

Everything that I dream of when I shouldn't.

I don't even care that her brother caught me staring, that's how enthralled I am by this girl.

"Your sister is beautiful." I finally take my eyes off the beauty in front of me and give Leo a smirk.

"Yeah, and you aren't allowed to touch her." He shoves me, almost pushing me off my seat, a smirk of his own playing on his face.

The bastard reminds me every chance he gets that his

sister is off-limits, but the both of us know that I would be a good choice for her. He's just too afraid to admit it, he will though, it will just take time.

Leo knows I would treat her the way she deserves and give her everything her heart desires. If I had the chance to give her the world, I would.

Never thought that at eighteen I would be having that thought process but even from a young age, I knew that Isabella Morales was special. Even with the two year age difference.

"Better me than that asshole over there." The words escape through my teeth as I see one of the kids, whose daddy probably owns half of Texas, approach Isabella and her friends.

The fuckwad looks like he just jumped out of a school brochure.

I'm sick of these preppy schoolboys that don't have to work for anything that they are given. The day I graduate and leave this preppy fucked-up world cannot come soon enough.

Whatever compelled my parents to send me to a school full of rich pricks that just flaunt their money is beyond me. I would have been perfectly fine going to any public school that the state of Texas had to offer. But I guess when you work with Ronaldo Morales, you take him up on his offer to send your only son to a high society school for extra protection. Like I can't take care of myself.

"I swear, all the threats in the world don't keep these assholes away from her." To anyone but me, Leo is one scary motherfucker, everyone at this ridiculous school knows not to mess with him.

When it comes to his sister, well, that's a whole different story.

"Maybe show them Ronaldo's dungeon and then maybe they won't even think about talking to her."

It's supposed to be a joke, but both of us know that everything concerning his father's "dungeon" is true.

You see, Leo and Isabella have a famous father of sorts. Famous in the sense that any mention of his name makes people that live in these parts of Texas fearful.

Ronaldo Morales is by far the most dangerous man that you can come across. Leo and I have known for a few years now just how dangerous. We may be only eighteen, but we weren't shielded from this world, we know exactly the type of business Leo's father runs.

We know enough that the two of us are weeks away from partaking in said business. The last two years, I've learned more and more about what our fathers do and have been trained to be just like them. Leo being molded into the man his father wants him to become a few years before me.

Come graduation, we will officially be involved in everything they are.

Once we walk across the stage at graduation, Leo and I will be a part of the Muertos Cartel. By force of our fathers and a partial decision from us both. No way was I going to let my one and only friend, someone who is like a brother, go through this life without me. He dies, I die right next to him.

Leo grunts, taking my mind away from the morbid path it was heading. "I do that, they talk and we will have a lot more than a few preppy assholes to deal with."

He's got a point there.

If anyone gets a wind of what our families are involved in, we will be seeing federal agents left and right.

"Like I said a few seconds ago, better me than those fuckers." I throw him a smirk, again I get shoved and my friend just shakes his head.

"Maybe one day you'll get my blessing. Maybe. If you prove yourself."

"I'll prove myself and I'll be standing there next to her, silently telling you I told you so." The grin on my face grows more when Leo just gives me a shake of his head.

He knows I will be doing exactly what I just said, it may take a few years, but it will happen.

The lunch bell rings, and we both get up from our seats and start leaving the school courtyard to head back to class. Before I leave, though, I turn to find Isabella. I give her a smile when I find that she is looking at me instead of paying attention to the asswipe that is currently trying to talk to her. With a wink in her direction, I turn and head to class.

The rest of the day goes by as slow as it possibly can with nothing exciting happening, and that's including the announcement of what the prom theme is going to be this year.

Who the actual fuck cares what the prom theme is? Isn't that a dance that students get all fancy for all so they can skip the dance and drink in a deserted parking lot somewhere?

No, thank you. I rather spend my prom night in San Pedro, Mexico, where I can actually legally drink. The perks of having multiple citizenships to different countries that have a drinking age of eighteen.

I make my way out of my last class and head to my locker to grab my things. It's not too surprising that I find Isabella standing in front of it, waiting for me.

"I see that you finally got rid of the preppy schoolboy from lunch." I approach her, giving her a smirk that says I'm just playing around.

"He's harmless. Was just asking about an assignment in a class we share." Isabella shrugs and I can't help but let out a snort.

"Yeah, I'm sure that's all that was." This girl doesn't know that every single guy in this school would kill to be with her. With me being at the top of that list.

She rolls her eyes at me, and I just go straight to opening my locker to grab a few things before going to find Leo and getting out of this place.

"So, did you hear about the prom theme?" Isabella asks once I have all of my things and we are walking side by side out of the building.

I nod. "It's some generic shit."

The comment earns me a small slap on the shoulder. "Once upon a time is *not* generic."

I raise an eyebrow at her.

She sighs. "Okay, maybe it is, but still, I'm excited for it and now I have a theme to work with to make my dress."

"I'm sure you will come up with something that will blow all the other girls out of the water," and she will. Isabella is only sixteen, but she is very talented when it comes to a sewing machine.

"Are you going?" It's the hopefulness in her tone that makes me stop walking when we get to the parking lot.

I have a feeling she wants to ask something completely different, especially with how wide her eyes are and how she's biting her lip.

"I wasn't planning on it." I give her a shrug and it just causes her to bite her lip even more.

"Why? It sounds like it will be fun." The hope is still there. I want to just come out and tell her to ask me what she wants to ask, but a part of me doesn't want to hurt her when I ultimately give my answer.

I give her a shrug playing it off. "It's not something that I see myself going to. You should though, you should go and have fun with your friends. Knock everyone out with one of your dresses."

I know for a fact that she will be the prettiest girl there.

Isabella continues to look at me with those brown eyes of hers, as if she is trying to figure me out. Probably contemplating why I'm not jumping at the chance to spend time with her, when I told her earlier in the day that one day she would be mine.

In due time, it will happen, but not yet.

Not now.

Finally, the brightness and hope in Isabella's eyes dims a little bit. "Yeah, going with my friends should be fun."

The small hint of disappointment makes me cringe a

little but all I can do is give her a small smile and continue our way to the car.

On our way to the Morales estate, because yes, I live there too, I have my whole entire life, I come up with a plan. One that would make Isabella happy and she'll get to go to prom. Hopefully.

When we pull up to the estate, the plan is all but set in motion, I just have to work on some of the finer details and then everything will be set.

I need to actually grow the balls to go through with it, but for right now, heading to the courtyard to map out my plan will have to do.

My feet barely step over the threshold of the courtyard when I hear my name being called.

Turning, I see my father standing in the corridor waving me over.

My relationship with my dad is nothing compared to the one that Leo has with his. I don't hate my father, just what he does, but our relationship is solid and I have mad respect for the man.

"¿*Si apá?*." I approach him, giving him a nod.

Cristiano Reyes is a very held-together man, especially since he is always dressed in a freaking suit. He stands a few inches taller than me and is literally a man I look up to.

"How was school?" he asks, waving me to follow him away from the courtyard. His accent thick as always. Makes me wonder sometimes how he and my mom got together.

I shrug. "It's almost over."

"Enjoy it while you can, you only get to be young once.

Then you're an adult and everything gets harder by the minute."

He's talking from experience. At a young age my father got roped into the cartel world and couldn't find a way out. According to him, the only time he was able to escape the Muertos was when he met my mother during a run and decided to stay with her.

For a few glorious months he said, she was all that mattered and the Muertos were as if they didn't exist. That is until they needed him back in Mexico. He came back, with my mother right behind him, and was once again entangled in everything Muertos. He has voiced in the past that he doesn't want this life for me, that I should go explore the world once I graduate but he knows that won't happen.

I'm already entangled in it. I may not be moving merchandise around just yet or have taken part in any deals, but I will. It's only a matter of time. I was born into this cartel, it's who I'm going to be and the only way out is if I'm one thing. *Muerto.*

"I'll try," maybe prom will be a good start to that.

He nods at my statement and continues to lead me through the estate until we reach a door that leads to the basement.

The dungeon.

I look at my father in confusion as he stands in front of the door, not moving to open it.

My whole life I have lived on this estate. My whole life, I have been surrounded by the inner workings of this Mexican cartel, but never has it gone this far.

Sure, I have seen men kill other men but never have I witnessed what has happened behind this door.

I've heard stories from Leo, but never have I seen them with my own eyes.

"¿*Apá*?" is that fear in my voice?

Am I scared?

Yes.

I thought I had a few weeks left before I was thrown straight into cartel life, now I have no idea what to think.

"I spoke to Ronaldo. He said since you are now eighteen, it's time to show you exactly how the cartel works."

Cristiano is a very calm man, nothing really ever is able to affect him. This, though, with this I can hear it in his voice that it's affecting him in ways he doesn't want me to see. The thought of me walking through that door angers him and if he had his way, he wouldn't be bringing me here. But he doesn't call the shots, Ronaldo does.

"I know how the cartel works." I square my shoulders, preparing for battle.

What battle exactly? I have no idea.

"You don't know it like this." The eyes that my mother says are exactly like mine, stare back at me and actually have me stepping back.

They are dark and hard and everything that someone should fear.

"This will not be the last time that you will step foot through this doorway, Santiago. If this life is really the life you want to live, you will walk through this door more times than you will ever be able to count. After I take you in there, you will finally figure out what your involvement will be in this. Just know that if you want to walk away from this, you have my respect wholeheartedly."

Something that Leo won't get if he walks away. No matter what I decide after walking through that door, my father will have my back. In Leo's case, Ronaldo will most likely have him killed for stepping away.

I look at the man standing in front of me and try to picture what his life, what my life, would have been if he hadn't fallen into the world of the Muertos.

I can't.

This is who he is, and it will be who I become.

After a few seconds I give my nod to my father, silently telling him that I understand.

With one final look at me and with an audible sigh, he walks to the door and unlocks it, opening it wide enough for me to walk through.

The doors close behind us, and the second that the darkness engulfs me, I hear it.

I hear the screams.

The begging.

The lives being taken.

I don't have to take a step farther to know that I won't be the same person I was a few seconds ago.

The more I hear the screams, the grunting and the gunshots, I know I will become a new person.

And that person won't deserve anything in this life and that includes asking Isabella to prom.

After what I'm about to witness, I don't deserve to receive any of her smiles that she throws in my direction.

I won't deserve her.

6

ISABELLA

I HAD HOPE.

Hope that he would finally break completely and do what I know he wanted to do.

Hope that the promise he told me in the hallway was going to come true sooner rather than later on.

Hope that once and for all my dreams were going to come to life and I had something to look forward to.

I had hope.

There was something in his eyes when we arrived back to the estate that day, something that looked like determination.

I thought that it might have had something to do with me.

It didn't.

How do I know?

Later that night, that determination was gone. It was gone and with it, the light that lived in his eyes was gone as well. In a matter of hours, it had seemed like he had changed. In the days to come, I also noticed he became harder, colder. Even toward me.

The hope I had in me started to dwindle.

With every day, every week that passed, it dwindled even more.

Until I finally got to the point where I was losing hope that his promise to make me his one day, would never come.

And now, weeks after those words were said, I have a feeling that I'm completely right.

I will never belong to Santiago Reyes, no matter how hard I had wished for it.

SANTOS

Twenty years old

I MADE HER HATE ME.

Two years ago, I had a plan set to ask Isabella Morales to prom. I wanted to do it. I was *going* to do it. But I made her hate me instead.

All because a darkness engulfed everything that I was, and I didn't want to cloud over her light with it. I didn't want to drown the very light that made Isabella her own person, because that's what I would have done.

So, I made her hate me. I walked into that basement and threw every single plan that involved Isabella out of the fucking window, because she deserved better than what I could give her.

The second I walked out that door, I became a different person. I no longer was the boy waiting for graduation to come, I became a man that wanted to embrace every last minute of his youth and forget that this was the life he chose to live.

A man that in the two years since I walked through that door, has moved more drugs and more bodies than I ever thought imaginable. And those numbers will just keep on growing from here.

Today, though, for a few hours at least, the drugs and the bodies will not take precedence.

No, right now the only thing that matters is watching a certain brunette *bella* walk across her graduation stage.

"Why is it so hot? And if this is a fancy school, why can't they have this shit inside where there's cold air flowing?" Camila's little voice takes my eyes off the stage centered on the field in front of us.

"Hey. Language." Why I agreed to babysit the eleven-year-old is beyond me.

"You say shit. You say a lot of worse words than shit, actually. Why can't I say them?" She has me there, doesn't she?

I guess this is what happens when you spend a lot of time around a kid.

"I'm allowed to say it because I'm older. But you aren't, so stop saying it." I should really watch what I say around this girl, she's like a parrot that repeats everything.

"But it's hot," Camila whines and I think if she was standing up instead of sitting, she would be stomping her foot. God, she reminds me so much of her sister.

"Suck it up." I say, turning to her and trying to give her the sternest look that I can.

Camila's eyes get all wide and sad and when she pops out her bottom lip and it trembles slightly, I cave.

"Fine. I'll take you for ice cream after this, just stop complaining. And stop with the bad words."

"Okay!" The sadness magically goes away and she settles into the seat next to me, like this whole thing didn't just happen.

If Leo thinks he has it bad with Isabella now that she's officially an adult, the man has another thing coming with Camila. She's had the both of us wrapped around her whole hand since she was five, now imagine the poor bastard that she ends up with.

"Where's Leo and my dad?" Camila asks a few minutes later.

That's a good question.

I volunteer to be put on Camila duty because Ronaldo had something very important to discuss and needed his son to be present. Fine by me, I was more than happy to skip any meeting and grab Camila and make it to Isabella's graduation early.

Now though, it's only about twenty minutes before the ceremony starts and Leo and Ronaldo are nowhere to be found.

"They're running a little late, but they'll be here." I give her the best reassuring nod that I can but I can tell that she sees right through it.

For the next fifteen or so minutes, I check the time on my phone more times than I can count. Isabella might hate me for distancing myself from her, but I know that if her brother isn't at the very least here, she will be pissed beyond belief.

It's only a few minutes before the ceremony starts, as everyone in the stadium is getting ready for the graduates to come out, that Leo finally shows up, taking a seat next to his little sister.

"It's about time you showed up," Camila snaps at him, not even bothering to look in his direction.

Leo looks at her with wide eyes and then turns to me as if to ask what has gotten into her. I just shrug. The girl is just something else.

"You look very pretty today, Camila," Leo says to his sister before leaning in and planting a kiss on her cheek.

Camila huffs and I have to fight to hold in a laugh. "I look pretty all the time."

The laugh that I was holding in finally escapes and Leo is laughing right next to me.

Our laughing earns us a narrow stare from our little companion. She looks like she's about to say something, but she is stopped by the start of the graduation music.

The graduates start walking into the stadium, and even though she is surrounded by other students, my eyes land on her right away.

Even when I separated myself from her for two years, I still have the ability to pick out Isabella from anywhere she might be. I have this type of awareness when it comes to her, and it gets stronger and stronger as time goes by.

The way I feel about her also gets stronger as time goes by.

For the past two years, I have kept my distance but

have kept an eye on her. If I had thought she was beautiful at sixteen, I was blown away as I saw how the beauty grew these last few years. Not only is she beautiful, but everything about her is radiating and seems to captivate me more every single day.

Every time I see a smile that isn't meant for me.

Every laugh that I hear.

Everything about this girl, this *woman*, has me wishing even more that she was mine.

But she can't be.

For the next three hours, we hear so many speeches that I'm positive my ears bleed at some point. Also, it's hot as fucking balls, which makes me agree with Camila that such a fancy school should have had this crap inside.

When they finally get to the student names, I want to jump up for joy because the torture of sitting in the Texas heat is almost over.

Every single family yells loudly when their student's name is called and when they get to Isabella, the three of us try to be as loud as we possibly can. We may not be a big group of people, but hey, we can make our presence known.

Once all the names have been called and the graduates throw their caps in the air, the event is over. The three of us make our way down to the ground level to find Isabella and get out of here.

The less time we have to spend at this god-awful school, the better.

"I need to find a bathroom," Camila says, tugging on both Leo's and my arms.

"Can you hold it?" Leo asks his sister, looking at the crowd surrounding us and possibly trying to figure out how to get to Bella and take Camila to the bathroom at the same time.

"I'll grab Bella. You take her." With a nod in my direction, Leo grabs Camila and walks her over to where the restrooms are.

I try to make it through the crowds as best I can until I finally reach the field and look around for the brunette that has captivated my mind for years.

Like earlier, I'm able to find her without difficulty. She's looking around for a familiar face, a bright smile on her lips until she meets my stare. When our eyes meet the smile she's wearing is still prominent until it isn't.

That has been the one telltale sign that I have that tells me that Isabella hates me, her smile easily disappears when I'm around.

I give her a small wave and make my way over to her.

Her eyes don't leave me as I close the distance between us. As I get closer, I see her take deep breath after deep breath as if she were trying to compose herself to face me.

I get a small smile, one that I've come to expect when it comes to Isabella, when I'm only about a foot or two away from her.

"You are officially done with high school," I give her a nod. Not really knowing what else to do or say.

This has been the process when it has come to communicating with her these last couple years. Everything that we say or even the way we interact with each other has felt awkward to the point where we just don't do it.

It's a little painful.

Isabella awards me with another small smile. "I am, and now out to the real world I go."

"The real world is not ready for Isabella Morales." The truest thing I've said to her in two years.

A small blush covers her cheeks at my words, but she tries to cover it as she takes off her cap and readjusts her hair.

Have I mentioned just how beautiful she is when her dark locks are flowing down her back? Seeing her hair like this makes me want to reach out and touch its smoothness. Makes me want to wrap my hand around the strands and bring her lips to mine.

Those are dangerous thoughts to have.

My mind is right, those are dangerous thoughts, especially when it come to Isabella.

But that doesn't stop me from taking a few steps closer and brushing a few strands of hair behind her ear.

A small gasp leaves her lips at the action.

This is the closest I have been to her since I told her that one day she would be mine.

My eyes stay with hers as the strands settle in place, with my thumb rubbing against the edge of her earlobe. We stand in this position for long enough to have Isabella lean into my touch. Her eyes are even closing and I have to fight with myself to not lean in even more and place my lips against hers.

A loud cheer is what finally breaks us apart, even making Isabella take more than a few steps back.

She looks at me with wide brown eyes and I just give her a nod.

We broke apart just in time because a few seconds later, Camila is running straight to us with Leo following a few steps behind.

"Congratulations!" Camila runs straight to her sister and wraps her arms around her waist, her head almost hitting Isabella's shoulder.

Isabella laughs and brings her sister in, placing a kiss on her hair in the process. "Thank you."

She lets go of Camila and soon she is getting the same hug and congratulations from Leo. When she steps out of Leo's arms, Isabella looks around, looking for someone.

"*Papá* didn't come." It's not a question but a statement of fact. By the way that her voice sounds, she expected Ronaldo not to make an appearance.

Leo shakes his head. "Something came up that he had to take care of. He said that he will be there tonight for your celebratory dinner."

Isabella nods, probably already knowing the drill when it comes to her father.

When it comes to his daughters, Ronaldo shows up when he wants to, not when they need him. From the look on Isabella's face, it looks like today was one of the days that she needed him to be here.

"Time for ice cream!" Camila announces, causing her two siblings to give her their attention.

"Ice cream? Who said we were going for ice cream?" Leo crosses his arms along his chest and looks down at the little girl.

Said little girl just smiles at her brother and turns to look at me, not saying a word.

Leo raises an eyebrow at me. I sigh. "She was complaining about how hot it was, so I told her I would take her for ice cream if she stopped complaining. She stopped."

Leo shakes his head and a sweet giggle escapes Isabella before she turns to Camila. "I'm up to get a few scoops of ice cream."

"Yes!" Camila grabs Leo by the hand and starts dragging him off the field.

Leaving me with Isabella.

Isabella gives me a small smile before starting to follow her brother and sister, but I stop her.

My hand lands on her forearm before she can move farther away from me.

She gives me a look of confusion, looking from where my hand is on her to my face.

After a few seconds, I finally let her go and give her a smile of my own.

"I didn't get the chance to say congratulations," I say to her, shrugging my shoulders.

"Thank you," she answers shyly. I can't remember the last time that she was shy around me.

"Of course. Being able to graduate high school and going to college is something to be proud of."

She nods, agreeing. "It is."

We continue to stand there awkwardly for a few more seconds before I wave for her to go ahead and start walking to catch up to Leo and Cam.

At some point, I have to hold her hand to make it through the crowd.

When we're almost to the parking lot, finally away from all the happy families celebrating that their kids graduated, I let her hand go but a few seconds after, I feel a hand on my forearm.

I stop walking and look down at the small hand lying on my skin.

Looking up, I find Isabella biting her lip nervously. Raising an eyebrow, I wait for her to speak.

"Thank you for being here. You probably had better things to do, but I appreciate you being here."

I look at the girl standing in front of me, and for a short moment I'm taken back to when she was twelve and she was looking at me like I was saving her world.

I give her a nod and the smile that is only meant for her.

"I will always be there for you, *bella*."

And I mean it.

8

ISABELLA

To some people, graduating from high school is a monumental steppingstone. They may see it as an official step into adulthood.

For me, graduating high school seems like an unnecessary event, especially if the people who should be the proudest of you, aren't there to see it.

My mom, because she lost her life too soon and my father, because he had something to take care of. That something had to do with the cartel, I knew it the second that I noticed that he wasn't there.

I had three other important people there for me, at least.

My brother.

My little sister.

Santiago.

The latter catching me a bit by surprise with his appearance at the stadium. I didn't expect him to be there.

In all honesty, I didn't think he cared enough to even show up.

But he did, and of course he had to go and make me feel all the feelings I had been suppressing when it came to him, they came back up again. All with a simple set of words.

I will always be there for you.

That, and he called me *bella*. I haven't heard him say that name in the two years since we last had a real conversation.

Hearing it in that moment did something to me that has me thinking about it even hours later.

During the "celebration" my father is currently hosting.

It's more of a full-blown party than a celebration. The ice cream we got after the ceremony is what I would consider a celebration. This party though, with *corridos* playing at full blast and tequila shots ringing out, is more of my dad showing everyone who holds power.

At least he cared enough to throw a party.

That's something, I guess.

I'm not ungrateful for it, I just wish that he showed he cared in a different way, not like this.

"You know, when it's one's party, that person usually is interacting with everyone and having fun. Not sitting around, looking like they would rather be somewhere else."

Even without having his words being directed at me for two years, his voice still brings butterflies to my stomach.

I take my eyes off of the pair of middle-aged men that

are making a fool of themselves on the dance floor and turn to face Santiago.

He's changed into a different button-down than the one that he wore to the graduation. The one earlier was a light blue one that did something to his eyes, but now he's wearing a black one that makes him look intimidating.

It's sexy.

Everything about this man is sexy.

I give a small smile. "I'm not really in the party mood. I would have been happy with just a small dinner or something."

Maybe I should have asked Mrs. Reyes to make me some of her chicken fried steak and her delicious gravy. That meal is a celebration right there.

Santiago nods, grabs a chair, and places it about a foot from me, before sitting down.

"I get it. I remember the party that my dad and yours threw when Leo and I graduated. Pretty sure I was hungover for a good two weeks after that."

Not that I would know. I left that party early. He had just stopped talking to me for no reason, and I didn't want to be at a party that was celebrating him when I was mad at him.

"You at least got to drink the night away. I've been told more than once tonight that I can't drink." What kind of bullshit is that? Telling an eighteen-year-old in Mexico that she can't drink, unheard of.

"Do you want to drink the night away?" Santiago leans in, making me feel like I can't breathe with his proximity.

There is a good foot between our faces but still, it's like being this close to him is impossible.

"I want to do anything that doesn't have to do with this party."

We look at each other for what feels like an eternity and I don't want it to end, but it does when Santiago nods and stands from his seat. I think that he is going to walk away from this conversation but he surprises me by holding out his hand.

"What are you doing?"

"Taking you to go do something that doesn't involve anything to do with this party."

His fingers wiggle in my direction and I'm tempted to slap his hand away, but after a few more seconds, I finally give in and place my hand in his.

He pulls me up and without any hesitation he walks us out of the courtyard and into the house.

I don't ask where he is taking us as he walks through the whole house, I just follow, trying not to freak out at how his hand feels in mind.

His grip is tight, like he's afraid that I will run away from him if he lets go.

His palm feels rough, like he knows what manual labor is and works with his hands every single day. Maybe he does, I don't know. I have no idea what this man does in his everyday life. All I know is that he didn't go to college after he graduated.

What does he do in his life?

The question is on the tip of my tongue but I don't ask it, especially when I realize where he is taking us.

"Leo's wing?"

My father's house is split into four different wings. The north wing is where my father lives with me and Camila, one wing is for the men that my father needs close by, another is for the staff that takes care of the estate and the last wing is Leo's. When he graduated high school, my father gave it to him to do what he wanted with it when he's in San Pedro and not Austin.

"Technically Leo's and mine. He gave me a room in his side when we graduated."

"How did I not know that?"

He shrugs and continues to walk through the wing until he reaches a door nestled all the way in the back.

Santiago opens the door without letting go of my hand and as soon as I walk in, I'm encased in everything that is Santiago Reyes.

His smell fills my nose and I want to stitch it to my brain so that I won't forget it.

Looking around, I see that he made this side of the wing like his very own apartment. There is a sitting area with a massive TV, there's even a small little kitchen with a fridge that I'm sure holds alcohol. Everything he might need, it's here.

My eyes continue to scan the space and I see two doors that I know lead to a bedroom and a bathroom.

He really made this place his own.

"Wow. It's like you have your own place." I turn to him and I find him already looking at me.

He nods. "I wanted it to feel like home, especially after spending so much time in Austin with your brother. So, I made this place home and it helps that my parents are only on the other side of the estate."

I nod, but I don't say anything. I just continue to marvel at everything that I haven't known about Santiago for two years.

I knew he still lived on the property part time, I just thought he was with his parents, not here with Leo.

There is something else that I don't know either...

"Why did you bring me here?" He leaves me standing there in the middle of what is considered his living room and heads to his small fridge.

"You wanted to leave the party." He opens the fridge and pulls out two beers before turning back to me. "So, I brought you here. Away from the party."

"Why?"

"What do you mean, why? Because I wanted to?" He gives me a confused look as he makes his way back to me.

"You didn't want anything to do with me for the last two years. Why now?"

It's an honest question.

For two years, he ignored me and acted like I didn't exist.

Why is it that all of the sudden, I graduate high school and he wants to spend time with me? It makes no fucking sense at all.

I can see him contemplating my question. I know he is trying to come up with the answer and coming up short.

Doesn't he know that all I want is the truth?

Like I gave him for so many years.

"I'm going back to the party."

I'm not going to deal with him, or him only wanting to be a part of my life when he wants to.

"Because for the first time in two years I want to be selfish and spend time with you."

His words ring out before I step over the threshold.

"How is spending time with me being selfish?" I don't turn to face him. I keep my head pointed straight ahead and my shoulders squared back, just waiting for him to speak.

"Me putting distance between us was to protect you, to save you. Seeing you today made me want to go back to a time where we could just be somewhere and not have a care in the world. So, when I saw you earlier, I decided to be selfish for one night."

I'm trying to comprehend what he is telling me, but it feels as if it's going in one ear and out the other. I hear the words; I know what they mean in a literal sense but what do they mean outside of that?

I turn slowly to face him again, stepping farther into the room and closing the door behind me once again. "Protect me from what?"

His facial expression changes. He cowers back and places the beers on the table before running a hand through his hair.

He's not going to answer.

"Protect me from what, Santiago?" I ask more forcefully.

I told myself earlier that I didn't know what this man

does for a living, but I guess I was blind to it. I know exactly what he does, I just need to hear him say the words. I need him to confirm it for me.

"Santiago."

His hands drop from his hair and he faces me. His posture, his face, his eyes, everything is telling me what I need to know.

"From me and whatever man I turned into when I officially became a member of the Muertos. Our lines were getting blurred that day, I was even going to ask you to prom, but when we got home, I got a firsthand glimpse of how exactly the cartel works. The second I found that out, I knew that I had to give up hope that one day you would be mine, because you deserve a hell of a lot better than who I was going to become. Who I have become."

He looks like he's in pain as he says the words. Even his eyes look like they have a tinge of sadness floating in them.

"My father is Ronaldo Morales, the damn fucking kingpin of the cartel. Did you think that maybe, just maybe, you didn't have to protect me from that? That you didn't have to push me aside like I was leftover food you didn't want anymore?"

Does he think I'm that stupid that I don't know what happens when my father's office doors are locked? Or when I see someone coming from the hallway that houses the door to the basement?

Does he really think that I have no idea just how powerful my father is?

"It's different with your father, hell even with your brother, you don't see it firsthand. You're sheltered from it.

You don't know the type of shit that goes on behind closed doors. You don't need someone in your life that is going to bring blood and drugs and weapons into your everyday life. You deserve a lot better than that. I don't give a shit that you're a fucking cartel princess, you deserve better."

I close the distance between us, my chest meeting his and getting my face within inches of his without actually touching him.

"What I deserve," —I stab a finger into his chest— "is someone that will put me first before any cartel. What I deserve is not to be walked away from and at least given a chance to prove that I'm a strong woman who can make her own decisions." Stab. Stab. Stab. "I wasn't even yours yet and you had already put the cartel first, and I deserve better than that."

I stab my finger into his chest one more time for good measure and that must have been the last straw of irritation for him, because he grabs my hand in an iron grip.

"I was trying to protect you." He growls out through gritted teeth, slightly pulling me closer to his body.

"I don't need fucking protection."

If he wants to growl, I can growl ten times louder.

The grip on my hand grows and the distance between our bodies closes.

We are the closest that we have ever been to each other.

I look into his eyes and get lost for a second, then I do something that I've been wanting to do since I was fourteen.

I kiss this man.

I kiss the man that I have been wanting to own my heart.

I kiss him, like I already handed it over.

9

SANTOS

I don't know how we got here.

Was it the confession as to why I wanted nothing to do with her?

Was it the anger in her eyes as she tried to get her point across?

Or was it the passion that was radiating off her body when she told me what she deserved and that she didn't need protection?

I don't know what the hell it was that got us here but there is no way in hell that I'm putting a stop to it.

This is a moment that I have waited on for years and I'm not letting it slip from my grasp.

Her mouth is sweet.

Her curves feel amazing against my palms.

The skin that's exposed is just as soft as I dreamt it would be.

"Tell me to stop," I say against her lips, my tongue dancing along hers.

"No," she's able to mutter out the word, all the while taking my bottom lip between her teeth.

My hands travel down from her waist to her ass. Her globes feel perfect in my palms, and I grip them as tight as I can to bring her body closer to mine.

"Tell. Me to. Stop." I grind her body against mine, the height difference helping me out when I lift her off the ground.

"No," again my bottom lip gets nipped at the word.

Whatever fierceness that she has in this curvaceous body of hers, is coming out as the seconds go on and I fucking love it.

I love pushing her buttons, and if this is the side of her that I get when I do, then I will continue doing it.

Lifting her up more, I give her enough leverage to wrap her legs around my waist, the dress that she is wearing getting pushed up and exposing her legs.

Fuck.

"You look beautiful tonight." My lips leave hers and travel down her jaw to her neck, sucking on any open skin that I can.

The second I saw her walk out onto the courtyard, she took my fucking breath away.

Her body was covered in a black silk material that accentuates every inch of her. Her hair was tied back, and she looked like the perfect symbol of a woman.

I wasn't the only one that saw her though, her father's men that filled the courtyard also saw her. I saw it in their faces that they were thinking perverted thoughts about their boss's daughter.

My taking her away from that party might have also been because of them.

"I didn't think you would notice," she sounds breathless and the way her hips are grinding against me. She wants more of whatever it is we are doing.

"I noticed." I place my lips on the space where her neck meets behind her ear and suck. I create a vacuum seal against her skin, ultimately leaving my mark. "I notice every fucking thing about you."

"I doubt that."

Isabella continues to grind her little body against me, giving me the opportunity to feel the heat coming from her pussy against my hardening dick.

"*Bella*." the fact that she doesn't believe me angers me. "There is nothing about you that I don't know."

The grip I have on her ass tightens, to the point that she lets out a yelp when my fingers dig into her skin, as I walk us over to my bed.

My lips separate from her skin for only a few seconds for me to lay her at the center of the bed before they are back to exploring every single inch of her.

"I noticed how your school skirt got shorter and shorter whenever I was around. I notice how good your body looks when you are wearing nothing but a string bikini. I notice when you cut your hair more than an inch. Noticed how you changed the way you do your makeup. Notice every piece of fabric that has covered this gorgeous body. I noticed every fucking thing about you, so don't tell me I didn't."

I don't give her the chance to say anything, I just place

my mouth on hers, harsher than necessary, and explore every inch of it that I can.

Her legs wrap around my waist again, one of her hands lands in my hair and she brings me closer to her.

"Santiago," she pants out when I pull away.

"You're wearing too many articles of clothing." I flip her onto her stomach, heading directly for the zipper that is holding her dress together.

Sliding the zipper down, I ask. "Is this what you want?"

Inch after inch of silky-smooth skin with a caramel tint to it, is exposed.

I see no bra as the zipper continues to go down the length of her back.

Isabella hums but doesn't answer my question.

"I need words, *bella*. Is this what you want?" The zipper reaches the edge of the seam and I let the fabric fall to the sides.

Isabella flips back over and faces me. Her face filled with determination, while her eyes are filled with lust.

She sits up and lets the straps of her dress fall, exposing her top half to me.

Her tits are fucking perfect.

The perfect shape and full enough to not only fit in my hands but in my mouth.

Her nipples are already in dark peaks, asking to be devoured.

Isabella must notice where my attention is because her right hand lands on her chest. She starts massaging it, digging her fingers into the skin, doing everything that I want to do to her.

Her fingers move to her nipple, and she starts to twist and pull at it, the movement causing my cock to grow harder.

"Santiago."

The way my name leaves her mouth is as if she's moaning, and what a sweet moan it is.

I pull my gaze away from how she is playing with her chest and up to her eyes. If I thought that her eyes earlier were filled with lust, I was wrong. Her eyes are filled with so much lust and desire, I have to find something to think about to keep my composure.

She holds my stare, but I see her take her bottom lip between her teeth. I see her hand traveling from her chest down her body, caressing the material of her dress. I see as her hand meets the edge of said dress and as she drags it up to her waist.

I see as she opens her legs just wide enough for me to notice that she isn't wearing any panties.

I see as she drags a finger along the exposed skin until she meets her inner thigh.

"I want this. I've wanted this for a very long time."

Fuck.

Moving my eyes from her to where her fingers are dragging along her pussy, I start to unbutton my shirt.

"Have you touched yourself in front of someone before, *bella*?"

Say no.

Say no so that I won't have to kill the bastard that witnessed something that should be mine and only mine.

She shakes her head. "No."

I nod.

Once my shirt is open, I move to my belt.

"Touch yourself, *bella*. Open those gorgeous legs of yours and let me see you fuck your pussy. Show me what you've wanted me to do to you for so long."

A small gasp leaves her lips at my words, but she listens. Her legs open wider, her dress bunching up at the waist, her heels digging into the bed, and her pussy out for me to see.

Dark curls cover her mound and every inch of her looks mouthwatering.

Slowly, her fingers move from the edge of her thigh to her folds.

I watch as she gives herself methodical strokes, and I hear exactly what those strokes are doing to her. She's starting to pant and when she circles her clit, a small moan escapes her lips.

"Does it feel good, Isabella?" She nods.

"Does it feel good knowing that I'm watching you fuck yourself with your fingers?" Another nod.

Watching her like this has started to become unbearable, so I finally cave and unbutton my slacks so I can take myself out and give my cock a few good strokes.

Isabella's mouth goes wide as she watches me, but it certainly doesn't go as wide as her eyes do when I take myself out and continue to stroke.

"Keep playing with yourself, baby." She does as I say but doesn't take her eyes off my cock. She even goes as far as licking her lips as she watches me.

I watch as she moves her fingers, moves them through her slit and circles her clit, over and over again.

She starts to get agitated, like she wants to ask for me to touch her, but she's not brave enough to.

Wanting to put her out of her misery, I climb onto the bed and settle on my knees between her legs.

Without warning, I grab the hand she is using and bring it up to my mouth.

Her taste meets my tongue and I'm in fucking heaven.

She tastes better than I thought imaginable.

I want more

"Fuck." I drop her hand and push her forward until her head is almost to the headboard, and I'm able to situate myself with her legs over my shoulder and my mouth on her pussy.

"Oh, shit," her hand goes straight to my head, pulling at the strands, holding me to her.

"You taste so fucking good." I take her clit between my teeth, and it causes her to let out a moan that fills the room.

I lick her, I tease her, I fucking devour her. I taste every fucking inch of her pussy, savoring every single moment of it.

Massaging her thigh one more time, I move my hand and start teasing her entrance. Another moan escapes her.

She lets out a gasp when I insert a finger and start moving it.

"So fucking tight," I say against her curls, moving my hand faster.

"Oh, fuck. Fuck." Her hips buck against me, her legs pushing tighter against my head.

I continue to eat her out as she bucks and thrashes against the bed. She's getting closer to a release, so I pull my mouth away from her, and start moving my fingers faster and harder.

"Come, Isabella." I press a hand against her stomach to hold her down and move the other.

"Santiago!"

"Come, *bella*." I growl and that was the trigger point because soon Isabella is holding my fingers as tightly as possible, her orgasm taking over.

"Oh my god." Her eyes are closed tightly, and her chest is moving up and down rapidly. I kiss up her body, helping her come down from the high.

After a few minutes, I finally pull away from her and take my fingers out of her. I'm about to put my hand in my mouth to lick away her release, when I notice specks of red.

They are bright and small, but I know it's blood. I've seen enough blood in my life to know it when I see it.

Was I too rough with her?

I don't think I was, unless...

"Are you a virgin, Isabella?"

Here I am on my bed with my cock out, between Isabella's legs and her pussy only a few inches away, and only now I'm asking this question.

I take my attention away from my hand to the woman bare in front of me.

All the lust that was there before isn't there anymore, fear is now in its place.

I don't say anything, I just wait for her to answer.

Finally, she nods.

Why did I think that she had been with someone before?

"Has anyone ever touched you before like I just did?" This time, she doesn't hesitate and shakes her head once again.

I nod, not saying anything.

"Are you mad?" Her voice is small and she sounds nothing like the woman that she is. Like the woman that was stabbing me with her finger earlier.

Am I mad?

No.

Do I wish I had known so that I could've been gentler with her?

Yes.

I don't answer her question, instead I bring my hand back to my mouth and lick it clean. Blood and fucking all.

After there is no sign left of her release, I lean forward and place my lips against hers, giving her a taste of herself.

"I'm only mad that I wasn't gentler with you," I say against her lips.

The shaking of her head is what makes me pull away. "I don't want you to be gentle. I want everything you have to offer."

"Isabella," I start to say but she stops me.

"No Santiago. I want everything."

Everything.

She wants everything.

Do I give it to her?

I don't even have to ask. I already know the answer to that question.

"You can have everything you want." It's a fucking promise that I seal with another kiss on her lips.

That's how we stay for a little while. Tangled around each other, kissing, groping, grinding. Everything you can think of that is an intimate action without sex, we are doing it.

Finally, I pull away, place my forehead against hers and breathe in everything that she is giving me.

"Are you sure you want to do this?" I don't want to push her into anything she doesn't want to do or rush her into a decision she might regret.

She nods. "There's a reason my virginity is still intact. I was waiting for you."

Not the words that I expected her to say.

It's a tall order, but I would give this woman whatever she wanted in the world.

I respond by kissing her again. I kiss with all that I can, so that I can show her that she means everything. She has always meant everything, even through the countless other women that have come around. It was always Isabella Morales that has always stood out. Now I have her in my arms.

When she is panting and squirming under me, I pull away only for a second to grab a condom from the nightstand.

Before putting it on, I rid us of all clothing that is in the way. The thought of leaving Isabella's heels on crosses my mind but after a few seconds, I decide to leave that for another night.

Finally, we are unclothed, with the condom on, and Isabella is under me as I look into her eyes.

I keep my eyes on her as I position my cock at her entrance and slide in.

There is pain coating her face as I slowly slide back out and repeat the motion until the expression is changed to one of pleasure.

I take a few seconds to control my breathing and also so that Isabella can get adjusted.

She leans up and places a kiss on my jaw. "Move."

So, I do.

I move until we are both panting. Until there is sweat dripping down my face and falling on Isabella. I move until Isabella's moans fill the room and I move until I feel her tighten around me.

And when she lets her release escape, I move until I can no longer hold it and let my own release go.

It was fast and hungry and everything that a woman's first time shouldn't be, but I will have to make it up to her.

We kiss some more and when I finally pull out of her, I see the blood. Without thinking, I take Isabella in my arms and walk her over to the bathroom. I get a hot shower going and wash away all evidence that her innocence is no longer intact.

After our shower, we head back to the bedroom and lie in bed until sleep takes over.

At least sleep is able to come for Isabella, for me

though, it was a long dark night overthinking more shit than I needed to.

It didn't help that every time I checked my phone while Isabella slept in my arms, there was a new message from one of Ronaldo's men talking about a new run.

A run that I'm supposed to be on.

I have one of the biggest drug runs in my life in a few hours. I should be preparing for it, not in bed with the kingpin's daughter.

This is why I put space between Isabella and me. Because instead of thinking of all the things I could be doing to her body when she wakes up, I'm thinking about how to make it out of this drug run alive.

I've made a lot of bad decisions in my life, and this might be the worst of them. I have a piece of Isabella that no other man will have and I'm going to ruin our night together when she finally wakes up.

It's for her own good.

The daylight comes too soon.

I want to be here when she wakes up, but I have to go. I have to go do cartel business.

After getting out of bed without waking her and getting dressed, I stand at the foot of the bed, looking at the beauty still tangled in the sheets.

I've wanted this for so long and I'm about to destroy it.

All because I'm choosing the cartel over her.

My phone dings once more, signaling that it's time for me to go.

I let out a sigh and walk over to the side of the bed that Isabella is on.

Leaning down, I place a gentle kiss on her lips.

She's going to hate me more than she did before, but this is what's best for her.

Isabella deserves more than a man that is dedicated to the cartel.

I just hope that one day she's able to find him.

10

ISABELLA

Twenty-Two Years Old

Life works in mysterious ways.

There can be curveball after curveball thrown in your direction or it can be as calm as the water in a lake.

For me, it feels like there has been a magnitude of curveballs thrown in my direction.

When I was younger, I used to think that my mother was killed because of something that I did. To this day, I still think that if I hadn't wanted to go to the fabric store so badly, then she would still be alive. Then there are days where I think that all the blame for my mother's death should fall on my father and my father alone.

If he wasn't so power-hungry and didn't have people after him or angry at him, then maybe she would still be alive.

This might make me twisted and a bit sadistic, but I

sometimes think that my life would have been better if it was my father in the ground instead of her.

Then I would have my mother to talk to.

Then the cartel wouldn't exists.

Then maybe I would be able to be with the man that I gave everything to.

Four years.

It's been four years since the faithful night of my graduation. Four years since I gave my virginity away to the one man that I thought would cherish it.

Four years since I had the best night of my life and woke up in a bed alone without even a note left behind.

That morning broke me into a million pieces. I sat there, in an empty bed, completely nude, surrounded by his scent, and cried.

Cried because he wasn't there.

Cried because in my head, it didn't mean anything to him.

Cried because I knew where he was, knew what he had chosen instead of me.

How did I know?

How exactly did I know that he had chosen the cartel over me? Because a few days earlier, I overheard my father and Cristiano talking about it. Talking about the logistics of the run and how Santos was the only one that could get the job done.

A part of me hoped when I fell asleep that night that he wouldn't go. I hoped that when I woke up, he would be there with me, and we would finally be whatever the hell we were fighting all those years prior.

But I was wrong.

And it fucking broke me.

It was after I left that room that I decided that I was never going to let any man make me feel that way again.

Not my father.

Not my brother.

Certainly not Santiago.

With my shoulders squared back and with my head held high, I did everything that was best for me and only me.

That's why a week after my graduation, I packed my bags and left my father's estate and headed to Austin. I needed to take the reins of my life and I had to do that outside of my father and the cartel and away from Santos, as I now refer to him.

Because Santiago is special to me, and Santos is not.

So I left. Of course, my father and my siblings fought me on it, and it hurt me so much to leave Camila, but I had to do it. It was the only way I was going to be able to find myself.

Austin was a compromise with Leo. It was far enough away from my father but close enough to him to be there if I needed him. I was okay with that. The University of Austin had an amazing fashion design department, so I was okay with calling Austin home.

Leo was able to find me an apartment and a car, and within a few weeks' time, I was set.

All without hearing a word from Santos.

That doesn't mean that he didn't try, I just wasn't strong enough to listen.

I was starting a new chapter in my life, I needed to put him behind me.

The first year outside of the walls of my childhood home was rough. It took some time for me to adjust to classes and to life in the city. It was different and I wasn't used to it. I also wasn't used to not having the constant protection that my father's men offered. It was scary but I was able to handle it.

By my second year in Austin, I was finding my footing and was even able to make a few friends. Friends that I could talk mundane things to and hang out with. It was nice to have people outside of my family that I could depend on.

My third year, I was fucking striving. My grades were up, and I was excelling at every single design that was put in front of me. I was even able to have Camila come visit me almost every month for some sister bonding time.

My last year though, that was my best year yet. I was at the top of my class and was able to take on two internships.

Now, I have a bachelor's degree in my back pocket and I'm currently standing in front of a boutique in Austin that is looking for an in-house designer.

I did something that my mother would be proud of.

I'm putting to use everything that she has taught me, and I couldn't be happier.

Closing my eyes, I face the sky and just take a deep breath.

Lo hice, Mamí, lo hice.

A smile forms on my face.

Eeeekk!!

Oh my god, this is really happening!

Okay, Isabella. Take a deep breath, you do not want to scare away the person who might be your future boss.

I take a couple deep breaths and try to center myself as best as I can.

I can do this. I can do this.

Squaring my shoulders, and I start to walk toward the door when I hear my phone ring in my bag.

Checking the time on my wrist, I see that I have enough time to see who it is. Pulling out my phone, I turn off the ringer and see who's calling.

Camila's name shines on the caller ID. She's probably calling to wish me good luck with this interview. Either that or to talk about something. I ignore it, I'll call her as soon as I'm done. My mind needs to be clear right now, and my sister is a talker, so calling her later is for the best.

After turning off my phone, and putting it back in my purse I head straight to the boutique.

My hand is slightly shaking when I reach for the door but my nerves calm down when I see a bubbly smile staring at me from behind the counter.

"You must be Isabella." The woman from behind the counter, the one with the bubbly smile, says.

"Yes. That is me." Her smile is infectious, I can't help but give her a bright smile in return as we meet halfway to shake hands.

"It's nice to finally meet you. I've been looking forward to meeting you all day. Especially with your designs."

Did you hear that? She was looking forward to meeting me!

"It's a pleasure meeting you as well. I've been excited since you called last week. I'm happy that you liked my designs that much." I try to keep my voice as level as possible, but the giddiness is trying to slip out.

No way am I going to scare this woman away. She is my ticket to making a name for myself.

"Liked? Honey, no. I absolutely loved them. I saw them and my mind was already planning ways to incorporate them next season."

I think I might love this woman.

"Well, I hope that you feel the same way with the ones I brought with me today." Fingers crossed.

"Why don't we go to my office, where we can talk more about this position, and you can show them to me." I don't know how it was possible, but her smile grows even more.

I nod, trying my hardest to contain my excitement. "That would be great."

Not even five minutes since I walked in, and I have a feeling that this will be the best interview that I will ever have.

I freaking love it.

"I KNOW YOU JUST GRADUATED, so you must be looking forward to some free time. So, how do you feel about starting the first of next month? Give yourself somewhat of a summer before you jump right into the grind. How does that sound?"

I'm already nodding before she can even finish getting the words out.

"I can most definitely be here the first of next month." I feel like jumping up and down, but I hold it in.

"Great. Welcome to the team, Isabella." Belinda, the owner and who I just interviewed with, says. A smile still on her face.

"Thank you so much for the opportunity. I promise that I won't let you down." I shake her hand once again.

"I have no doubt that you will be a great addition to the team."

And with that, I'm free to go and free to jump around without my now new boss getting tempted to fire me.

I'm able to make it to my car before the smile I have on my face finally causes an explosion through my whole body.

I can't believe that just happened.

I just got a job as an in-house designer, at twenty-two. That is crazy.

Mamí, I'm going to be making dresses for a living. Tears start to form in my eyes, wishing she was actually here for me to share this with her.

She would have been so proud, so happy to see that I turned something that I did with her into something I absolutely love.

The first dress that I make for the boutique, I will honor my mother with it.

I wipe the tears away and then remember that Camila called me earlier.

I should call her back. She's going to freak out when I tell her I got the job.

Pulling out my phone from the bottom of the purse, I turn it on and wait for my reception to come back on.

When it does, I'm surprised by the number of missed calls that come through with Camila's name. She must have been super excited to talk to me.

Or something is wrong.

I shake that thought out of my head and hit her name and wait for Cam to pick up her phone.

"Isabella?" She finally answers after the fourth ring.

"Hey, sorry I didn't answer earlier. I was about to walk into my interview, but guess what? I got the job! You are now talking to the new in-house designer at Boutique B! Isn't that awesome?"

I squeal into the phone.

"Isabella." My sister's voice comes through the phone and instantly all the joy that I was feeling flushes out of my body.

This is why she called so much.

"What happened?" Something is wrong, I can feel it in my gut.

Camila lets out a sob and I want to reach through the phone and just hold her. I don't say a word, just wait for her to speak.

"Cristiano Reyes was killed this morning."

11

SANTOS

DEATH IS a hard pill to swallow.

An even harder one when you witness it firsthand and there's not a fucking thing that you can do about it.

You can't pull out your gun fast enough.

You can't run over to the person falling to the ground, with a pool of blood forming at their chest, because you feel numbness over what you just witnessed.

You can't do a fucking thing but hold your dying father in your arms and pray to any God that would listen to save him and to take you instead.

But that's exactly what I did.

I witnessed my father get shot right in front of me and I couldn't react fast enough, and because of that, he's dead.

I watched as all the life left his body. I heard the words he said telling me to do anything to stay alive and keep my mother safe.

Watching him die the way he did, was the hardest

fucking thing I'd ever done in my life. No matter how hard I screamed or cried, nothing was going to bring him back.

But just because he's not coming back, that doesn't mean that I can't go after the fucking bastards that took my father away from me.

I don't give a shit how much blood I will have on my hands, but I will find the cowards that shot the bullet, and I will make them pay with a slow tortured death.

"*Té vas a matar.*" You're going to kill yourself. Leo's words come, taking me out of the bloodthirsty headspace that I'm in.

I look up from the screen that is currently taking all my attention, to my friend.

It's been nearly ten hours since I held my dead father in my arms. Eight hours since I had to go to my mother and tell her that the love of her life was dead and I didn't save him. Four hours since I started looking through all the camera footage that I could find to track down who the murderer is.

"If you were older and had the resources we have now, you would have done the same thing when Rosa Maria was killed."

If it wasn't for Ronaldo stepping in and putting a stop to Leo's crusade of finding his mother's killer, he would probably be in a box six feet under right now.

"I would have, but his body isn't even cold. Put this shit on the back burner and go be with your mom."

He's right.

My mom needs me right now, more than anything.

But I can't seem to move away from the screen.

I shake my head. "I need to do this. I need to find the fucking bastards."

"You will and I'll fucking help you, but right now there are other things that are more important." He's getting angry at me, I can hear it, that still doesn't make me stop.

"Let me do this. Just for tonight. Come the morning, I will take care of everything else."

I look at my friend, practically begging with my eyes for him to let me do this.

Things were different for me than they were for him when it came to my father.

I actually had a relationship with him.

My father respected me, he fucking loved me.

Those are things that Leo doesn't have with Ronaldo.

After a long second though, he finally nods, giving me this one thing.

I throw a silent 'thank you' in his direction and go back to the task at hand, finding the bastards that killed my father.

For the next two hours or so, I go through every piece of security footage that I have found from the truck stop we were at this morning.

We were doing a run.

It was one of the first runs that he and I had done together in a while.

Everything was going as planned. We had successfully moved a truck from a warehouse we have in Austin, filled with Colombian cocaine. Five thousand kilos were on their way to be sold and my dad and I were headed back to Austin so that he could come back to San Pedro.

The only logical explanation that I have is that we were being followed. That's the only way the gunmen knew where to find us. Where we were vulnerable. They were probably waiting for the right moment to go through whatever they had planned.

Mine and my father's plan after dropping off the shipment, was to drive through to Austin. But the gas gauge on the box truck we had was giving us trouble, so we needed to pull off.

It was supposed to be just ten minutes.

Ten minutes and we would be back on the road.

We weren't even there for ten minutes before the shots started to ring out.

They took me by surprise, and when I turned, I knew my reaction time was too slow.

My father was already falling to the ground.

Blood was coating the asphalt.

I couldn't comprehend a thing, and when I finally did, I ran over to him. I held his body as tightly as I could, trying to stop the blood from escaping.

For a few minutes, I thought that it was going to be okay. He was speaking, but his eyes wouldn't stay open.

When I felt his body go limp, that was when I knew he was gone.

Police arrived after that.

Followed by the paramedics, but they were too late.

I was questioned about every last detail.

Did I see who did it? No.

Did you hear a car drive off? I wasn't paying attention. Thank you for reminding me that I need to be vigilant at all fucking times.

Whose truck is this? My father's.

Who was driving? I was.

Were you hit? No, only him.

It felt like hours were spent there, answering question after question from the police. At one point when they were loading my father's body to be taken away, I told them to fuck off.

Pendejos.

And they did, but only for a moment. They will come back to ask questions. I know they will. Especially when it comes to light that Cristiano Reyes had cartel ties.

Somehow through all the shit I was able to call Leo and he was there in no time.

Now we're combing through video after video trying to find something, anything.

All the footage from the truck stop is showing us nothing, and the only thing that we see is the aftermath of this morning.

After two more hours of looking, we move from footage of the shooting to any footage we can find of the truck and who might be following us.

"Dark-gray suburban." Leo points out the vehicle on the TV screen that we currently have playing all the videos.

I look at the other videos from last night. At every location that the truck passed that had a camera, the suburban passes a few seconds later.

"Motherfuckers!" I grab the nearest object and throw it against the window.

"How? How the actual fuck did I miss this?!"

"You're not going to notice everything." Leo is trying to calm me down but fuck that.

"We have been trained to notice every single thing. Feds, other cartels, everything. How the fuck did I miss a fucking Suburban following us?"

This shit doesn't make sense.

How can I be so blind?

We were tailed from the second we left the drop-off point. I should have noticed something.

"Maybe Cristiano noticed. Maybe he noticed and that's why he made you stop. He knew what was coming."

He would have told me if that was the case.

Wouldn't he?

Not if he thought that you were in danger.

Did he risk his life, in order to save mine?

"Go to your mom, be with her. We'll deal with this in the morning."

If I do this in the morning, or right now, it will only have the same outcome.

But he's right, I have to go be with my mom.

The woman just lost her husband and I haven't been with her all day.

I nod, all my emotions finally fighting to get the best of me. "Thanks, *hermano.*"

Leo nods. "Whatever you need, I'll be there. Cristiano

was a lot more of a father to me than Ronaldo ever will be."

The father he needed at times. He doesn't have to voice it for me to know that he is just as fucked up by this as I am.

But we're cartel men, we don't show emotions.

Without a final word, I walk out of the room and head to my mother's quarters.

Yesterday I was having dinner with both my parents before we left, and now I'm about to console one for the loss of the other.

A fucked-up world we live in.

When I reach my mother's room, it's silent. The screams of agony that I expected to hear, are nowhere to be found.

Pushing the door open as quietly as possible, I look inside the room to find my mother lying on her bed, wearing one of my dad's shirts, sound asleep.

The day's events must have finally caught up to her if she found sleep.

I walk into the room and grab the blanket at the foot of the bed and place it over her small body.

Her small stature was always something my dad made fun of. He was six-three, and she was four-eleven, and he couldn't figure out how they came together.

I tuck the blanket in at her sides and lean down to place a kiss on her forehead.

"*Duerme, Mamá. Dile a Papá que tanto lo quieres en tus sueños.*"

Tomorrow the sorrow and the screams of agony will

most likely make an appearance, hopefully she gets all the sleep she deserves.

I leave the bedroom and head straight to the kitchen, where I know the liquor is kept. I need something to keep myself from wanting to do more research on the dark-gray SUV.

Grabbing the fullest bottle of tequila that I could find, I leave my parents' part of the estate and head out to the garden. One of Rosa Maria's pride and joy.

I find a bench and just look up at the sky.

It's once I'm surrounded by the darkness, with a bottle in my hand, that I finally let all the emotions that I have building inside of me flow.

The tears come out in an angry rage, and I'm not doing anything to stop them.

I lost my father.

The one person that made sure I had a good life and made me into the man that I am today is gone.

The man that showed me how to shoot a gun and to defend myself is no longer on this earth breathing and laughing through his day.

The individual that I respected more than anything in this fucked-up world will no longer walk it again.

He warned me about this before. When Rosa Maria died, he told me that death can unexpectedly happen to anyone. That's why every time I went on a drug run, he would tell me he loved me and to stay safe and be vigilant.

Of course, I didn't follow the last part when he was with me. I wasn't vigilant enough. If I was, he would still be here.

Fuck this world.

I place the opening of the bottle to my mouth and let the liquid flow down my throat, living for the burn it brings.

I don't know how long I sit there drinking the pain away, but it's dark and the crickets are out chirping.

The sound of the crickets isn't loud enough for me not to hear the footsteps approaching.

They are light and approaching cautiously. I don't look up to see who it is, but when the individual gets closer and I catch the scent of their perfume, I know exactly who is here with me.

The princess has finally returned to her kingdom. It only took a tragedy to get her here.

A squeak leaves the bench when she sits down. She takes the space on one side of the bench while I take the other. We sit there in silence, neither of us saying a word.

I haven't spoken or seen much of Isabella since that fateful night she gave herself over to me. And it was for her own good.

"This is what I meant about protecting you." I break the silence before taking another drink from the bottle.

I was protecting her from a lot of things.

Myself.

The drugs.

The enemies.

Death.

"I know." Her voice is like sweet nectar that adds to the pain.

We go back to sitting in silence.

There is so much I want to say to her, but right now is not the right time to say them.

"Santos?" I close my eyes when I hear the name. Never has Isabella called me Santos, not even when she hated me. Hearing it now tells me just how much I broke her and how much anger she might hold towards me.

"Yeah?"

A hand lands on my forearm and gives me a squeeze. "I'm so fucking sorry. Cristiano deserved more."

Out of everything that has happened today, those last three words are what break me.

Cristiano deserved more.

I no longer am able to hold the tears at bay and a sob escapes.

Isabella's arms wrap around my shoulders, and she holds me as I cry over my father.

I hold her arm closest to me with so much tightness it no doubt will leave a bruise.

We both cry for the man that we knew and cry out the pain that comes with losing someone so close to you. Not only are tears shed for my dad but for Rosa Maria as well. They are tears for two parents that should be here.

We sit there for a while, until we are both finally able to compose ourselves but don't let each other go.

"Isabella?"

"Yeah?"

"I'm so fucking sorry I left you that morning."

More silence follows the words. They needed to be said. Maybe if I hadn't left, today wouldn't have happened.

Maybe my father would still be alive.

Maybe if I had stayed, I would gone to him and we would have figured out a way out of this life together.

Maybe if...

I can't go back and change it now.

"I know."

12

ISABELLA

I KNOW the pain that comes with losing a parent. It's one of the most unbearable things that someone can go through. Especially if the parent was taken away in such a gruesome fashion.

When I finally digested the words that Camila sobbed through the phone about Cristiano's murder, I drove down to San Pedro right away.

I could have stayed in Austin, but every part of me needed to see how Santos was doing. Not only him though, but his mom as well.

After my mother died, Amelia Reyes stepped up as a mother figure for me and Camila. She was there in those moments when we really needed a mother. She guided us in a way that my father never would have. We spent countless hours and days with her, it felt like we were her own children at times.

It was during that time that I saw just how much love

Amelia had for her husband and how much her husband cared for her.

Cristiano treated her like a queen and my first thought after thinking about how her son was doing with this was how hard did the news must have hit her.

She loved that man more than her heart would allow and I couldn't imagine what she was going through.

My relationship with Cristiano was something similar to the one I had with Amelia. He was like a second father to me and my siblings. When my father wasn't around, he was. He always made sure we were taken care of and protected and never looked at us just as his boss's kids. He also treated us like we were his and showed us what a father's love should feel like without being our father.

The whole ride to San Pedro, all I could do was think about a conversation I had with Cristiano when I decided to move to Austin.

"Austin va a estar bien para ti." Cristiano's voice fills the room as I fold the last of my T-shirts.

I turn to find the man leaning against the doorframe, as if he doesn't have any other important things to do.

"Do you really think that? That Austin would be a good fit?"

I've been having my doubts all week. Austin is a big city, and I can't help but think this move is a mistake.

Cristiano nods before giving me a smile. "I do. You're too big of a force to be held in place here in San Pedro. You need something better and bigger, and I think Austin will be able to give you that."

I smile at his words.

Finally, someone that supports this decision. Leo and my dad haven't been seeing the bigger picture of it all, they just complain and complain about the whole thing.

"Thank you. I really needed to hear that." *I give him a smile as I put a folded T-shirt in the suitcase.*

He nods and looks like he is about to leave but he surprises me when he steps into the room, comes over to me and places a hand on my shoulder.

"Build yourself up to be the person you want to be, Isabella. Don't let any person, any man, even my son, bring you down." *Another squeeze to my shoulder and Cristiano steps back to leave the room.*

I'm left standing there in shock.

How...?

"H-how did you know about...?"

Did Santiago tell his father that we were together for one night?

That has to be the only way he knows, right?

Cristiano stops at the doorway and looks back to me, a small smile playing at the corner of his lips.

"I've seen the way that my son has looked at you for a few years now, Isabella. I'm not blind. I also might have seen the two of you sneak off the night of your party. It didn't take much to put the two things together when I saw him the next morning and then you decided to leave. Mis disculpas por sus acciones."

He's apologizing for his son.

I can't form a response, so all I do is stand there and give him a smile, silently telling him that I appreciated it.

That day played over and over in my head so many

times that by the time I crossed the border to San Pedro, and arrived at my father's estate, I wanted to run out of the car and go find Cristiano. I wanted to tell him that it was because of that conversation that I started to forgive Santos little by little.

But of course, I couldn't, because he wasn't there.

It hit me like a ton of bricks, and instead of going to find Cristiano, I went to look for Amelia. I half expected her to be surrounded by people, by her son, but the only other person I found with her was Camila.

I spent hours with the two of them and helped console Amelia as much as I possibly could. Eventually she fell asleep, and Cam and I let her be.

After crying our own tears when we headed back to our side of the estate, I was supposed to fall asleep, but that didn't happen. So I went for a walk.

That's when I heard the silent cries.

I turned the corner and saw Santos sitting there by himself, crying into a bottle of tequila.

Without thinking about it, I went to him.

It took a few years to think about fully forgiving him but when I saw him break over his father, I couldn't hold any more anger toward him.

I held him in my arms as tight as I could and shed my own tears when I heard just how deep his pain was.

That was hours ago, now I'm currently lying on a bed, on top of the covers, looking at the boy that held me when my own mother died, as he sleeps

He looks peaceful and much older than he looked the last time I saw him.

I shouldn't be here, especially after everything that happened when I last stepped into this room. But I couldn't leave him.

He was drunk and mourning and shouldn't have been alone, so I stayed.

As I watch his chest rise with every single breath he takes, I contemplate leaving more and more.

I'm almost done convincing myself to leave this bed when he shifts and turns to face me. His eyes finding me right away, holding me still and anchoring me to the mattress.

"*Buenos días.*" His voice is filled with sleep and reminds me of everything that I ever loved about this man.

"Good morning." I tuck my hands under the pillow and just look at him.

There are dark bags under his eyes which makes it seem like he could sleep for a few more hours.

"You stayed." It's not a question.

I give him a small nod. "I wanted to make sure that you were okay. I also thought that you shouldn't be alone."

He continues to look at me, not saying anything, not moving. His eyes just continue to bore into mine. Finally, after what feels like an eternity, he shifts and a hand lands between us. With his eyes, he silently asks for me to take it.

I hesitate for a second but ultimately place my hand in his.

"Thank you for being here." His rough palm meets mine and like that night many years ago, I marvel at the feel of it against my skin.

I give his hand a squeeze. "You've always said that

you'd be there for me. This is me being there for you." I leave out the part where I want to say that I will always be there for him.

I would though. Given everything that we have been through together, I would be there for him in a heartbeat for however long that he needed.

Santos closes his eyes and holds my hand tighter. "I've fucked up so much when it comes to you."

He has.

But if he hadn't, would I be the woman that I am today? Would I have gone to Austin and gotten my degree, and been able to get the position that I did?

No.

Because my world revolved so much around wanting to be with this man that I didn't realize how fighting to be with him would have changed the person that I needed and wanted to be.

"We were both young," I squeeze his hand back. "I don't think that either of us knew what we wanted or needed at the time."

Santos shifts so that he's lying on his back, still with my hand in his.

"I knew what I wanted," he says up to the ceiling, pausing before he continues. "I still know what I want. You."

When he turns his head to face me again, I see the sincerity of his words in his eyes.

It renders me speechless for a moment but finally I'm able to shake my head and form words.

"You don't mean that." I'm sure that he has been with plenty of women these last few years that I don't even compare to.

"I do. I meant it all those years ago when I told you that I was going to make you mine, and I mean it when I say I want you now."

He's mourning.

That's the only reason he is saying these words.

But he sounds so sure. How can that be?

We were in high school when he first let his feelings be known. We haven't so much as been on a date or anything like that, so how can he be so sure that he wants me and wants to be with me?

How do you know you wanted to be with him?

I don't know. When it came to him, there was always something about the way he presented himself that I was attracted to and felt pulled in by.

Is that how he felt about me?

"You probably only think that you want me because I'm Leo's sister and you have known me my whole life."

The thought of him thinking about me as a sister has always been something that I thought about, much more after we slept together.

Did he leave because he realized I was like a sister to him?

"I haven't thought of you as Leo's little sister in a very long time. You are a lot more than just his sister." His eyes are bright and there is this warm gold color that pops out with the morning sunlight.

A color I wish I could see every single morning for years to come.

"Why are you telling me all this?" I involuntarily scoot closer to him, my body mere inches from his. I'm close enough that I can feel his heat, and by the way his grip on my hand grows, he can feel mine too.

He lets out a long sigh and I watch as he closes his eyes again.

"I guess it took losing my dad for me to realize that there are a lot of things in this world that I don't want to lose. One of those things being you."

Words that I've wanted to hear since I was sixteen.

"I don't want to lose you either." My voice is small but it's loud enough for the words to mean something.

He shifts, letting go of my hand and wrapping his around my shoulder, bringing me closer to his body.

We lie intertwined like this for a few minutes. The only noise filling the room is our breathing.

"Everything in me is telling me that I should walk away from you forever and let you live."

I press my head deeper into his chest, listening to his heartbeat. Feeling his words vibrate through his chest as he speaks them.

"I don't want you to walk away."

It's the best time as any to put my heart on the line, right?

"What do you suggest then? I don't want you to suffer like my mother currently is. You deserve a whole lot more than that."

I untangle myself from his body and sit up on the bed and look down at him.

"Amelia made that choice when she met your father. My mother made the same one. Let me make mine. You've left me before because you were protecting me from this life, because I deserved better. Well, guess what? This is the only life that I have known. If I want to be with someone that is part of the cartel, then I will, because that's my choice. And if that choice comes to bite me in the ass, then so be it. I will suffer the consequences, just as long as I get to be with you. Because guess what Santiago, I love you. I've loved you since I was sixteen. I loved you when I was supposed to hate you and I still love you now. So, if you want to walk away, fine, walk away, but know that if you walk away on last time, I don't know just how much longer my love for you will be intact. Because you're right, I do deserve better. Now I just need to know if you are going to give it to me."

My chest feels like it's on fire from my confession, but every single word needed to be said. He needs to know how I feel and where I stand.

Santos sits up, scooting closer to me, his nose almost touching mine. I can feel his breath against my lips, almost as if it were a whisper of a kiss.

My gaze stays with his as he leans in and places a chaste kiss on my lips.

It starts off sweet and slow but then after a few seconds, his hands land on my hips and I'm straddling him. His tongue is sweeping across my lower lip, asking for entry. I happily open up and marvel at the feeling of his mouth on mine and his hands on my body.

He pulls back slightly, placing his forehead against mine. "I love you too."

I can't help but smile at his words and place another kiss against his lips.

When we pull apart, there is one uncertainty that is stopping me from continuing with the moment.

My father.

"If we are going to be together, we have to figure out a way tell my father." I cringe slightly at the words.

It's not something that sounds like a joyful experience.

Santiago nods and lets out a sigh. "He won't approve. He will most likely have me killed."

It may seem drastic but there's a possibility of it happening.

I think about the scenario. One where we go to my father, and I tell him that I'm stepping into a relationship with one of his men.

If I'm being honest with myself, it's not something that I really want to do.

So what if…?

"What if we don't tell him?"

"Isabella." he starts but I hold my hand up stopping him.

"No, he doesn't have to know. We don't have to tell anyone. It could just be between the two of us for a little bit."

His grip on my hip tightens and I'm sure if he wanted to, he would roll his eyes at my suggestion.

"For how long? How long do we keep it a secret? Until we're thinking of marriage? When we start thinking about having kids?"

"You want to have kids with me?" I give him a smile, really liking the idea of having a baby with his eyes.

This time, he does rolls his eyes. "I thought that was a given."

I press my lips back on his and give him a bright smile when I pull back but the smile doesn't last long.

Because he's right, of course he's right.

"We'll tell him when we think it's the right time. When the both of us know exactly what's going on between us. For right now, I just want to be with you for a little while and not let my father, or even my brother, interfere."

"Keeping this from Ronaldo will be easy. Your brother, on the other hand, that will be hard."

I nod. "I know but I think we can do it."

He stays silent for a little bit, just moving his hand up and down my hips, finally he breaks the quietness of the room.

"Are you sure this is what you want? You want to hide this?"

No, I want to scream it off the roof of this estate that this man is officially mine, but this is the best option for the both of us right now.

My father will hate it no matter when we tell him.

And given that his father only died twenty-four hours ago, he needs to be in the right mind set to have a conversation with the kingpin regarding his daughter.

I nod. "Yes, I want this. I want this with you."

"Then you can have it."

He seals the deal with a kiss, and before long, we are getting lost in each other, but only for a few minutes.

Only enough to forget about the pain that is going to come once we leave this room.

13

SANTOS

Twenty-Eight Years Old

THE DARKEST DAYS of my life were the days that came after my father's murder. And I say murder because that's what happened. He was murdered. It was an act of violence that was meant to send a message.

Well message fucking received.

The funeral was two weeks after the shooting, all because the Criminal Investigation Division comprised of Texas Department of Public Safety special agents wanted to conduct a thorough investigation. After two weeks, they concluded it was a random act of violence, and released my father's body to my mother.

Random act, my fucking ass. There was nothing random about it.

But I didn't question them on it.

One, because my mother was in pain and I wasn't

going to drag it out anymore for her to suffer, and two, I would find the *pinche pendejos* myself.

So, I stood at my father's funeral with my crying mother at my side, and acted as if I didn't give a shit who shot her husband down.

After the funeral, the only thing holding me together was Isabella.

She was like an angel that fell from the sky at the right moment.

According to my mother, my dad had sent her because he didn't trust anyone else to watch over us. I might have agreed with her on that statement.

From the second we left the room, after deciding to keep whatever was going on with us a secret, she was by my side, making sure I ate and bathed. Not only did she look after me, but she looked after my mother as well, and for that, I will be eternally grateful.

As the days went by, my mom became more and more adjusted to my father's death. She smiled more, actually ate, and was able to get out of bed. The one thing that didn't stop was her falling asleep in his clothes. I asked her about it, and she told me that smelling his scent every single night was the one thing that kept the tears at bay, so I dropped the subject after that.

The one thing that really did surprised me about my mother was that three weeks after the shooting, and a week after we laid my dad to rest, she decided to move back to Canada. The woman spent nearly twenty-eight years in Mexico all because of her husband's choice of career, and now she has nothing holding her here.

I wanted to fight her on it. I wanted to tell her that I was here, she had me, but I knew where she was coming from. So, I agreed to let her go. If she felt safer in Canada, away from the cartel, then so be it.

I'm not going to lie, having my mother in another country and my father six feet under, hurt. I wasn't used to them not being around and even at twenty-four, as a grown adult, I admitted that I needed them more than anything.

The only thing that was holding me up at that point was Isabella. She was the only thing keeping me from stepping into a black hole.

The black hole of finding my father's killer.

I was able to hold myself off for a few weeks. I was able to go back to Austin and spend time with Isabella. I was able to go on runs and make deals with street level drug dealers in the city. I was able to function, but the second Isabella started her new job, all that went to shit.

Not having twenty-four-hour access to Isabella, made me go slightly insane.

At first, it was just one more look at the camera footage.

One more look turned into countless hours, and the hours quickly morphed into sleepless nights.

Every single night after Isabella fell asleep in my arms, I would leave the bed that we shared, and I searched for at least a speck of an answer.

I searched and searched until I found the speck.

It was small, so small that it took me weeks to see it, but I found it.

A hand hanging out of the window of the dark-gray

SUV. Nothing else about the individual was visible, just the one stupid-ass hand.

Nothing should be special about a hand, except that this one had black lines running all along it.

A tattoo.

I studied it. I looked at every fucking line and shape and now four years later, I would know if I saw it in person, I would be able to pick it out from far away.

Four fucking years and all I have been able to go on is a fucking tattoo.

That's how far I've gotten in finding my father's killer.

Finding more became an obsession, one that Leo had to step in to stop.

I was turning into someone completely different, and it was affecting me in my work with the cartel and my secret relationship with Isabella.

I don't know what it was, but one day I finally realized that there was more to life than getting revenge, so I stopped looking.

Not everything has been peachy, as Camila would say, but things are good.

In the time since my father's death, I've climbed up in rank within the Muertos. I'm no longer a soldier that does drug run after drug run. I call shots, I make deals and Leo and I are making the Muertos more money than anyone else before.

Not even Ronaldo himself.

I have the nice suits, the nice townhome, the sports cars, the money to take care of my mother for the rest of her life, and of course I have the beautiful girl at my side.

The only downside of having said beautiful woman is that I can't claim her as mine outside the four walls of my place.

That's right, four years later and we still haven't come clean to Ronaldo about our relationship.

You may be thinking, Santos, four years is a long time.

No shit.

I've been ready to tell Ronaldo and the whole damn world that Isabella Morales is mine, but every single time I bring it up, she tells me 'not yet.'

Not yet.

Four long-ass years and I still get a 'not yet.'

If I didn't love this woman so much, I would find her infuriating.

This whole thing is becoming harder and harder to keep behind closed doors. We each have our own place here in Austin, we aren't able to go out to dinner in public and Leo is starting to look at me funny.

It's like he knows I'm fucking his sister every night and he is planning on how to cut off my dick at his earliest convenience.

I swear, every time he enters a room, I jump just a little waiting for him to attack.

If I could tell him, I would, but of course his sister doesn't let me.

Like I said if I didn't love her so much, I would find her infuriating.

Maybe I do, slightly, but I would never voice it out loud. I like my balls too much.

But since there is a small velvet box hiding in my closet

currently burning a hole through my socks, I need to broach the subject again.

Her cuddled up in my arms, watching a Disney movie should serve as a good distraction, right?

"*Bella*?" I stroke her hair, trying to get her attention away from the TV screen.

"Hmm?" She hums against my chest, telling me that she is falling asleep.

"I'm going to call a meeting with Ronaldo." The statement must have woken her up because right away she sits up and looks down at me with a confused look.

"*¿Porqué?*"

I shrug. "I just think it's time. It's been four years, *bella*."

She just continues to look down at me, like I'm an alien or something. Her mouth is even slightly open, like she doesn't know what to say.

At least she hasn't said 'not yet.'

Isabella's mouth finally closes and opens as if to say something, but nothing comes out.

It might be best to pull all the stops here.

Shifting off the bed, I head to my closet and dig through the bottom sock drawer of the dresser I have in there. I feel around until the sensation of velvet crosses against my fingertips. The small velvet box.

Toying with it, I leave the closet and head back to the bedroom. Isabella is still sitting there, with even more confusion coating her face.

That confusion is replaced by surprise when I show her the box. Her brown eyes go wide and her mouth drops open even more.

"This is why I want to meet with him," I don't open the box, just hold it out between us. "To get his permission."

Hesitantly, she reaches for the box and I let her take it from my hand. She looks down at it like it's an explosive device or something. I can see by the look on her face she is fighting the urge to open it.

"It's okay, you can look inside," again I'm met with wide eyes, but she doesn't move to open the lid.

"You're really thinking about this?" Her voice has a shakiness to it and I can't help but give her a smile.

I nod, taking a seat next to her on the bed. "Have been thinking about it for a while. Finally bought that a few months back. I was just waiting for you to tell me it was okay to finally talk to your dad."

She looks down at the ring box one more time before shaking her head and handing it back to me.

"You should take it back then."

What the fuck?

"What do you mean, 'take it back'? Isabella, I can't just take the ring back."

"Santiago."

"No, don't 'Santiago' me." I get up from the bed and start pacing the room. I can feel the anger bubbling inside of me. "I want to marry you. Spend the rest of my life with you, however long that is. All I have to do is talk to your father, and you don't want me to? Do you really want to spend the rest of our lives together in hiding? Because that's one shit of a life."

I must have been so distracted with the pacing that I

didn't notice that she had gotten up from the bed and walked over to me.

It's her hands landing on my face that stops me in my place. I look down at the woman that took me out of all the dark places and think about how far we have come. No way am I letting her get away so easily.

"You didn't let me finish," she leans up and plants a small kiss on my lips. "I meant to say it as in, you should take the ring back and keep it safe until you have that meeting with my father."

This woman is going to give me gray hair.

"You know you should've said that, instead of trying to give me a heart attack." I place my hands on her hips and bring her body closer to mine.

She's wearing a short silk nightgown that leaves very little to the imagination. I fucking love it.

"Maybe I like it when you get all mad like that. It makes you all that much hotter." She throws her hands around my neck and starts to play with my hair.

Hair that she told me to grow out a bit because she likes running her fingers through it.

"Really?" I can feel my eyebrows raise on their own, questioning just how hot does one look when getting mad.

"Hmm," she takes her bottom lip between her teeth. Instead of thinking of releasing it and taking it between mine, I lean down and do just that.

I suck on her plump bottom lip and marvel at the sweet moans that she releases.

"What else do you like?" I move my mouth away from hers and start trailing kisses down her neck.

"I like when you get all growly and your voice gets super deep. Like it when you're on the phone working and how you sound when you're in charge. So hot."

I nip at her collarbone and pull back slightly, just to take her face between my hands.

"Do you now?" I raise an eyebrow at her and give her a smirk.

She nods, taking her bottom lip between her teeth again, but this time the lip biting is accompanied by a slight blush coating her cheeks.

My sweet innocent *bella*.

"Then maybe we should bring out that little toy that you use when I'm not around."

On the nights that I'm out doing whatever Muertos business that I'm doing, Isabella likes to tease me that she has a toy that she uses to get her through the night.

Naturally, one night while we were at her place, I looked through her drawers and found said toy. I may or may not have bought the same toy to have here.

For her to use, of course.

I may have also come home and caught her using it once or twice and she puts it away right away, but she has never used it with me right in front of her.

Now I thinking that it's time.

"You want me to use the toy? In front of you? Don't guys get jealous of that sort of thing?" She's cute when she's all flustered.

I drop my hands from her face, and move them slowly down her body, until I reach her ass and dig my fingers into her covered skin.

"The only time I'd get jealous is if there was another man near you and trying to go after what's mine." I lean down and place my mouth close to her ear, "And you are in fact mine, *bella*."

Digging my fingers deeper into her ass, I lift her up and walk us over to the bed.

She lets out a yelp as soon as she lands on the mattress, and I walk over to the nightstand on her side of the bed.

We don't live together, but a lot of her stuff is here.

I find the little silicone toy easily and test to see if it's powered.

I was gone this week to do a job in Tijuana, of course it's powered up.

"That smile you're wearing tells me that you're up to no good."

"Always, when it comes to you, *bella*."

With the toy in hand, I get on the bed, spreading Isabella's legs open and getting situated.

She is looking at me with wide eyes, a tinge of fear swimming in them but the lust is overpowering it.

"Trust me, Isabella. This will be more for your pleasure than it will be for mine. Since you said that you like it when I was in control and all."

She nods, leaning back and relaxing.

I turn on the toy, the smile that she said I was wearing growing.

Her legs are open and nothing is in the way, and I don't hesitate to put the toy on her uncovered pussy.

A sweet moan rings out over the vibrations, and I watch as she throws her head back and her eyes close.

"Tell me what you think about when you are using this." I run the little device up and down her slit, her arousal coating the silicone.

"I-I—" she stutters a bit, letting out a moan before she can let out a word.

"Tell me." I press the toy to her clit, this time I'm gifted with a whimper.

Her breathing is getting labored but she is able to speak. "I think about you." She pauses to let out a moan. "Doing things to me."

"What am I doing to you?"

"You lick me." I can do some licking right about now.

I move her nightgown farther up her body, exposing her stomach and finally her breasts.

Her glorious full tits stare back at me asking for attention, but at the moment I have more pressing things at hand.

"What else do I do?"

I move the toy from her clit down to her entrance, teasing her a bit before I move the toy farther down and circle it around her puckered hole. The second she feels it there, her eyes spring open.

"What else do I do, *bella*?" I ignore her stare and continue to move the toy, applying more pressure.

"You fuck me," she's breathless, her chest moving more rapidly.

"How do I fuck you?" I move the toy back up, covering the toy even more with her arousal. She liked the pressure she was getting.

"With your tongue." Moan. "With your fingers." Whimper. "With your cock." A tremble.

"I can do all three."

She's on the edge of combustion, I can tell by the way her legs are shaking and I haven't touched her yet.

I pull the toy away from her body and leave the bed.

"What the fuck are you doing?" she groans out.

I just give her a smirk and start to undress. "I'm in control, remember?"

I undress as slowly as possible, making her more and more impatient.

"Take the nightgown off," I order and within seconds, she whips it off and she is left sitting there completely nude.

Absolutely fucking gorgeous.

"Get on all fours." Again, she complies and her delicious ass is staring back at me as she turns to face the headboard.

I stalk over to the bed, climbing on and taking my place behind her. I want her mouth wrapped around my cock and watch as her lips form a perfect O as she takes me in, but right now I need to fuck her, so fucking her mouth will have to wait.

A loud slap rings through the room when my hand lands on her ass cheek.

"Fuck," she lets out as I smooth a hand over the red skin.

With all the foreplay, I'm all ready to go. Watching Isabella on a brink of an orgasm is a special sight that will forever be engraved in my head.

I thrust my cock a few times through her folds to coat myself, and when Isabella releases another moan, I slide into her, enthralled with how tight she feels around me. At how hot she feels wrapped around my cock.

"Fuck, *bella*. Every time with you feels better and better."

I thrust into her pussy over and over again, the movements getting closer to that edge. Leaning forward, I cover Isabella's whole back with my front, snaking an arm around to her front and rubbing circles against her clit, getting her to the edge with me.

"Santos!"

"I'm no *santo*, baby. When it comes to fucking you, I will be everything but a saint."

I grip her hips in my hands and pound into her. Pound until she can't hold herself up any longer, and her legs are shaking underneath her.

"I'm going to come." Her voice is muffled by the pillow her head is lying against, but I heard her loud and clear.

"Fucking do it. Come all over my cock. Milk me with all you have."

She pants my name out one more time before she does exactly what I told her to do. Her pussy tightens around my cock, and I can no longer keep myself together and fucking lose everything that I have inside of her.

"Fucking hell." I slide out of her and throw myself onto the side of the bed, so I don't smash her with my weight.

Isabella settles in my arms, sweat covering both of us and our breathing is erratic.

We are lying there just catching our breaths when I realize that the movie is still playing.

Great, I now have the memory of fucking Isabella while a singing fish watched us.

"Santiago?" Isabella breaks the silence and takes my mind off of the damn fish.

"*¿Si, mi amor?*"

"Do you really want to marry me?"

I smile at her question. I guess I wasn't clear enough.

Sliding down so that we are face-to-face, I take her face in my hands and plant a kiss on her pouting lips.

"With everything that I am."

Her dark brown eyes look back at me, and even in the dark, I can see the glistening of the tears wanting to come out.

"Then set up that meeting with my father."

I give her one more kiss, and once again get lost in everything that Isabella has to offer.

Come tomorrow morning, I will set up a meeting with the kingpin to ask permission to marry his oldest daughter.

Should be fun.

14

ISABELLA

Eleven Months Earlier

IT TOOK a handful of years for me to realize just how much my father dictated what I did with my life.

I guess that's what happens when you are no longer under his bubble twenty-four-seven, but even then, he still calls the shots.

For all intents and purposes, I know for a fact that I don't live or have the perfect life. I also know that the life I live is not a life that I would wish upon my greatest enemy.

There was a point in my life I thought that the world that was handed to us by my father, was something that I would be forever grateful for. Forever cherish and hold near and dear to my heart. Then I learned the truth on how and why we had the things that we did.

There wasn't anything that me and my sister couldn't ask for during our teenage years.

Clothes.

Cars.

Jewelry.

Money.

Whatever request that came out of our mouths, our father gave us. Even Leo stepped in, especially when I moved to Austin and needed a car and my own place to live.

Those men have handed us almost everything, Leo being the one to put up more of a fight, but nothing compared to the leniency of my father.

At an early age, around the time of my mother's death, I realized that the life that surrounded me was one filled with not only death but with blood as well. Add the drugs, the weapons that my family moved around, and the drug money associated with it, and it would feel like a prison at times.

Especially these last four years, when I got a much deeper look into the business that my father has perfected.

It's a dark one and makes me look at my father differently.

I'm not going to lie, there have been times in my life where I wanted to escape, I couldn't. Because no matter how hard I try, I will forever be tied to my family's name.

Not even as I draw one of my designs on paper, do I see the day when I will be able to go against my father's word and live the life that I want to live, with the person I want to live it with.

There will always be an obstacle in the way and the obstacle is my father and this cartel.

I shake my head and go back to concentrating on the design in front of me.

It's been a month since Santiago came to me and told me that he wanted to call a meeting with my father.

A month since he told me that he wanted to propose.

I was happy.

I was so freaking ecstatic that my dream of spending the rest of my life with this man was going to come true.

Then my mind reminded me that there was a reason why I was holding out on telling my father about my relationship.

Throughout the years, the jokes of him being killed and castrated were just that, jokes. A part of me though, a very big part, knew that it could happen. My father could kill him or have him killed and I wasn't going to let that happen.

So, I kept it a secret.

If I could keep it from my father forever, I would but it was the look of disappointment in Santiago's eyes and the anger that radiated off his body that convinced me not to.

I guess I should hate my father even more because he's dictating this too.

Because we're going to tell my father, I thought that it would be best for me to come to San Pedro and make it seem like I was here to spend time with him. To lessen the blow, in a way.

I asked the boutique if it was possible for me to work from home, and they agreed. So here I am in San Pedro, trying to come up with new designs and patiently wait for the day that Santos finally speaks to Ronaldo.

It's been a fucking month and still no conversation has happened.

I hear the door to the room, the room that was once my mother's old sewing safe haven and I turned into a drawing studio, open. There are only three people besides me that have access to this room.

My brother and sister.

And *Santiago*.

The boy that has occupied not only my head but my heart for as long as I can remember. My whole heart. Of course, I would give him access to my safe space.

As I listen to the footsteps, I know exactly who it is.

I continue to draw as I wait for him to approach me and do the one thing that he always does when we're here and alone like this.

Like second nature, the footsteps stop behind me, and within seconds I feel a featherlight touch on my shoulder, moving my hair from one side to the other. I feel his lips on my skin next, he places a soft kiss on my shoulder blade that is exposed by my shirt before pulling back.

"You would look beautiful in that," he says, most likely looking over my shoulder at the dress design that I'm working on.

I shrug, looking down at the drawing. "It's not something that I would be able to pull off."

"You most definitely can." He places another kiss on my shoulder and I can't help but to lean back and melt into him.

There is something about being in this room and being in his arms like this that makes me feel safe.

Like everything is going to be okay. All I have to do is not leave the comfort of these walls or the comfort that comes from him being around me.

Maybe once we are out to my father, I will be able to experience this feeling outside of this studio. Maybe I will be able to feel safe as we walk down the sidewalk together or have dinner out in public.

But there is only one way that I would be able to feel that.

"Have you talked to him?"

I know the answer before any words can leave his mouth. The tension coming off him tells me everything I need to know.

He hasn't.

I turn to face him.

Santiago lets out a sigh. "I started to, the words were about to come out, when he stopped me."

My brow bunch together. "He stopped you?"

I look at him and there is something about his expression that is throwing me off.

Why does he look so pissed off? Like the conversation with my father made him angry beyond comprehension.

He nods. "That's why I'm here. He requested for me to get you. Ronaldo wants to see you."

If any other person was here, instead of the man standing in front of me, telling me that my father wanted to see me, I wouldn't question it. But the way the tension is rolling off him, my whole body is on high alert.

"Why does he want to see me?"

"He didn't say," again, his expression has me wanting to ask questions.

I continue to look at the man standing before me with a questioning look, and after about two minutes, I finally stand up.

"Okay."

Maybe my mind is going haywire and my father requesting to see me is a good thing. Maybe he knew what Santiago wanted to speak to him about and decided to stop him for a reason. Maybe he somehow found out about our relationship and about Santiago wanting to propose and this is him giving us his blessing to get married.

That can be a legitimate possibility, right?

My father is capable of doing that and letting me marry this man, right?

Everything in me is telling me no.

That's not the kind of person that Ronaldo Morales is, but a girl can hope.

Really hope.

Or maybe the reason he is summoning me has nothing to do with me and my relationship at all. Maybe it has to do with planning an event or something.

My father definitely loves to drop events I want nothing to do with on my lap.

I keep myself as composed as possible as we walk through the estate and to my father's office.

So many scenarios are running through my head and all I can hope is that it's the one scenario where Santiago makes it out of this meeting alive.

When I approach the office, I knock on the gigantic

wooden door and wait for a second before it opens and we get waved in by my brother.

I knew that Leo was here because Santos is on the property but why am I being summoned to a meeting that he's present for?

Nothing is making sense.

As I pass the threshold, my whole body is on high alert.

Because inside the office, are two other men besides my father and brother. Two men that I have never seen before and don't look familiar at all. The more I look at them, the more I can see that they are father and son.

But them looking alike doesn't tell me who they are or why they are here.

Let alone why I'm here.

"You wanted to see me?" I give my father a smile, trying not to alert him to tension that keeps riding up within me.

"Close the door, Santos," my father orders and seconds later I'm closed into a room that holds the five men and myself.

I keep myself composed as much as I can, but that's on the outside. On the inside, I'm filled with fear and maybe a tinge of curiosity.

As soon as the door is closed, my father holds out a hand for me to take, which I do.

"Isabella, I want you to meet Frederico and Emilio Castro. They run a small cartel out of Jalisco." He waves at the two men standing at the edge of the room.

I want to let out a snort.

Small cartel. It's only small because Ronaldo Morales

won't let any other cartel grow as big as his. The Muertos Cartel runs Mexico, and he will do everything in his power to keep it that way.

But what do these men from a small cartel in Jalisco have to do with me?

"*Mucho gusto.*" I offer them a small smile, because right now that is all I can muster.

The older man approaches me and my father and starts looking me up and down as if he were assessing me. Like he has X-ray vision and can see through my clothing and can see every single flaw that I have. I step into my father's hold slightly as if to shield myself from this man's gaze.

After what feels like the longest thirty seconds of my life, the man finally meets my questioning stare and gives me a bright smile. One that twists something in my stomach.

"It's very nice to finally meet you, Isabella. Ronaldo has spoken very good things about you. I can see that he was right when he described you as a beauty."

The man, Frederico if I had to guess, has a thick accent, one that mirrors my father's. That tells me that this man has spent the majority of his life in Mexico and only speaks English when absolutely necessary.

He has dark hair that has sprinkles of gray and a full beard with a mustache that covers most of the smile he is giving me. Something about this man doesn't sit well with me.

"This is my son, Emilio." Frederico waves over to the younger man. He's bulky, not like my brother and Santiago, but enough to hold his own. I can't see his facial features since they are covered by the shadow of the cowboy hat he is wearing, but I can feel his eyes on me. Like his father's, his gaze makes my stomach churn. "Hopefully he learns to treat you in the way you deserve."

My attention diverts from Emilio back to his father.

What did he just say?

"I'm sorry? Treat me the way I deserve?" I look from Frederico to my father, trying to get an answer.

What the fuck does Frederico mean by that?

When I turn back to the man in question, his smile grows even more, this time into a more sadistic one.

"Yes, since he will be your husband."

Everything around me goes black. As if I'm in a tunnel and my eyesight went straight to the little light of hope at the edge of the darkness and then it disappeared.

Husband.

He's going to be my husband?!

I turn to my father for some answers, anything that tells me that I'm not hearing this correctly, but all he does is give me a nod and then he tightens the hold on my hand that he has in his.

"Emilio and Isabella will be getting married. Think of it as a merger of sorts. The Castro cartel and the Muertos coming together. A marriage will solidify the agreement," Ronaldo announces to the whole room, as if this was grade school and he was explaining an assignment to the whole class.

I can't breathe.

No noise from the room is reverberating, all that I can

hear is my erratic heartbeat and how it feels like it's about to jump out of my chest.

I need to get out of here. I need fresh air. I try to pry myself out of my father's grip in a discreet manner, but he just keeps tightening it, holding me in place.

He's not going to let me go.

Turning, I catch sight of my brother and Santiago standing at the edge of the room, looking like they are ready to go to war.

They didn't know.

Both of them look beyond furious, with scowls on their faces and fists ready to be swung.

Santiago more so looks like he wants to tear this room apart and drag me out of here and get as far away as possible.

As I turn back to my father, for the first time in my life, I actually fear him.

If I don't go through with this, what would he do?

I try and try to open my mouth to yell at my father that I won't be going through with whatever arrangement he has set up with the Castros, but I can't seem to speak.

"You two will get engaged in the coming weeks." My father gives me a pointed look as if he were telling me that I have no say. "In the meantime, Emilio will be working here at the estate, give you some time to get to know each other."

Tears spring in my eyes, but I don't let them escape.

This is not what I expected to happen when Santiago came to get me. The only marriage that I thought my father would be speaking of was one between me and his loyal soldier.

But no, he called me in here to tell me that he was giving me away to another man. To another family.

All because he wants more power.

More money.

My father has arranged a marriage for me, and I have no say.

Instead of marrying the man I love, I will be marrying a man that I know nothing about.

A man that could be ten times more evil than any other man in this room.

Now not only am I the daughter of a cartel kingpin, but I'm also now owned by the cartel completely.

There will never be a way out.

15

SANTOS

Is there a word that can describe being beyond pissed off?

Rage?

Fury?

Wrath?

Whatever the word is, that's how I'm feeling right now. Everything inside of me is fucking boiling at Ronaldo's words.

Marriage.

To a fucking stranger.

What kind of sick fuck arranges for his daughter to marry a man she doesn't even know, all because he wants more power?

If you ask me, he's basically selling his daughter off, and if I wasn't the man that I was, I sure as hell would be charging across the room and beating the shit out of him.

It's already taking everything that I have in me to keep myself composed to not go to Isabella and take her in my arms.

But I can't.

Because no one standing within these four walls knows exactly what is happening between me and Isabella.

They don't know how I fully feel about her.

I don't even think that Isabella knows the extent of my feelings for her either. She knows I love her, that I want to marry her, have kids with her, but maybe she doesn't know everything that is in my heart, body, and soul.

Isabella doesn't know that she is everything to me.

She is everything that I want but cannot have, apparently. All because her father views me as nothing more than a man that will do his bidding and as someone who doesn't deserve his daughter.

Yet someone like Emilio Castro does.

The man, if you can even call him that, is fucking scum. He is a sick bastard from what I can tell, one that is probably only in this because he wants his daddy to have more money that he could inherit.

This is all a money grab for Ronaldo and the Castros with Isabella in the middle of it.

Not even an hour ago, Leo and I were in this office discussing business with Ronaldo. After the meeting, I was going to talk to him and Leo and tell them about me and Isabella. They were both there and they had a right to know what was going on behind closed doors. After that conversation was over, I was going to ask for her hand, like the good traditional boy my mother raised me to be.

I was ready to form the words when our meeting was cut short by the Castros showed up. It wasn't out of the norm to have a smaller cartel come and speak to Ronaldo, but I found it strange when I was asked to get Isabella.

Why would she be involved in cartel business?

But I got up and went to retrieve her anyway.

Now I'm fucking regret it.

I feel my fingernails digging into the skin of my palm as I catch a glimpse of Emilio's smug expression as he looks at Isabella.

If I could beat the look off his face, I would, but like fucking always, I have to keep myself composed.

Be the man in the shadows that my own father had raised me to be.

"*Ahora.*" Ronaldo claps his hands, finally letting go of Isabella and calling for all the attention back to him. "Santos, please escort Isabella back to her room. We have business to discuss."

It takes me a second to move from my position but I finally nod and do my duties as a soldier.

Escorting the princess back to her quarters.

You would think I wasn't as important as Leo to this cartel by the way Ronaldo talks to me sometimes. Or that my father didn't dedicate his life to this *familia*.

Before I'm able to wave at Isabella to come to me, Emilio steps forward, taking the hand that Ronaldo had a grip on and grabbing it. I watch as the fucking bastard brings her hand up to his mouth and places his lips on her skin.

I see fucking red.

He's planting his good for nothing mouth on what is mine.

But his lips on my woman isn't the only thing that has me seeing red.

It's also the fucking intricate lines that are adorning his hand.

Lines that I have seen before.

Lines that I have spent countless hours studying.

Studying and committing to memory.

I spent years looking at these lines, at this design, hoping that I would find the person who they adorned so I could kill them the same way that they killed my father.

In cold-blooded murder. Maybe with a little more added torture somewhere.

Fuck.

I now know who killed my father, who pulled the damn trigger.

The fucker is standing right in front of me, with his hands on the thing that I cherish the most, about to be engaged to her, and I can't do a fucking thing about it.

I can't cause a scene; I can't voice my theory. I just have to be the good soldier that Ronaldo thinks that I am and leave with Isabella.

"It's a pleasure to finally meet you, Isabella. I can't wait until we are married, to know you even better." He gives her a wink.

Isabella recoils a bit and I fight not to lunge forward and sucker punch him in the nose.

She needs to leave this room. The further away she is from this bastard the fucking better.

I place a hand on Isabella's elbow signaling that it's time to go. When she looks over at me, I completely ignore the tears I see forming in her eyes. I need to get us out of this office before showing any emotion.

Isabella's tears aren't the only thing that I ignore.

Leo is fuming where he's currently standing. He might want to kill his father and Emilio just as much as I want to. Leo loves his sisters and would do everything he could to protect them, crossing his father might be one of them.

I wouldn't put it past him.

Ignoring my friend, I walk his sister out of the room and let the men discuss business. Whatever the fuck that means. It most likely has to be something concerning the future nuptials if I'm not included. No fucking way would Leo let his father discuss cartel business without me present.

The second the doors close behind Isabella and me, there is a silence that encases us like a bubble. That silence follows us all the way to her side of her father's estate.

There are so many things that I could say to her right now, but it's as if I'm not able to form a single word.

I don't even reach for her, and take in my arms while I tell her everything will be okay. We just walk to her room, and I break with every shaky breath I hear her release.

Once we reach her studio, she pushes the doors open and storms in, and being the sad little puppy that I am, I follow, closing the door behind me.

The second that the door clicks, Isabella releases a sob that shakes her body completely. Her face turns red with anger and she looks like she wants to strangle someone. Or she needs someone to hold her.

Yet, I don't move.

Because I'm a very stupid man, but I don't take my eyes off her. I watch her as she goes through whatever emotions that she needs to go through. What her father just told her is life changing and it's a lot to digest. I don't blame her for how she is currently feeling.

She finally calms down, and that's when she meets my gaze.

Her brown eyes are red rimmed and filled with tears, her bottom lip is shaking and so are her shoulders.

I should move.

I should go to the woman that owns every single inch of me and hold her as tight as I possibly can. But I just stay rooted in place.

"Say something," she whispers, the shakiness of her body radiating to her voice.

There is so much I want to say.

Things like I will talk to her father and try to stop this. I want to say that I'm not going to let her marry my father's killer.

So many things want to leave my mouth.

But I don't say any of it.

Because I need to come up with a plan. A plan that gets her out of this mess and protects her like I have been trying to do for most of my life.

So for the moment, I just sigh. "What's there to say? Ronaldo wants you to marry another man. There's not much I can say to keep it from happening."

My voice sounds hard and by the way Bella flinches, she heard it too.

"We can go to him. We can tell him that I won't marry

Emilio. Who I marry is my choice, not his. We can tell him that you want to propose and ask for his blessing. Maybe once we tell him that we're together, he will stop this whole marriage thing." She is determined and I couldn't be any prouder of her.

But if anyone is going to go up against her father, it's going to be me. I'd rather be the one to put a stop to whatever plan Ronaldo has, then let his daughter get hurt in the process.

If someone gets hurt, or dies, it will have to be me.

No way in hell am I going to let Isabella get involved in the crossfire.

And the way to keep her safe is to let her believe that I don't give a shit about this.

I shake my head, about to regret every little thing that comes out of my mouth, but I have to say it. It's for her own good.

"It's done, Isabella. I had my chance, and now it's gone." *Please know I don't mean a word.* "There is no changing Ronaldo's mind. You'll be marrying Emilio and that is that."

I watch as more tears spring from her eyes. I'm hurting her with what I'm saying. I know I am, but the words need to be said. I need to have her believe that whatever we had going on between us is over now.

I blame her father for making me do this.

I blame him for driving me to this point, where I have to break his daughter's heart and throw everything that we have built these last few years away.

"What are you saying? That you're not going to fight

this with me?" Her voice breaks and my heart shatters with it. "You're going to just sit there and watch as I marry another man?"

The real question that I'm asking myself is, can I watch her marry another man?

I don't even think about it long, I know the answer.

I can't.

And I fucking won't.

I will try my damned fucking hardest to not let that wedding happened. I don't care if I have to kill Emilio myself, it won't happen.

But I can't do that I can't go after Emilio and kill him, if Isabella is near me in anyway. She needs to stay as far away from anything that I might do, I can't have her dying on my watch.

"As long as your father is at the helm of this decision, yes, that's what I'm going to do." The lie flows out of my mouth more easily than I thought it would and by the look in her eyes, she believes it.

More tears roll down her cheeks. I turn to walk out before she can say anything.

"Santiago!" she yells out, stopping me in my tracks.

With a hand on the doorknob, I turn slightly to face her.

Her face is redder than it was before and if I thought that she wanted to strangle someone before, she definitely wants to now.

"I hate you."

And I believe her.

With one final look at the woman that owns every inch of my heart, of my soul, I nod and leave the room.

For the third time in my life, I have made this woman hate me with all that she has, but this time I don't know if she will forgive me.

All I can do is hope that the memories that we made together are what hold her together while I do everything to get her out of this shit. No matter whose blood I spill.

Even if it happens to be Ronaldo's.

Isabella Morales is mine and she is sure as hell not going to marry another man.

Especially one that I know murdered my father.

16

ISABELLA

It shouldn't have been that easy.

After everything that we have been through, walking away from me shouldn't have been that easy for him.

Yet it was.

Never in my wildest dreams did I ever think that all it would take was for my father to say that he was marrying me off. Or the man I truly wanted to spend the rest of my life with would be able to walk away without a backward glance.

But he did.

My father told me that he was marrying me off and Santiago just left me standing there, crying every tear that I had, and walked away.

I fucking hate him.

But I love him so damn much.

Did these last four years not mean anything to him?

Was it really that easy to walk away from me?

No, there has to be something more.

Something else has to be a factor, because I cannot believe that Santiago would give up on not only us, but everything we've built over this. The Santiago that I know, would have stood up to my father and fought for what we had.

The man that I know, wouldn't have done this.

I know there is something more at play here, I will find out exactly what that is. I don't give a shit if he acts like he wants nothing to do with me.

Why are you worrying about this? You're marrying someone else.

Not if I have a say in it. I've been through too much shit in my life, no way in fucking hell am I adding this to the list.

So, what am I going to do?

Talk to my father, or at least attempt to talk to him.

Maybe, just maybe, if I go to him and he sees that I really want no part in this, he will call the whole thing off. Maybe he will realize that he doesn't have to marry off his daughter to gain more power and money.

You know that's not going to happen.

A girl can hope, right?

I'm strong, and I vowed once in my life already that I wasn't going to let any man in it, make me feel like shit ever again.

It's time to stand up to my father.

Like any other time that I have attempted to speak to my father in his office, the one and only place that you will find him, I square my shoulders and take a deep breath.

You can do this, Isabella.

You can do this.

Here goes nothing.

I lift a fist up to knock on the wooden door, but before I can make contact the door opens. Standing in front of me is the man I was about to ask to speak to.

"*Papi,*" I give him a bright smile, as if nothing in the world could be wrong.

He looks me up and down, probably wondering what I'm doing here, about to knock on his door.

When it comes to interactions with my father, we usually keep them to his living quarters, the patio, the dining room, or the kitchen. If me and Camila want to speak to him, we will do it then. Leo is the only one that gets the benefit of the office.

Camila and I do not venture over to his office unless we are asked to.

Like I was when he told me I was going to be marrying Emilio.

"Isabella, *todo está bien?*" He gives me a concerned look. I let my smile grow a little more and try to act like everything is fine.

"*Si,*" I give him a nod to convey it. "I was just wondering if you wanted to go for a walk with me. It's a beautiful day out and all."

As much as this office is his safe space, it's not mine. I'd rather not step foot into the one place where my world came crashing down. I need to be in my own space and walking through my mother's garden is one of the places that I can do that.

He gives me a look that tells me that he doesn't believe

that everything is fine and knows that I'm full of shit, but eventually he gives me a nod.

"*Estará bien.*" A curt nod and an offered elbow later, me and my father are walking through the estate and heading straight to the garden.

Taking walks like this is something that I have missed dearly. Before my mother died, these kinds of walks were almost a daily occurrence. Usually it was just me, my mother and Camila, but there was always the rare occasion that my dad would join. It was those walks that always put a big smile on my face.

It was during a time where I thought of my father as just dad and not something so formal.

It was always those small moments with my father that I always enjoyed and to this day, treasure. But when my mother died, and the cartel became a more prominent focus for him, these types of walks became things of memories.

I honestly can't remember when the last time I spent time with my father like this was.

"It really is a nice day today." He guides us to the garden and soon we are surrounded by colorful roses and the ever-bright *flor de muertos.*

My mother's favorite.

I nod. "I can't remember the last when me and you went for a walk like this."

He is silent for a few seconds, and I watch him as he ponders my statement.

"*Años.* I think the last time we did this was when Camila was still running around."

Sounds about right and given that Camila is about to turn nineteen, it's been almost ten years.

"I've missed it." This time the smile that I give him is one that reaches my eyes.

I guess a part of me misses being the small little girl that looked up to her father.

Do I still look up to him?

Sure, but I just wish he lived life differently and wasn't dedicated to being the most feared man alive. Maybe then we would have an actual father-daughter relationship and I wouldn't feel like a transaction.

Ronaldo just nods and continues to walk us through the garden.

"What's on your mind, Isabella?" my father asks as we walk deeper through the path.

"Nothing," I say a little bit too quickly and when I hear a small scoff coming from his throat, I know that he doesn't believe me.

"*Dime la verdad.*" Tell me the truth. I guess it's time to have this conversation.

I take my gaze away from the man next to me and speak. "I don't want to marry Emilio Castro."

The words leave my mouth, and it feels like the pressure that was sitting on my chest finally elevated a little bit.

But that pressure returns when my father stops walking and somehow turns me to face him.

Anger swims through his eyes. His mouth is in a tight line and the hand that I had through the crook of his elbow is being tightly held by his.

"Are you trying to embarrass me?" he says through his teeth and if I could step back from him, I would.

I start to shake my head. "No, *Papá*."

There's more that I want to say but I don't.

"Then what? I made a deal with the Castros. *Ah la chingada,* I will not be going back on my word."

His grip on me grows tighter, a lot more than how he held me when he broke the news of this deal. This grip is at the point of pain, and it has me cowering under my father.

"I don't want this," I try to start but the words are cut off when the grip he has on my hand is moved to my upper arm.

My father holds both my upper arms in his hands, almost shaking me, trying to knock sense into me.

"*No mi importa*. I don't give a shit what you want or don't want. You will marry Emilio. You will marry him, fuck him, be the perfect housewife to him, and give him however many babies he wants. You will do that for this family. You will do that for me, for this cartel. Because without this cartel, you would have nothing. It's time to show how grateful you are for this life that I gave you."

Grateful.

How can I be grateful for a life that I want nothing to do with? A life that I wish with everything in me never existed.

His grip on my arms tightens even more. I can feel his fingernails penetrating through the fabric of my shirt and hitting my skin.

"*Papí. Por favor.*" I feel tears start to run down my cheeks. "Please don't make me marry him. Please!"

He lets me go and takes a step back, but only for a second. I watch as my only living parent takes a step forward, swings a hand back and strikes me on my cheek.

I feel a pain, one a lot stronger than his nails digging into me, radiating from my jaw all the way to my temple.

The tears that were rolling down my cheek a few seconds ago are coming down a lot more freely as I cradle my aching face.

He hit me.

Never in all my life has my father hit me.

I look at the man in front of me and all I see is annoyance and anger and no sympathy or remorse.

"You will do as I say." he grinds out through his teeth, not looking like my father at all. No, the man in front of me isn't my father, he's the drug lord, the kingpin. Right now he doesn't give a single fuck about his crying daughter that he just slapped. No, all he cares about is that she is scared to the core so that she can uphold her end of the bargain.

"And if I don't?" It's stupid of me to say the words, to even try to stand up to him, but I can't help it. He had to know that I was going to defy him in some way, and he had to come up with something to make sure that this agreement was upheld.

With not even an ounce of care in his expression, he lifts his hand and cradles my face, placing his palm against my throbbing cheek.

"*Entonces.*" For a split second his face changes, it looks slightly sincere, but it's gone too fast before I can really know. "I think that Camila would make a good wife for Emilio."

He gives me a sadistic smile to get his point across.

No.

No, I will not let that happen. I will not have my sister be a part of this in any way. Camila is young, she deserves to explore the world, go to school and paint every single thing that she wants to paint. She deserves a lot more than marrying a strange man, all because I don't want to.

I won't put her in that position.

I'm shaking my head just thinking about it. "No. Don't bring Camila into this."

"Then do as I say. Marry Emilio and your sister will not have to do the job that is meant for you." Again, anger coats his face.

With his hand still cradling my face, I feel his fingers move up until they are wrapped around a strand of my hair. That's when he pulls.

The pain that was radiating from my jaw to my temple, is now all the way through my skull, like a million tiny shards being pulled out of me.

"As long as you go along with the plan, your sister is safe to do what she wants." He pulls harder and I need to control my breathing before I hyperventilate. "So will Santos."

The mention of Santiago's name has my eyes snapping open and meeting my father's.

He knows?

"Did you really think that I wouldn't know that the two of you have been sneaking behind my back, committing an act of betrayal? I've known since the very beginning. And if he's smart, he will stay away from you from now on and not mess this up for me. If not, then he will be sharing a box with Cristiano."

One last pull of my scalp and he finally lets go of me, causing me to stumble to the ground from the pain.

"You're my daughter, Isabella. I'm the one that says who you will spend the rest of your life with. I don't give a fuck what you want." With that, he leaves me there on the garden floor, not even allowing me to say another word.

I lie on the cold concrete floor for a good while. With the cold ground against my cheek, I realize something.

My father dictates a bigger part of my life than I had originally thought.

Now, I'm going to marry a man that I know nothing about, that is not the man I love.

Why?

Why am I not going to fight my father?

Because I need to save my sister, and I need to keep Santiago alive.

Because I know that my father means every single word that he voiced.

I won't be a defiant daughter, and I will try my hardest not to make my father's promises come true.

I have to.

17

SANTOS

Ten Months Earlier

THE URGE TO kill Emilio Castro grows with every passing day.

Every single time that I hear him speak, every time he enters the room on Ronaldo's tail, the urge to grab the gun that I have hidden in my waistband and shoot him dead, is there.

I want to kill him for killing my father.

Kill him for entering the deal to marry Isabella.

Today, though, the urge to kill him comes from the fucked-up bullshit that he pulled yesterday with casino owner, Sterling Chambers.

For weeks, Leo and I have been planning on coming to Las Vegas to speak with Chambers and have him agree to the deal that we put together. Chambers wanted to make a name for himself and what better way to do that than to work with the Muertos Cartel. We're able to give our customers the best cocaine in the world, of course, anyone would choose to work with us.

We had a plan in place, both Leo and I agreed on a price to offer Chambers and it was all going accordingly.

I should have known that the plan was going to go to shit when Ronaldo informed us a few days ago that Emilio was going to come to Vegas with us.

I was already in a shit mood since I had spent that morning with Leo in the estate's basement, torturing one of the men that had talked to the *federales* and turned one of our runs to shit.

Don't get me wrong, I can spend hours breaking every single bone in a man's body to hear them scream, because I'm a sadistic bastard like that, but this was different. This was someone that stood by my side, a man that at times had my back and I had his.

To top it off, the fucker got sloppy one night with some tequila and confessed all that he had said to the feds to me. I listened as he blabbered all about doing it because maybe then he would become the kingpin.

I had two options, tell Leo what Adolfo had spilled or keep it to myself. The answer was simple, I didn't care if I saw Adolfo as a brother, my loyalty to Leo was a whole lot stronger. So, his secret was soon out there and after a failed drug run, he was strapped to a chair, fighting for his life.

When Leo finally told me to light him up, it was like a damn Christmas miracle.

So, when Ronaldo brought up the subject of Vegas and Emilio, I just nodded and fucking agreed.

Now here I am, in fucking Las Vegas, nursing a hangover, trying to figure out a way to not let our deal with Chambers go to shit.

It doesn't help that Leo is nowhere to be found this morning.

That's a lie, I know exactly where he is. All cuddled up with the brunette from the club.

Last night we decided to go to find a distraction, well I decided for us because no way in hell was I going to be staying in our room. Just watching Emilio disrespect Isabella repeatedly with the string of pussy that walked through the door made me want to kill the man even more.

So, we went to the club. While we were there having a few drinks, two women that we had helped back to their room earlier in the day had shown up. Instantly Leo's attention was taken by the dark-haired beauty, and I can't blame him.

When the beauty's friend had come over to invite us to join them, I agreed. Just because I was having a shit time, didn't mean I was going to keep my friend from enjoying himself right next to me.

We went to sit with the two lovely ladies, and Leo went straight to the brunette, and I hung out with her friend. Then the two of them left and then it was just me and the friend, Aria, left to our own accord. I had noticed the closeness of her body to mine, and the way her eyes danced whenever I said something, and, of course, the beauty that she was.

But I wasn't going to touch her, and I told her as much. Even with whatever was going on between me and

Isabella, I was still loyal to her, and I sure as hell wouldn't touch another woman that wasn't her. I thought that Aria was going to fight me on it, but she just smiled at me and told me that she was fine with that.

The rest of the night consisted of us just talking. Yeah, talking. She told me about her life, and I told her the PG-rated version of mine. I might have even told her some things about me and Isabella. She was a stranger and I sure as hell couldn't have that conversation with Leo.

It was good.

But that was last night.

Now it's time to handle business and I have no idea how to do that.

That's why I'm currently sitting at a damn blackjack table at seven in the morning, just hoping that something will come to fruition.

Anything that will save our asses if our deal with Chambers goes south.

The dealer lays a card in front of me, and I groan when I see a twenty-four.

Fuck me.

Throwing a few black chips to the dealer, I grab my drink and leave my chair.

I guess I can take a gamble with my life and my choice of career but can't catch a break at the blackjack table.

Walking through the casino, I try to figure out what to do with myself. Finally, the smell of food stops me, and I end up at this restaurant that serves French and Mexican fusion for breakfast. It's an odd combination but hey, it works. Coming from a man with a French Canadian mother, the food is fucking mouthwatering.

Without even thinking, I walk in and grab a table.

Once the waitress comes by and grabs my order, I pull out my phone and the small leather-bound journal that is burning a hole in my back pocket.

The pages are frayed and almost all the small pieces of paper are filled with words that would mean nonsense to anyone but me. Anything that has to do with my life and job is written on these pages, in a coded manner of course. It is a combination of three different languages that only I know how to decode. Even Leo looks at me weird when I bring the book out.

I open the book to the section that I have dedicated to Emilio and his family.

The tattoo was the turning point in finding out that he was the one that shot my father, but I have yet to find out why.

The only theory that I could come up with is trying to make a name for himself and for the Castros' cartel. Taking down someone from the Muertos makes your name known in this world, but that would mean you have to step out and take the light, let every single person know what you did.

Up to this point, the only person that knows what Emilio did, is me. It's not even something that I have mentioned to Leo, because I know if I do, Leo would be the one to pull the trigger, killing the bastard.

The only person that gets to hold a gun barrel to the fucker's head is me and me only. I need to be the one that pulls the trigger and sees all the blood drain from his worthless skull. And after he's dead, I will continue to rip his body apart and treat him to the ruthless death that my father endured.

Maybe I can confront him and kill him before Ronaldo calls for a ring to be put on Isabella's finger.

"Well, if it isn't an old face." A male's voice takes me away from the words jumping out at me from the journal.

When I look up, I have to do a double take at the man in front of me.

Dressed in a well-tailored suit, stands Elliot Lane looking like he comes from the wealthiest family in the world.

Because he does, the lucky bastard.

"Definitely not a face that I thought I would be seeing so early in the morning," I throw back, giving him a smirk.

"Not disagreeing with you there." He gives me the cocky smile that I'm sure had the girls going crazy when we were in high school, before holding out a hand to me.

Standing up, we give each other a back slap before he takes the seat across from me at the table.

Elliot Lane.

He's a rich kid from Chicago, comes from a family that owns more than a few multimillion dollar businesses. His family is the type to socialize with senators and former United States presidents. How I came to know him was because his uncle shipped him off to Texas for high school.

The preppy academy that housed me and Leo for four years before cartel life took over.

"How the hell have you been, Santos?" he asks as soon as I'm back in my seat.

I give him a nod. "Keeping alive."

Elliot knows what Leo and I do for a living and who we do it for. This man is very knowledgeable in what types of things the Muertos Cartel has their noses in. Coming from a family like his, he holds a lot of knowledge about certain things, and makes it so that everyone knows not to cross a Lane.

Come to think of it, I have no idea what he does. I know he helps run the family business, but to what extent? The man is only twenty-seven.

"Heard about your old man. My condolences." His tone tells me that he is being sincere.

I nod, holding out a drink to him. "Same to you. Heard about your dad passing away while he was overseas a few years back."

Elliot's face drops slightly. "Thanks, man. Yeah, the man didn't know when to quit, but he did his country proud."

The way he says the words has me asking. "Not his kids?"

Elliot's father was a marine. Every time I saw the man, I almost shit my pants, he was that intimidating. I heard a lot of stories about him while we were in high school and whenever he was in Texas to visit his son, Eli always had a big smile on his face, like he was his hero or something.

Maybe that view has changed.

Eli shrugs. "I'm proud of him, but he left his four kids

for his brother to raise. Can't help but resent the man sometimes."

Well, fuck.

I don't know what to say to that, and thankfully I don't have to because the waitress comes by and asks Elliot if he wants to place an order.

After he does, we sit in silence for a few minutes. Eventually, he breaks it when he points to the object in front of me.

"Didn't realize that Leo's right-hand man was a journal keeper." He takes a sip of his coffee, but I can see the teasing smirk he's wearing.

Asshole.

I look down at the journal that's in front of me, reaching out and slapping a hand on the pages, and closing it before he can read anything from it.

"Even the darkest man has deep shit to write down."

Half true but I'm not going to just come out and say that I write down how to kill people in this journal.

"You write your deep shit in code?"

He notices everything, doesn't he?

"A man has to have his secrets." I'm not Adolfo that talks about everything the cartel does when asked.

Elliot nods, drinking more of his coffee.

"Who are the Castros and how do they tie in with your father?"

I tense at his question.

How?

How the actual fuck did he read off the open page?

My writing is small and a mess, something that

Isabella reminded me every chance she gets, and every other word is in a different language.

How?

Elliot must have noticed how tense I get because he leans back in his chair and holds up his hands.

"Sorry. It's something that I can't help. I notice a lot of the small details, a habit that my sister hates. I noticed it when I approached you and given that I know some French, I was able to read some before you closed it."

I can get up from my chair and walk out of this restaurant and stop this conversation from happening.

Or...

I talk. There's a reason why I haven't talked to Leo about this. Maybe this is my opportunity to come up with an idea to get rid of Emilio for good and get Isabella out of the arrangement Ronaldo cooked up.

Letting out a sigh, I open the journal and place it in front of my breakfast companion.

He doesn't ask what I'm doing, just gives me a curt nod and gets to reading.

I sit there as he reads page after page that I have written. Everything that I know about the Castro family and Emilio is on those pages. Every theory that I thought of as to why they went after my father and even the theories as to how the deal between Ronaldo and the Castros came about.

A part of me can't help but wonder if the relationship between the two cartels has gone back years or if it's something that just recently happened.

Elliot reads the pages for a few minutes and then finally looks up, letting out a whistle when he's done.

"And I thought that the shit that I had to deal with was complicated. This is a whole other level." He slides the journal back to me.

I guess this asswipe is smart enough to decode my writing.

Grabbing the journal, I pocket it, not taking my eyes off him. "I guess that's the cartel life for you."

Elliot nods. "I guess so."

We go back to silence and it's enough time for the waitress to come back and bring us our food. We continue with the silence while we eat.

"I'm guessing Leo doesn't know what you found out, given that the arrangement with his sister is still intact."

I nod, chewing through my chorizo and eggs. "I need to find out more information first, like why the fuckers went after Cristiano. Then maybe I will tell him."

"Makes sense, I would do the same. Especially if my sister were involved."

Is it weird that this is the first time I hear him mention that he has a sister? I know he mentioned her earlier but before today, all I knew was that he had brothers.

"Have you come close to figuring it out?" Eli throws out there before I can say anything.

I shake my head. "Nothing definite. The closest thing that I have is that they wanted to just kill someone to make a name for themselves. If that were the case, then my father would just be another casualty."

"But you know there is more." It's not a question.

"There has to be. Especially now that the Castros are making deals with Ronaldo Morales. There had to be something that brought this on. This whole arrangement has more to it. More than money and power and I have no idea what. All I know is that I have to get Leo's sister out of this before it's too late."

"Will—" Elliot starts, but he takes a bite of his food before he can continue. Finally, after endless chewing, he starts again. "Will the Castros' hurt Isabella?"

I don't want to think about that happening.

I don't want to sit here and come up with stupid ass scenarios where Isabella is put in danger and I can't do anything to save her.

"Everything in me wants to say no, but the reality of it is, I don't know. I sure as fuck hope they don't."

I will kill anyone who dares to touch Isabella Morales.

Again, we go back to eating in silence. I look up to my companion every once in a while and see that he has a look of contemplation on his face. Whatever he is thinking of, must be a hard pill to swallow.

His face looks like he's constipated, and he is trying to plan out his next shit.

"Let me help you find anything on the Castro family," Elliot finally offers when we were almost done with our meals.

I place my fork on the plate in front of me and look at the man.

"How would you do that? This is a cartel we are talking about; I doubt that all their information is out on the internet."

If it was, I would have found it by now.

The look of constipation leaves his face and it's replaced with a smirk.

"The Castros don't have as big an operation as the Muertos, right?" I nod. "They had to get sloppy somewhere. Hell, you were able to find the tattoo, you and Leo would never let that happen if you were in their shoes. They're a small cartel. If they messed up somewhere or they talked about your father in some way, shape or form, I will be able to find it. Let me help you."

I think about it.

He does have a lot more resources than I have access to. The possibility of him finding something is somewhat high. Even if he finds a speck of information, it can be beneficial.

That is if he's able to do it.

Am I willing to take that risk?

To trust someone outside of my circle of cartel brothers to help with this? To help find any information as to why my father was killed?

It's worth a shot.

I give him a curt nod. "Okay. Do it. See what you can find on Emilio Castro."

We shake on it.

I just made a deal with a billionaire playboy. Hopefully, it doesn't come and bite me in the ass.

"If you ever need anything else from me, let me know. I'm only a phone call away." He hands me a business card as we handle the bill. Well, he handled the bill. Of course, I was going to let the billionaire treat me to breakfast.

I take the card from him and hold out my hand to him. "Thank you."

He gives me another nod as we walk out of the restaurant.

"If I find anything, I will give you a call." With that, he walks away, and I'm left there thinking about how I didn't even give him my number.

He'll figure it out.

I head back to the casino, contemplating sitting at another table while I wait for Leo to text me when he's done with his activities. I'm about to give up the search for a table when I overhear a group of young women talking.

"You did *not* see him!" a girl in a pink dress exclaims to one of the other girls in her group that is wearing a shirt that is definitely a bra.

"I did! He was having breakfast at the restaurant around the corner." The one that I was just at?

Well, shucks, I missed a celebrity sighting. Poor me.

"You should have seen him. He looked so dreamy in his suit. You know he has them tailored to fit his body perfectly."

"What kind of guy wears a suit at eight in the morning and in Vegas?" the girl with the pink dress questions.

A pretentious asshole, that's who.

Okay, I need to get away from this conversation. I feel like I'm becoming Camila when she talks about Harry Styles or whatever his name is. I don't have time to deal with little girl shit.

"Elliot Lane." The girl in the bra shirt says in a dreamy sigh.

Lane is considered a celebrity? Since when?

I should go up to these girls and tell them I had the pleasure of sharing a table with him.

Okay, now I'm really sounding like Camila. I need to get as far away from this conversation as possible.

"He's like hella rich, right? Like he can buy this hotel and still have billions left over?" another girl in the group voices.

"Yeah, and he's completely single." Bra girl says to her.

Some of the other girls say something, but I block it out, concentrating on what was just said.

Elliot Lane is rich. If not him, his family. They run all different types of businesses all around the world and must deal with some shady shit.

No family is that rich without having skeletons in their closets.

Maybe they would be willing to add a different type of business to their lineup.

I leave the women and try not to kick myself in the ass for not thinking about this earlier.

I may not be able to figure out why Emilio did what he did four years ago, but I can make sure he doesn't screw up the deal with Chambers. Make sure we have a backup plan.

Pulling out the card that was handed to me not ten minutes ago, I dial the number and wait for the rich fucker to answer.

"Miss me already?" he says when the ringing finally stops after a few rings.

"I need to call a meeting. You, me, and Leo. To talk business." I get right to the point.

"Are you going to tell me what it's about?"

"Nope. Not until we are all in the same room." No way am I discussing this in the middle of a busy casino.

After a few seconds, Elliot lets out a sigh. "Okay, my room. I'll text you the number and the time."

"Okay." I hang up the phone and waste no time in texting Leo about our meeting.

Emilio might have taken something important from me and is trying to take something else, but he isn't going to touch this.

There's a reason why I'm a high-ranking soldier with the Muertos and he is not.

The fucking asshole will not see me coming.

18

ISABELLA

Eight Months Earlier

I CAN TELL you the exact moment when I realized that I was unhappy with how my life was going. The moment is ingrained into my brain.

It was the moment that my brother walked into my father's estate with his wife that he married in Las Vegas.

Yeah, you heard that right. The man that hasn't had a serious relationship in his life, got married one drunken night in Vegas and now she's fucking here.

Serena Davidson.

I swear if I hear her call herself a Morales, I'm going to flip out on her.

You like her.

Okay, I might not dislike her so much now, especially after she told me and Camila how she told Leo the almighty, no, when it comes to a divorce and her reason behind it.

I might have gained a few ounces of respect for her after that.

But it was when she pulled me aside when that respect grew even more.

I'm about to walk out of the room and follow Camila out when I feel a hand on my shoulder.

Turning slightly, I see Serena's well-manicured nails on me and she gives me a sheepish smile.

I swear if she is about to tell me that she wants to change the flowers we just picked out for her stupid wedding, I'm going to punch her.

"It's not my place, but there's someone, isn't there? Someone you wish your father would have chosen for you to marry?"

Earlier when we were picking flowers for the wedding my father is forcing me to plan for Serena and Leo, I said something about choosing who she got to marry.

Leo and Serena might have been drunk off their minds in the middle of the night, but they still had the choice. They had the choice to marry who they wanted to, even if it was a complete stranger.

They had a choice that I don't have. All because my father is forcing my hand and taking that choice away from me.

I look at my now sister-in-law and contemplate telling her. I've held my relationship with Santiago inside for years, so it would be nice to have someone to talk to.

Is Serena that person?

Maybe she is.

I close my eyes and give her a nod. With one nod, I silently confess my love for Santiago to a woman that I don't even know.

"It will work out. I don't know how, and I don't know when, but it will work out. You will one day find yourself with the man you love."

My head is already shaking before she can finish her sentence. *"You have no possible way of knowing that."*

I want to believe that it will happen, I want to have faith that her words are true, but I really don't want to get my hopes up.

"If that man is anything like your brother, then I know for a fact that it will happen."

"And what type of man is my brother?"

I swear to god if she tells me what kind of man he is in bed, I'm going to actually punch her

"The type of man that will act like a villain to everyone else but a prince for you and only you. Saving you from the dragon if need be."

Saving me from the dragon...

It's been a few weeks since that conversation, and every day I think about it. Serena is right, in a way. If the man that I love, is anything like my brother, he will fight for me.

But is he doing it right now as we speak?

I have no idea.

It's been almost four months since my father announced that I was going to marry into the Castro family.

Four months of silence from the one person I want to hear from.

The only interactions we've had have been ignoring each other while in the same room.

Take the night that Leo brought Serena over, we were

in the courtyard together, but the man didn't say a word to me. I did catch him staring more than once, which is what I wanted when I picked out the silk white design to wear. But that was all.

Did I want him to look at me and whisk me away so that he could have his way with me? Maybe.

But Santiago Reyes would rather grind his teeth all the way to his gums than claim what is his in front of my father.

No matter how badly I wanted him to.

I have to have faith though. I have to have faith that Serena is right, and he is the man that is fighting for us. Maybe he is and he's just not telling me about it.

I don't know, but that is certainly not something that I want to be thinking about right now.

"Attend? Like go out into the town square?" Serena's voice rings through the room.

We are currently setting up the sitting room here at the estate for the *Dia de los Muertos* celebration. It was my mother's favorite tradition and every year she would honor the family members that we lost too soon. She would set up an altar every single year and would partake in all the activities and festivities that were put together by the people of San Pedro.

Every year, Camila and I try to honor her during the celebration as much as we can. This year we decided to include Serena. Olive branch and all that.

Don't worry, a part of me still thinks that she's a gold digger at times, but a gold digger that I kind of like. It's weird, I know.

"It will be safe and nobody will know who you are. I promise." I try to convey as much sincerity in my statement as possible. Just because I don't like her most of the time doesn't mean that I'm not going to do my part and help my brother protect her.

A few weeks ago, there was an incident where Serena was followed while she was in Austin. From what Leo told me, it ended in a shoot-out with a few men dead. Ever since then, Serena has been spending a large amount of time here at the estate and that's how I can somehow tolerate her now.

She gives me a look of concern and eventually gives me a nod.

With a small smile from me, I turn back and finish up my portion of the altar.

I'm so enthralled in the flower making that when I hear my name, it takes me off guard, especially when I hear the voice that says it.

"Isabella." His voice sounds far away, but even then, I still feel it caress every single inch of skin that I have exposed.

"Yes?" I don't turn to face him. I can't. This is the first time in months that he has addressed me. I can't turn and show him what hearing him say my name does to me.

"Your father wants to see you." My back gets more tense when he says those words.

The last time my father wanted to see me, he announced that I would be engaged to Emilio soon.

Why is he summoning me now?

I try to remember back to that lovely meeting, and all I

can hear my father say is that in a few weeks' time, we would be engaged.

Is that time now?

It has to be, it's the only reason that he would be sending Santos to come get me.

Fuck.

"Isabella." Santos's voice comes out in a no bullshit way. Instead of turning to him and giving him an answer, I continued doing what I was doing.

Even as I hear the impatience in his voice, I still don't turn.

I'm not going to be answering a man that has not said a word to me in months.

I know he's up to something, but he still threw us away like pieces of trash that didn't mean anything.

Four years together meant something.

"*Bella*!" he yells out the name and I go absolutely still.

He called me *bella*.

He knows what that name means to me, he knows how much hearing that name affects me, and he used it on me to get what he wants.

Fuck him.

He doesn't deserve to say that name. Not right now at least.

I close my eyes and I take a few deep breaths, trying to collect myself before I turn to face him.

Very briefly, I catch a glimpse of Serena, who is staring at me like she is wondering what is happening. I can see her putting together the puzzle pieces in her head.

"*¿Qué quieres, Santiago?*" He called me *bella*, I have every right to call him by his full name.

He looks at me with ferocity. His lips are in a tight line and his jaw looks like it's about to break with how he is grinding his teeth.

"Your father wants to see you. Now," he grinds out.

I don't make the effort to even move an inch, I just continue to stand there, staring at the man that left me when I needed him most.

I know why my father is calling for me. I know what will happen the second I step foot into his office, and I just want to drop down to the ground and let out the sob that has been brewing in me for months. But I don't.

Because that is not the woman my mother raised.

Going with Santiago right now is going to break me beyond repair, but I have no choice, so I nod.

I nod and walk out of that room with him right behind me.

The walk to my father's office is similar to the one we made all those weeks ago. The only difference is that back then I had the hopes that maybe, just maybe, it would be me and Santos getting engaged. Not what I think is about to happen.

"You called me *bella*," I mutter out, not bothering to look at the man.

"You were ignoring me. I had to get your attention somehow." I can hear him grinding his teeth out of annoyance from where I am. Good. Let him be annoyed.

We could be figuring out this whole fucked-up situation together, but no, this man had to leave me, throw everything we've built together away, and for what? To be mad at me for being in this situation?

Fuck that.

"Well, you've been ignoring me since all this shit started so I guess karma came and bit you in the ass."

He doesn't say anything, he just continues to grind his teeth as we walk through the estate.

When we finally make it to my father's office, my suspicions about why I was called in here are right.

In the office is Emilio and his father sitting on the armchairs in front of my father's desk and Ronaldo himself sitting behind the wooden piece of furniture, with not a care in the world.

"Thank you, Santos. You can go." My father waves a hand of indifference at my companion, excusing him.

He must nod and walk out of the room.

When I hear the wooden door click closed, I try to hold myself together as much as I possibly can.

Not one man in this room has my best interests at heart. The one man I could depend on, who I know would try to save me from anything, was just dismissed and now I'm left to the wolves.

Actually, no. Calling these men wolves is too generous. They deserve something more, something more fearful, something more predatory.

Vultures.

These men are vultures, and they hunt two things. Money and power.

I continue to stand there by the doorway, waiting for someone to say something.

It takes me by surprise when Emilio stands up and approaches me.

There's a look of smugness on his face and his mouth is curved up in a smirk that makes my stomach queasy.

Emilio Castro is a handsome man, that much I will give him but there is something about him that comes off as seedy or maybe it's the predatory side. I did say he was a vulture, after all.

"You look beautiful as always, Isabella." He reaches for one of my hands and brings it up to his lips.

I want to cringe at the action. I want to take a step back and get as far away from this man as possible, but I can't.

Even the way he says my name unsettles me.

This good-guy thing is a front. Ever since my father announced the agreement, Emilio has worn a mask. Since he has been spending a lot more time here at the estate, becoming one of my father's trusted men, we've crossed paths a time or two.

If my father is around, he acts like the perfect gentleman that would make any Mexican mother proud.

But when there is no one around that he needs to impress? The mask comes off.

Every single time that I have ran into him, he reminds me of what he will do to me when we are married.

He tells me that he won't touch me before, but once the vows are said, that I'm all his. That I should get used to being on my knees.

That I will be his bitch forever and nobody will take me away from him.

Every single time I hear him say those words, I want to puke. I want to puke and then let the tears flow.

But I just take his verbal abuse and walk away, keeping the words he tells me locked up inside of me.

The thought of telling Leo always comes to mind, but I never do it.

Why?

Because my brother will kill Emilio and if the Castro heir is dead then that means that the deal is off. Which means that my father doesn't get what he wants, and he will probably retaliate and hurt me or Leo in the way that he only knows how. By hurting the people we love the most.

Serena, because no matter if my brother hasn't voiced it, he loves her and would be devastated without her.

Santiago, because I would be devastated without him.

And I won't let that happen.

"Thank you." My response is small, but he was still able to hear me by the look he's giving me.

"Now that you are both here, I think it's time to get to business." Frederico claps his hands as if this were a joyous occasion.

Business.

That's what this is, just business.

"And what business is that?" I'm playing stupid and it's only to show my father that I'm playing along.

"*El compromiso.*" The engagement.

Tears start to well up in my eyes, but I keep them at bay.

I give my future father-in-law a tight smile, vaguely aware of my hand still being held by his son. "Are we going to do the proposal in private?"

I throw it out just to throw it out there. It's not like Emilio and I even spent any time together. You would think that if you wanted your daughter to marry someone, you'd at least have them date first, but no.

"No, you will do it here. No need for a proposal or privacy. My son is going to take care of you," Frederico promises, but with the way his son has been speaking to me, I highly doubt it.

I nod, no need for me to respond.

The faster I get this over with, the faster I can go to my wing here in the estate and cry.

"*Ahora*, Emilio, give her the ring so that we can be done with this and talk about bringing on the Castro men into the Muertos."

Emilio does as my father says and pulls a ring box out of his pocket and hands it to me. He doesn't even bother opening it, he just hands it to me as if it's an inconvenience for him.

I don't look at him as I take the box and open it. The ring is beautiful and if it were under any other circumstances, I would be jumping up and down for joy.

But there is nothing joyful about this.

A lump forms in my throat as I take the ring out from between the cushions. Tears start to slide down my cheeks as I slide the ring onto my ring finger.

This is it.

I'm engaged to Emilio Castro.

I'm going to marry him.

Everything that I know and love about my life will be gone.

All because this is what's best for the cartel.

Fuck the Muertos Cartel.

19

SANTOS

SOMETHING COMPELLED me to wait for her as soon as I closed the door.

Maybe it was the look that came across her face when she first entered the room. Or maybe it was how her body tensed up when Ronaldo dismissed me.

Whatever it was, I stayed. And now I'm on pins and needles, waiting for the door to open and for her to come out.

I was called into Ronaldo's office earlier by the man himself. He wanted to see how things were going with a few dealers in Austin. Nothing out of the ordinary. But then, of course there was a knock on the door and in walked Emilio and his father.

The second he met my murderous stare he gave me a smirk that I wanted to punch off him. Killing him was the next best option.

Ronaldo must have noticed how tense I got when the

Castros made their appearance because within seconds, he dismissed me to go get Isabella.

Once again, I was sent away to escort the princess into the office, this time though, the princess hates my guts.

I've been keeping my distance from her. Not because I wanted to, but because if I was around her, I would have done something stupid. Like possibly getting her killed if Emilio doesn't marry her. I wouldn't put it past the Castro family to retaliate if something happened to him. So, the best way to keep Isabella safe is to stay away from her.

Especially given the information that Elliot was able to find out on Emilio.

Looks like the blood prince to the Castro cartel is in deep, with some money issues. So deep that he started to use the cartel money and stopped paying for the merchandise that the Castros were getting from Belize. And when you don't pay for your product, people start coming after you.

According to Elliot, the fucker probably made a deal with someone wealthy to take down a member of the Muertos to be able to pay for his debts. He just wasn't able to find out who exactly.

I have a theory but until I have more information, I will not say anything.

Right now, I have to concentrate on finding a way to take down Emilio and stop this fucking marriage from happening.

Maybe it's time to get Leo involved.

Just as I'm thinking of how to tell Leo about the dirt

that I have on Emilio, the door to Ronaldo's office opens up.

My eyes land on her right away. They scan her whole body, check to see if there is anything that will have me bursting through the door and killing anyone that laid a hand on her, but I don't see a thing.

The only thing that grabs my attention is the redness of her eyes. She's angry, on the brink of tears, trying to hold all her emotions in.

I want to instantly go to her, but I hold myself off. Wrapping my arms around her and consoling her will not be a good idea, especially when her father is on the other side of the door.

She doesn't notice me at first, she just looks ahead at the living space in front of her, not really paying attention to her surroundings.

It's when I clear my throat that she notices that I'm there.

Instantly, her defenses go up. There's my stubborn, resilient girl. "Why are you still here?"

I shrug. "I figured I brought you over here, might as well walk you back." *I want to make sure you're okay.*

"I don't need an escort in my own house." There's a bite to her tone and she starts walking toward her wing, bumping me in the shoulder with a little too much force along the way.

"Your father seems to think so." She turns to face me, anger radiating off her more than it was a few seconds ago.

"I don't give a shit what my father thinks." Finger stab to the chest. "I can walk through my own house." Another stab. "I don't need you to walk me anywhere." Stab. Stab. Stab. "I don't fucking need you for anything."

I grab her by the wrist and stop the assault that her finger is doing to my chest.

"That last part is a fucking lie," I growl through my teeth.

She needs me.

She needs me just like I fucking need her. To breathe. To stay alive. I fucking need her for everything.

She's able to escape the grasp I have on her and shoves me with all her strength.

"No," she growls, just low enough for only me to hear. "I don't need you. Want to know why? Because you hurt me. You've hurt me more than once before and you are hurting me now. I don't need you."

What the fuck?

Where is this coming from?

Yes, I hurt her. I'm the first person to admit that when it has come to Isabella Morales, I have done more wrong than good. But I did that fucking shit to protect her, to make sure she got the life with someone that deserved her.

But now things are different. I'm fucking different.

She walks away from me, and it takes me a few seconds to comprehend what is happening before I'm following behind her.

I reach out and grab her by the elbow, bringing her to a stop and making her look at me. "What is going on with you? Why the hell are you acting this way?"

"Why? Why?" If looks could kill. "I will tell you why I'm acting this way, Santiago Reyes. This is fucking why!"

Isabella lifts her hand up and that's when I notice the piece of jewelry adorning her finger.

A diamond ring.

Of course, that's what the meeting was about. How I fucking missed that memo is beyond me.

"You're engaged." It's not a question. She's fucking engaged to Emilio Castro.

She's engaged to a fucking killer.

My plan to stop this fucking wedding from happening, just got put into hyperspeed.

"Yeah, I'm fucking engaged to a man that isn't you. Because you were a coward and couldn't go to my father to talk to him. So much for loving me."

She's hurting.

I know this woman well enough to know when she is hurting and when she lets the hurt take over, she says spiteful things.

It doesn't matter if it's me, her sister or her boss. If the hurt runs deep she will let you know exactly what she feels, even if you know that she doesn't mean it.

"I do love you."

Saying the words during this type of argument is not a good move, but I had to say the words. It doesn't matter what she feels about me right now, she has to know that I love her and that will never change.

"Then prove it. Do something about this. Don't just stand there and let this happen. Don't let me walk down that aisle while you stay silent. Do something. Please Santiago, do something to stop this."

I will try.

But I don't voice it.

I just continue to stand there in silence while the woman I love breaks further into the hurt that I have caused.

"I guess your silence is all the response I need." Without a final look in my direction, she walks away and I let her.

I won't let Isabella marry that man.

I will kill him before he gets to call her his wife.

———

ISABELLA

My chest burns so much from all the anger that is boiling inside of me.

I want to reach into my chest and pull my heart out so that it would stop hurting so much.

I blame Santiago, I blame my father for making me feel this way.

This is a point in my life where I really wish that my mother was alive so that she could wrap her arms around me and make the pain stop.

If only she were here.

If only she hadn't been killed.

So much for the promise I made to myself about not letting men hurt me like this ever again.

I guess I'm just a weak girl that will let every single person she knows, walk all over her.

The weight of the ring adorning my left hand feels like it's pulling me down and making the whole situation much worse.

This is my life, and it feels like there is nothing I can do to change it.

I need to run, to get away from here.

I need to do something because I feel like I'm about to explode. There are so many emotions running through my body and I hate it.

I hate feeling so out of control like this.

So I walk. I walk as far away from my father's office and Santiago as I possibly can. I won't be able to get very far but it still would put a good distance between us.

My emotions start getting in check, or at least I think they do. Everything comes running back out when I run into something. And that something is my brother.

"Whoa there," he places his hands on my shoulders, trying to keep me steady.

The second I look up at him, I want to lose it. I know he sees how I look right now and the worry line forming between his eyebrows tells me that he doesn't like it.

"Isabella, what's wrong?"

I try everything in me not to let my emotions take over. "I just got engaged to Emilio."

As soon as I say the name, everything that I was holding in, every emotion that was being kept at bay, seeps out and eventually I find myself in my brother's arms, letting every bit of pain out.

Everything I am holding in, I let it out in sobs, soaking my brother's shirt in the process.

I just want the pain to stop.

Why can't it stop?

———

A BRIGHT LIGHT that is entering the room is what wakes me the next morning. After a few seconds of me trying to fight it and trying to go back to sleep, I realize it's the sun that is shining brightly and it won't go away to let me enjoy these last few seconds of solace that I have.

I slowly open my eyes and I see that I'm in my room at my father's estate, and Camila is sound asleep right next to me.

Leo called her last night after finding me wandering around and I cried all the tears I had in my body onto his shirt.

For a few long hours, I was held by my two siblings, both of them telling me that they would do everything in their power to figure out the situation. Hearing them say the words made me cry harder.

I will admit, though, being held by two people that love me so unconditionally was exactly what I needed. I didn't know that that was what I was missing until I experienced it.

Eventually the tears stopped. Leo left me and Camila to check on something and me and my sister just lay in my bed, having a silent conversation, until we both fell asleep.

Now morning has arrived, and I don't want to get up

from this bed, because I'm scared of what awaits me once I leave the comfort of this mattress.

So, I watch my little sister sleep.

Her almost white hair is all over the place and it's like a sheet, making her look like an angel.

Camila is the rebel that I will never be. She lets me dress her up in my designs, but she makes each and every one of them her own, what with her Docs always on her feet.

She takes risks that scare me, but those risks are making her a young woman that our mother would have been proud of.

Camila will do great things in this life, but she just needs to get out of these four walls to be able to achieve them. No way in hell will I be letting our father do to her what he is doing to me.

My marveling over her must not have been as silent as I thought, because she begins to stir and eventually, I'm met with a sleepy brown-eyed gaze.

"It's not creepy at all to wake up and find someone staring at you." She closes her eyes again, but she scoots closer to me, placing her head against my shoulder.

"I have a beautiful sister. Sue me if I want to stare at her for a few seconds before she wakes up and turns into something out of a horror movie."

The comment earns me a pinch to the hip, and I can't help but let out a laugh.

I stop when I notice Camila staring up at me with eyes full of wonder.

"What?" I ask her curiously.

"That's the first time I've heard you laugh in a while. I've missed it."

Has it really been that long since I've laughed at something?

I try to think about it, but the only thing that I can come up with is that my sister is right. I haven't laughed in a very long time. I think ever since I found out I was to wed Emilio.

My mood is somber and I slide down the bed a bit to wrap my arms around her.

"It has been a while," I murmur into her hair.

She nods against my shoulder and wraps her own arms around me.

"Leo will figure it out, you know," she says, pulling back slightly to look me in the eyes.

"What will he figure out?"

"A way to stop that wedding. He will figure it out and end whatever arrangement dad has. It will happen."

She's hopeful. I can see it in her face and hear it in her voice.

I want to be hopeful right there with her, but a big part of my brain is telling me that I shouldn't. That this whole situation will take a lot more than Leo figuring it out.

"I hope you are right." I give my little sister a smile and wrap my arms around her again. Eventually she falls back asleep, and I stay awake with my thoughts keeping me company.

I do hope she's right.

But at this point I'm not sure how much hope I have left.

20

SANTOS

Seven Months Earlier

"Do you really think icing out your wife is a good idea?"

I watch as Leo finishes getting dressed in his office, all because he's been avoiding Serena.

Want to know why he's avoiding the brunette beauty he married one drunken night in Vegas?

For the same reason that I've been avoiding Isabella for almost five months. To protect her, to leave her out of this world as much as possible.

I, at least, haven't been sharing a bed with the woman I love. This bastard goes to sleep with his wife in his arms every single night and doesn't spend an ounce of time with her during the day. He even has me taking the woman to work because he can't deal with it.

What kind of bullshit is that?

You should be asking yourself the same question.

I do. I ask that very same question every single day.

Maybe Leo and I aren't meant to be in serious, committed relationships, since we keep finding reasons to hurt the person we love. And yeah, the snarly bastard that is supposed to put fear into people is in love with his wife, who would have thought?

"It's the best option right now. She'll realize soon enough what this life really is and when she does, she'll want to walk away, and I will let her."

He would. Leo would rather break watching Serena walk away, rather than let her stay here and be in constant danger.

Why do you think I went along with Isabella to keep our relationship a secret for so long? Because even if she was the kingpin's daughter, she's still in constant danger. Her father is one of the most hated men in the drug business, anyone would go after her for that alone. Add in being with someone that is a part of her father's cartel, she would have a bigger target on her back.

"And if the opposite happens?" I raise an eyebrow to my best friend. Surely, he thought all of this through.

He stops tying his tie midway and looks at me like I have three heads. "I don't fucking know. I've been trying to get this woman to divorce me for months now, all for her own good, and nothing makes her sign the papers. I've killed men in front of her for fuck's sakes and she still wants to stay married to me. Who in their right mind thinks that's sane?"

Seems to me like Serena and Leo are cut from the same cloth. They are both fucking stubborn, no wonder they got married on a whim. They are made for each other.

"Serena apparently." I give him a small snort and the man gives me a look like he wants to murder me.

I want to see him try; he would be lost without me.

"I hope one day you find a woman that's a pain in your ass, then you will know the shit I go through." He rolls his eyes at me before pulling his tie out of its place before throwing it on the ground.

That woman is already in my life.

Isabella.

And my situation is a lot more complicated than his.

I don't voice it though, as much as I want to, I continue to keep my relationship with his sister to myself.

After a few seconds, Leo's little temper tantrum is all but forgotten when he picks up his tie from the floor and goes back to trying to tie it.

It takes him a good five minutes to get it but hey, he gets it done.

You would think that a man that wears suits on occasion, would know how to tie a tie a little quicker.

"Are you going down to the square?" he asks as he pulls his jacket on.

I nod. "Was planning on it. My mom wanted me to go place a few flowers for her on my dad's grave."

It's the *Día de los Muertos* celebration tonight. Growing up, this tradition wasn't something that particularly grabbed my attention. Then my father died and that first year, Isabella showed me what partaking in the celebration can do to help you cope with the death of a loved one.

I'm going to be honest here, I didn't think that it would help but that first year after his death, I set up a small altar with my mother. She surrounded it with his favorite food and drinks and placed pictures of him everywhere she could.

It was a nice way to honor him, and we've been doing it ever since. It has changed a bit since my mother has been in Canada, but we make it work in any way we can.

This is the first year that I will be placing flowers on my father's headstone without Isabella at my side.

"Serena wants to do the same for my mom." Leo gets a somber look on his face, and I know every bit of him wishes that Rosa Maria was here.

Eventually we both get situated. Leo finishes getting dressed and makes his way over to grab Serena. I follow him out of the office and head over to my parents' old living quarters and grab the flowers.

I didn't bother dressing up like Leo did. My plan is to just place the flowers on the grave and head home to bury myself in a bottle of tequila.

"Santos!" a female voice calls out my name as I'm about to pass through the security gate of the estate.

Turning, I see Camila running over to me. In one hand, she is holding the fabric of her traditional style dress and in the other, she is holding a mountain of flowers.

I stop and wait for her to make her way over to me.

"Here. Take these," she says, handing me the mountain of flowers as soon as she's about a foot away from me.

"Got enough flowers here?" I have to make sure I have a good hold on all the bunches, or they will fall to the ground.

"I was supposed to have more, but that was all I could

carry," she sounds out of breath, and my guess is it's from the running.

"You good?" I ask her, nodding at her to follow me to the square.

"Oh my god, this dress is so heavy and hot," she fans herself with her hand. "Is my makeup okay? I feel like I'm sweating and it's all melting off."

She closes her eyes and has me inspect every single inch of her well-decorated face paint.

This girl is seriously an artist. Her face is covered in different shades of black and a few specks of reds and blues, all of it coming together to make it look like an actual skull.

It's impressive as hell.

"Not a line out of place," I tell her and she lets out a sigh of relief.

"*Gracias a Dios*. I had to do not only my and Isabella's makeup but also Serena's, so I was in a time crunch, and I was worried that mine would look like shit."

I snort. "Nothing you do looks like shit."

"Aw! You gave me a compliment; you really must love me!" She gives me a bright smile, all the while I just roll my eyes at her.

"I love you like an annoying cat that won't go away."

That causes her to scuff. "Excuse me. I'm not an annoying cat. I'm more like a puppy that will forever be your companion."

"You're too fucking much."

This is my relationship with Camila. Leo acts like the

overprotective brother that he is and with me she gets the type of brother that will spar with her wit.

She's a real pain in the ass but she's the sister I never had.

"You still love me.," she sticks her tongue out at me. Something must have caught her attention because she pauses and looks around. "Where is Isabella? She's always with you during this."

Have I ever mentioned how I hate how observant the Morales can be sometimes?

I shrug, trying to act as indifferent as possible. "Your sister and I aren't talking at the moment."

It's more like she hates my guts and thinks that I don't love her because I won't fight for her. Little does she know that's all a complete lie. I will fight for her until I die.

"Because of the engagement, right? She should be happy about celebrating an engagement with you. Instead, she's miserable and depressed over the engagement with Emilio."

Camila's statement makes me stop in my tracks.

How the fuck...?

How the fuck does she know about me and Isabella?

I know for a fact that Isabella didn't tell anyone that we were together, not even her sister.

So how the actual fuck does Camila know?

"How...?" I start off the question, but I can't seem to form the words to finish it. My mind is fucking blown, I can't even form concrete thoughts.

"How do I know that you and my sister were in a relationship for four years?" I nod.

Pretty sure my mouth is wide enough to let a few bugs in.

"Yes," I'm able to get out.

Camila shrugs. "I've known for a while. I noticed the way you two would act around each other when there were people around. So, my suspicions were always up, but I finally was able to confirm it a few years ago when I had a sleepover at Isabella's apartment and you called her. She thought that I was asleep, but I wasn't. I heard her tell you that she loved you."

Again, I hate how observant the Morales are.

I scratch my head, trying to make sense of everything. "How did you know about the engagement?"

I think if Isabella had told Camila about it, she would have told me.

"When she moved back here, I would find her looking at Pinterest boards that featured weddings and putting together mock-ups for a wedding dress. It wasn't hard to put two and two together. Especially since this was before anything with Emilio came up."

Well, fuck.

"You didn't tell anyone, did you?"

She shakes her head. "No. Not even Leo."

I'm sure that if she had told Leo, I would have heard something by now.

Or maybe he would be planning your slow, torturous death.

I shake that thought out of my head and concentrate on the matter at hand.

"Does Isabella know that you know about us?"

Again, she shakes her head. "I never told her. You get that special title."

"Great." I don't know why this is taking me so much time to comprehend. So, what if Camila knew, or should I say knows, about what went on between me and her sister.

That's one less person to tell, right?

But if Camila knows, what are the chances that Ronaldo does too?

What if everything was set up with the Castros because he knew and wanted to keep me from marrying his daughter?

Is Ronaldo even capable of doing that?

Yes. He is very capable of doing just that.

But confirming that he actually did is a whole different story.

I start walking again and right away Camila is at my side.

"That's why you guys aren't talking, right?"

I sigh. I could lie to her right now but then I would have to add that to the list of lies or lies by omission that I have racking up against me.

So I nod. "I might have told her that I wouldn't go against your father's word on this. What's done is done. She thinks that I don't love her, that I'm choosing the cartel over her, that I won't fight for her, but that's not even close."

"Then what are you doing?" There is curiosity in her voice. I think about not spilling everything to the nineteen-year-old but since I can't go to her brother with this, I might as well tell her.

"I'm protecting her. There are a few things that I need to take care of, and I can't do them with her at my side. That would put her in danger, or worse yet, killed. I can't do that to her. It was better for me to walk away and let her believe that I was throwing away four years together, and not have something happen to her."

We begin to approach the town square, so I guide us through a path that has fewer people going through. I don't need some random individual hearing this conversation.

"So why not be honest with her and tell her exactly what you are doing? You telling her could have saved her a whole lot of heartache." Great, the teenager is the voice of reason.

"No shit, but if I had told your sister, she would want to be involved in every single detail. No way will I have her present while I put a bullet through someone's skull."

Exactly what I want to do to her fiancé.

"I still think that you should talk to her." She gives me a stern look before she takes a bouquet of flowers from my arms and walks straight to the cemetery.

I, of course, follow behind her and watch her place a bouquet of flowers on all the gravestones that have no decorations around them.

This is something that Camila does every single year. I asked her about it once and she told me that every single life should be celebrated, not just the ones that we were close to.

I find it admirable.

Camila and I walk through the whole damn cemetery

until the only flowers that are left are the ones for my father.

We walk over to his gravesite together, and we both come to a stop when we see someone in a similar dress to Camila's sitting in front of it. I don't need to see who it is that is honoring my father, I already know.

"I'm going to go back to the estate and grab more flowers," Camila shoves me, not even moving me an inch. "Go talk to her."

Before I can say anything, Camila is leaving me there to interact with her older sister all by myself.

Isabella looks absolutely breathtaking, even from fifty feet away.

I make my way to her in a slow manner, avoiding all the other people around us, keeping my eyes on her and her alone.

She must have heard me approaching because she looks up when I'm only a few feet away.

Like Camila, her face has an intricate design adorning it. The only difference between their face paint is that Isabella's is a lot more colorful. She even has jewels around her eyes.

"I can leave," she says taking my attention away from her face.

She's already pushing herself off the ground, where she was kneeling before I can answer.

"It's fine. He would have been happy that you came by to visit him. He always loved hearing about any new designs you had come up with." I wave for her to sit back down, which earns me a small, sad smile.

I don't want that shit.

I want the smile that takes over every single inch of her face and brightens up her eyes like no tomorrow.

She nods before extending a hand to me, silently asking me for the flowers I'm holding.

Without a word, I hand them to her and crouch down next to her, watching her place the flowers in an intricate pattern. Only a clothing designer would be this intricate with her work.

"Were you telling him that I'm an asshole?"

Isabella lets out a small laugh as she continues to place the flowers.

"I was telling him about my job. A few years before he died, he told me to build myself into the person that I wanted to be, and I was telling him that I did it."

This time the smile that captivates her face is a real one, one that I haven't seen in weeks. I never realized just how much you can miss seeing a smile until now.

"I didn't know he told you that." I keep my eyes on her, not wanting to miss a single thing that she does.

Isabella nods. "Right before I moved to Austin. He said that Austin was going to be a good move for me."

Even from the grave, the old man keeps surprising me.

"He was right. Austin was a good move." She was able to grow into her own person and not depend on her father's hand. Even if she did have me or Leo at her side most of the time.

Once again, she gives me a sad smile, and I hate it. I want the smile from only a few seconds ago back.

I don't move my eyes away from hers and she meets my gaze straight on.

As I get lost in her eyes, I think about what Camila said earlier. If only I had talked to Isabella, then I would have saved her a lot of heartache.

She's right.

I think it might be time to talk to her.

A piece of dark hair falls out of the bun that she is wearing, and I can't help but reach out and tuck it away.

Her eyes go wide at the action and even more when I slide my thumb along her cheekbone. But it's the gasps she releases when I place my palm against her cheek that get me, and I'm gutted even more when she leans into my touch.

"Do you want to go talk?" I ask as my thumb moves back and forth along her skin.

Her wide eyes look back at me in fear. Fear that is probably there because she doesn't know what a conversation between us might hold. Fear that I will break her heart once again.

The brown eyes that I love so much stare at me for an endless amount of time until finally they close, and she nods against my hand.

I drop my hand, only to hold it out for her to take. There is hesitancy there, only for a second, but it was there before she finally places her hand in mine.

Once she is steady on her feet, she goes to pull away from me, but I don't budge. I continue to hold her hand tightly in mine, not giving a shit anymore.

Isabella looks at me, as if she wants to ask what I'm doing.

Without giving her the answer she is looking for, I guide her out of the cemetery, avoiding the throngs of people.

Her hand stays in mine all the way back to the Morales Estate.

21

ISABELLA

To say that I'm not a little shell-shocked is an understatement.

I knew he was going to be at the celebration. He's been going for the last couple years, albeit with me, but still, I knew that he was going to be there.

Did I think that he would find me at his father's grave?

No. I thought that I could go over there, talk to Cristiano for a few minutes and then I would be able to make my way back to my mom's grave.

But of course, that didn't happen.

I was so enthralled with talking about how much I love my job, and telling the gravestone how much I hated my father for what he is doing to me, that I lost track of time.

When I heard him approach, yes, I heard the man approach, he has a very distinctive way of walking and even with dirt I can always tell when it's him. Anyway, when I heard him approach, I tried to not show any emotions, well, at least not any that will show that I was hurt or angry.

It was nice talking to him without any screaming matches or wanting to throat punch him, even if it was for a few minutes.

It also felt nice to just look into his eyes and get lost in them.

All of it felt sort of normal.

Then he placed his hand against my cheek and I tried not to melt away.

When he offered to talk, I wanted to say no. Because if we went somewhere to talk, it was possible that we were going to yell at each other some more and I was going to leave hurt yet again.

Yet, I still agreed.

I agreed and I spent the whole time walking from the cemetery all the way back to the estate with my hand in his.

The only other time he has held my hand in public was when I graduated high school as he guided us through the crowd. This time felt different. Like I had to keep checking over my shoulder that my father or any of his other men weren't watching us. I even tried to hide the hand-holding with my dress as much as possible.

The fear of someone seeing me with Santos while I was supposed to be engaged to another man was real.

I don't really care what complete strangers think but if it were my father, that would be another story.

Even now, as we walk through the estate and head to my wing, I'm still worried about running into him.

Santos guides us to my studio and when we walk through the door, that's when he finally lets go of my hand.

The second that his palm is no longer next to mine, I miss it.

I watch as he closes the door behind us and when he turns back to face me, he gives me a small grin. One that doesn't reach his eyes.

Never has this man not given me a smile that hadn't reached his eyes.

A part of me hates it.

I give him a similar smile back before he drops my gaze and looks around the room, which is a complete mess.

I'm still working from the estate. Mostly to please my father, and just in case he wanted to drop another bombshell on me. Maybe this time, instead of marrying an heir to another cartel, I would be turning into a drug mule or something. You never know with the man.

"This dress is beautiful," Santos says about the current white dress that's on my mannequin.

"Thank you," I'm used to receiving his praise on my work but for some reason, getting his praise for this dress feels wrong.

"Serena's wedding dress?" He grabs one of the lace sleeves, inspecting it.

The wedding that my father is putting together for Leo and Serena is a good reason as to why I'm currently working on a wedding dress.

But no dice. I started this dress before Serena was even in the picture. Even before I was even promised to Emilio, for that matter. I started thinking about the fabric, the silhouette, every design aspect for this dress the second I saw the ring box that he had hidden in his closet.

Seeing the box gave me an idea. I could picture the ring that was inside in my mind and started working on a dress right away

But that was months ago. I haven't touched it in weeks.

Because this is the dress that I'd be wearing if I ever married Santos. And I say if, because at this point, it will never happen.

I just nod and give him a quick yeah, keeping the truth to myself.

He continues to look around the room and a part of me feels a little uneasy.

Before everything, having him in here felt right. It was my favorite thing combined with my favorite person all in one place.

Now it feels a little off.

Or maybe it's just me.

"You wanted to talk?" I have to bring it up, otherwise I will be going crazy hoping he doesn't see any of the other designs that are scattered around the room.

Like maybe the lingerie I had drawn out for our would-be wedding night. I may or may not have photoshopped the drawing onto my body for reference. Sue me.

He turns to face me and this time, instead of keeping his distance from me, he approaches me, only leaving a small space between us.

Santiago isn't even touching me and I feel him all over my body.

"Have I mentioned how beautiful you look tonight?" he offers and I have to take a step back. I'm not doing this.

"Don't do that." I hold up a hand when he takes a step toward me.

"Don't do what?" He seriously can't be this stupid.

"Don't tell me that I look beautiful. We both know what happened when you told me those words all those years ago. And we also know what happened after. So please don't make this worse. You wanted to talk, so please just talk."

Am I being harsh? Maybe, but this feels like a violent cycle that has no end. He wants to call me beautiful, fine I'll let him, but he can do it after he says everything he brought me here to say.

I'm standing my ground because I'm sick and tired of this shit.

He nods and I think he's going to take me seriously but then he speaks.

"It's not a lie though, you do look beautiful."

Oh my god.

I'm out.

With a groan and an eye roll thrown in his direction, I turn to leave the room.

"I'm sorry!" He yells out before I can even take a step.

I turn slightly, not fully facing him, seeing that he is still standing where he was a few seconds ago.

"I'm sorry, *bella*. I'm so fucking sorry."

The way the words are rolling off his tongue, he's not saying sorry for his comment a few minutes ago. No, this is a different kind of sorry.

I don't move from my position. "What exactly are you sorry for?"

There's a lump already forming in my throat. The conversation hasn't even started and I'm already feeling emotional.

"Everything. For hurting you all those years ago, for leaving you that morning, for making you think that I didn't love you and for giving you the impression that I didn't believe in what we built together."

The hurt in his voice makes it almost near impossible to move or to not go to him and tell him that I accept his apology.

But I have to be honest with myself here.

I don't accept it, and I won't accept it until I hear why he did what he did. Why he walked out of this very room and told me that he wasn't going to with me.

I deserve at least that.

"Then why did you? Why did you walk away from me when shit got tough? Why didn't you stay to fight for me? Why did you walk away?" The more I ask the questions, the angrier I get.

What makes me want to blow a gasket though, is the fact that Santiago just stands there, not saying a word.

So much for talking.

"I can't do this."

The lump that was forming in my throat has become so big that I can't take it anymore and let the tears release.

This time when I turn around and walk, I am able to make it to the door before he actually speaks.

"Because the second I saw Emilio Castro, I knew that I

needed to figure out a way to get you out of whatever arrangement your father put you in. I needed you to stay safe, and the only way to do that was to keep you out of it. Keep you out of everything that I was about to plan."

I turn to the man standing in my studio. The look in his eyes is all I need to see to know that he is telling me the truth.

Chills run up my arms, just thinking about the reason why he would want to get me out of anything that had Emilio involved.

"Who is he? Why did you have to think of a way to get me out of this?"

So many scenarios run through my mind, each one worse than the one before it.

"Isabella."

"No, tell me. I have a right to know the kind of person he is. If I'm going to marry this man, I have a right to know."

I'm standing my ground. He knows who this person is, and I'm going to make him tell me.

Surprisingly, Santiago moves toward me and doesn't stop until his body is only inches away from mine and my face is being held between his hands.

"Tell me. Please."

I beg him.

Santiago moves his thumbs along my cheeks, wiping away the tears that have escaped.

"Emilio Castro killed my father."

22

ISABELLA

There's a coldness that runs through my veins as I try to digest what I was just told.

Emilio Castro killed Cristiano Reyes.

So many questions are running through my mind.

"H-how do you know he did it?" I grab on to Santos's wrists, trying to not only hold his hands to my face for comfort but also to keep myself steady.

"You might not remember this, I don't even think I told you, but the day he died I spent hours looking through footage trying to find something. Anything that would lead me to his killer. I didn't find anything that day, but something did stick out a few weeks later."

I knew he had gone down a dark hole after Cristiano died. It was around the time that our relationship started, so I was noticing a lot of things about him.

How he had dark bags under his eyes from sleepless nights. How red his eyes were every single morning, that told me that he spent hours looking at a computer screen. I saw every single sign, but I chose to ignore it because in my head it was his way of coping with his father's death.

If hunting down his father's killer was something that he needed to do, then I would look the other way.

As the years went on, though, the dark bags started to disappear, and the red eyes stopped. At the time I thought he had given up, but now I'm thinking something different was up.

Maybe something caused him to stop looking.

"What? What stood out?"

Santos removes a hand from my face and shows it to me.

It's covered with multiple tattoos. All varying in size and all making him look like the badass that he is.

"A tattoo. It was in a few pictures, a little blurry, but I was able to make out the lines and the design. I stamped it into my memory, studied the design for years. Didn't have much luck finding the person who wore it until…"

He stops and I'm left wondering when he realized who it was.

That's when I start thinking.

The first time that I met Emilio, I noticed the tattoo. Something about the way he held his hands made me remember the intricate pattern that was placed on it. For a second I even thought it was pretty but the design didn't suit him. That type of tattoo was made for someone who could own it. Like my brother or Santos.

The way he was standing in that room that day would have made his hands only visible to me. That is until he…

Holy crap.

Until he came up to me and grabbed my hand to place a kiss on my knuckles.

Santos would have seen the tattoo then.

"Until you saw it in my father's office. The day he announced the arrangement with the Castros," I finish his thought process.

There's a second of hesitation, but soon he's nodding.

Fuck.

Who is my father making me marry?

"Does anyone else know?" Surely if my father knew that Emilio was the one that gunned down Cristiano, one of his most loyal men, then he would call off this fucked-up arrangement, right?

Right?

Santos shakes his head. "You are the first person I've told."

Holy. Shit.

I can think of at least one other person he could have told first besides me and that's my brother. He would have known how to deal with this. Me, on the other hand, I'm trying really hard not to hyperventilate right now.

Breathe, Isabella.

Take a deep breath and try to center yourself.

"I think you should tell Leo," I mutter out, tightening the hand on the wrist that is up and still cupping my face.

"I know, but before I went to your brother, I had to tell you. So that you could know why I'm doing what I'm doing."

He leans forward and places his forehead against mine. This is the closest we have been to each other in months.

I watch him as he closes his eyes and takes in a deep breath. His hands travel to my waist and bring my body closer to his.

This is something that I've missed.

The proximity.

I've missed being this close to him. I've missed his hands on me and being able to take in his scent.

I've missed it all when it comes to this man.

I want to get lost in the feeling of his hands on my body and forget about all the shit that I have been through these last couple weeks. But we aren't done talking.

"What are you planning on doing?"

A feeling that he has been up to something has been stuck in the pit of my stomach for weeks. This is finally my chance to know what it is.

Santos keeps his forehead against mine, with his eyes closed, until he finally pulls away, his forehead showing signs that my makeup rubbed off on him.

He doesn't care though, he just looks at me. The way he's eyes are looking me isn't in a sweet way. It isn't a look that I'm used to seeing.

Then I realize why it looks different.

He's not looking at me as if he were Santiago Reyes, the man that I've known all my life. The man that I shared four amazing years with.

No, the man before me is looking at me as if he were Santos. The cartel man that is deadly and will kill anyone that gets in his way. The man that is seeking revenge for his father's murder.

This man before me terrifies me.

"Figuring out a way to end this arrangement and kill Emilio the same way he killed my father. In cold blood."

He means it.

Every last word.

He will no doubt come up with a plan that ultimately ends Emilio's life.

I nod, instead of saying anything. What is there to say?

No, don't kill Emilio?

Even I, a person that doesn't want anything to do with any cartel business, know that when you go after a member of this family, there will be consequences. Those consequences come with the possibility that you won't get to live the next year of your life.

How Emilio has gone this long without being killed is beyond me.

I can't help but wonder if my dad knew about this. If he did, why hand me over to the Castro family on a silver platter?

It doesn't make sense.

I go back to what Santos just said. He said figuring it out. Meaning that he hasn't come up with a plan that will work to put a stop to all this.

"You said you were figuring it out? What is there to figure out? Just kill the bastard and be done with it."

If Emilio is dead, I don't have to go through with the marriage.

But what if Ronaldo just finds someone else for you to marry?

I swallow down that thought process.

"It's a lot more complicated than just shooting the asshole in the skull," Santos growls out.

"How? How is it complicated?"

"You're involved, Isabella. Whether I like it or not, you're involved. In a few short weeks, you're set to marry the bastard and then you will be tied to him forever. If I do anything, anything at all, I have to make sure that you are as far away from this as I can get you, that you don't know every single detail. What happens if I kill him and the Castro cartel decides to retaliate? And what if they decide to retaliate by killing you? That shit can't fucking happen. That's why I distanced myself from you, to fucking protect you. There are eyes everywhere. If the wrong person saw us together, it would get back to Emilio or worse, your father, and there would be even more consequences to pay."

I take an audible breath.

The more I listen to him speak the more I realize that things are in fact, complicated.

But there is one more thing to add to the complications

"My father knows."

He looks at me like I have gone crazy, like the words that just left my mouth were something of make-believe.

"Please tell me that's a joke." If only.

I feel my eyes close and I shake my head.

"I went to him a few weeks ago to tell him that I didn't want to marry Emilio. He told me that if I didn't go through with it, then Camila would be the one marrying him. That I had to do what he said if I wanted her to be able to continue living her life. Then he warned me that you should stay away too."

Santos scrubs his hands over his face and lets out a frustrated groan, which sounds more angry than frustrated. I'm definitely not telling him about the face slap I received courtesy of my father, that just might send him over the edge.

"Did he say how long he's known?"

"Apparently from the very beginning."

I still can't figure out how he knew for that long.

Did he see us together?

I don't see how that would be possible since we spent ninety percent of our time in Austin. If we were in San Pedro, we could act like we would when we were teenagers, before my hopes were up, and Santos was still speaking to me.

Did he have someone following us? That would seem more likely but why would he need to have someone following his own daughter?

Besides, Santos is one of my father's most loyal next to my brother, why wouldn't he want him to be with his daughter?

Nothing makes sense.

"Camila knows too."

That takes my mind off my father.

My sister knows?

"How do you know that?"

"She told me tonight. Apparently, she noticed the way we looked at each other, whatever the fuck that means."

I can't believe that Camila knew about us and didn't tell me.

That bitch.

If I would have known that she knew about me and Santos, I would have gone to her when I needed to talk and not held everything in.

"I'm not worried about Camila. The one that has my mind working overtime is Ronaldo. He's not the type of man to stand back with something like this."

"What are you thinking?" I ask.

I know the man well enough to know when his mind is spinning. And right now, with a murderous glare in his eyes, I know that it's spinning out of control.

"There's a deeper reason as to why he is taking over the Castro cartel and why he wants you to marry Emilio so badly."

He's right.

This all can't be about the money and power that this arrangement is going to bring to the Muertos. There has to be something else. Something bigger and my father is using me to get it. But what is it?

Thinking about all this takes me back to the day of the walk with my father and what he said about Santos being right next to Cristiano.

He needs to know.

"This may be nothing but that same day that he told me about knowing about us, he said that if you do anything to stop this, you'll be in a box next to your father. I think—" I stop. Can I say the words? Can I put this thought process out there? "I think my father had something to do with Cristiano's death."

This is something that I thought about for a while. And the more I think of it, the more it makes sense.

But how does the Castros tie into all of this and how does it come back to my father?

The room is still for a few seconds, with Santos just standing before me, until he finally nods.

"I've thought the same thing."

Four years ago, I never would have put Cristiano's death on the man that brought me into this world. Now, I can't help but think that it's true.

"So what do we do?" Because as much as he doesn't want me involved, I am.

Santos looks at me and when he makes his way back to me, his eyes don't leave mine. Once there, only a few inches away from me, he takes my face between his hands again.

"Do you trust me?" His voice is a whisper against my lips, my hands instantly going to his waist.

"With everything that I am." Even through the immense amount of pain that he has caused to my heart, I still trust him.

"Then let me continue to figure this out. I'll go to Leo, and we will figure this out together. But you can't be involved in this any more than what you already are. Let me do this for you. Let me keep you safe."

My eyes close at his words and I can't help but lean into his touch.

How much longer do I have to continue going through this?

What if I still have to marry Emilio and this becomes my life forever?

I swallow everything down.

"Okay but do it quickly. Please."

"I will try my fucking hardest."

He pulls back slightly, only to lean forward again to place his lips against my forehead.

I'm pressed against him so tightly that I can feel all that he wants to say all with only this one kiss.

Finally, he pulls back, fully this time, and rubs my cheek with his thumb, wiping the tear that must have escaped away. He gives me a small smile and starts to walk out of the room.

"I don't even get a real kiss goodbye?"

It feels like it has been forever since I have felt his lips against mine. You have no idea how much I miss his mouth on my skin, kissing, licking, nibbling on every single inch of me.

"As long as you have another man's ring on your finger, I won't touch you."

With that, he leaves.

And I'm left standing there wondering if I can find a way to break that last promise.

23

SANTOS

I'VE SAID THIS BEFORE, but Emilio Castro is a fucking dead man.

This time, I'm not talking out of my fucking ass. No, this time it's an actual possibility that I'll finally get the chance to kill the fucker once and for all.

Why might Emilio finally meet his demise?

Well because he decided it was a good idea to go after Serena and her friend Aria, have a few of his men kidnap them and possibly kill them.

The fucker wasn't counting on Serena calling Leo and leaving a horrifying voice mail that notified him that she'd been taken. He also didn't realize that his men were so stupid that they didn't notice a federal agent outside of the building.

Thankfully Leo has a tech-savvy hacker in his back pocket, courtesy of Elliot Lane, that was able to get us in contact with said federal agent. Which led us to where Emilio was holding the women.

Now there are five men dead downstairs, Emilio is writhing on the floor from a fucking bullet that went through his leg, and Serena and Aria are getting taken to the hospital by Leo and Agent Madden.

Yes, the federal agent worked with us.

As long as he doesn't arrest me for what I'm about to do to the fucker crying on the floor, I'm good.

"Take care of it," Leo orders as he carries an almost passed out Serena out the door.

I give him a curt nod, not taking my eyes off of Emilio. I'm so focused on him, I don't even realize when Madden leaves behind Leo.

Emilio's whimpers fill the room.

Such a fucking pussy.

A real cartel man knows how to take a bullet, if he was anything like Leo and me, he wouldn't be on the floor curled up in a ball asking God to save him.

I guess that goes to show that he's not a real cartel man. Not even with all the shit he yelled out about his family deserving all the power and money.

The only reason that Leo didn't kill the bastard is because he threatened Isabella's life.

If Leo killed him, his men would kill her.

No one goes around threatening my woman's life, and when I'm done with this fucker, he will be begging me to end his.

I crouch down in front of him and he must know what is coming, because the second he notices me in front of him he squirms back.

The fucker doesn't even move a few inches before I

grab him by the thigh and press my thumb into the wound.

His screams fill the room.

Blood covers my hand, seeping into the carpeted floor, but I don't give a shit. Let the neighbors hear him, he'll be dead before the cops arrive.

"Did you really think you were smart, *pendejo*?" I tighten my grip on his thigh and, as expected, his screams grow louder.

"I don't know what you're talking about," he pants out through gritted teeth. Trying his hardest not to succumb to the pain.

"*Si sabes*," I give him a sadistic grin, taking my hand away from his leg and giving his face a few slaps.

Love taps, if you will. Love taps that cover his face with the blood from his leg.

"I don't," Emilio groans again.

Without warning, I grab his face, digging my nails into his cheeks like I did his leg. The pussy squirms even more, trying to get away from me, but he's not going anywhere. It's just going to be me, him, and the dead bodies down on the first floor.

"So you didn't take Serena and her friend from their apartment?" My nails puncture his cheeks. "You didn't tell Leo that if he killed you that your men would go after Isabella? You didn't do any of that?"

My nails are so deep into his skin that little beads of blood start to come to the surface.

Good.

Emilio looks me straight in the eyes, not saying a damn

word. His eyes got darker at the mention of Isabella's name.

Confirmation.

"Ah, so you did those things." Another love tap, this time just a little bit harder

"I'm not telling you shit," Emilio spits outs, the droplets of his spit landing on my face.

This fucker isn't going to make it out of here alive.

"You see, that's where you're wrong." I shift myself so that my boot is closer to his leg. "You threatened the one person that you had no right to threaten. That right there is reason enough for me not to let you leave this room alive."

My foot lands on his thigh.

I barely even make contact, when his screams start to fill the room again. This time, there is no doubt that the neighbors are hearing him.

I apply more and more pressure onto the leg until I watch Emilio's eyes roll back into his head, finally starts to succumb to the pain and passing out.

Looks like this fucker can't take pain very well.

Standing up to full height, I look at the piece-of-trash man lying at my feet. He looks pathetic, and I could kill him right here, but I have this feeling in my gut that tells me that I should put him through some torture just a little bit longer.

I tend to trust my gut.

Shaking my head, I crouch down and pick the bastard up and sling him over my shoulder. He's such a heavy bastard.

On the way down the stairs, the dead bodies that are scattered all over the first floor grab my attention for a few seconds.

They will be disposed of properly and then it would look like not a single soul was in here.

I will take care of the bodies and the house, but first I need to get back to San Pedro to set Emilio up for a long weekend getaway with me.

It's time this fucker pays for every last thing he has done.

———

Bodies disposed of? Check.

House catching fire by aerial fireworks? Double check.

Emilio tied to the chair with a few broken ribs and being deprived of food? That would be a triple check.

Five days.

That's how long it's been since Emilio and his men took Serena. Five days since I tied him to the metal chair that he's currently occupying.

I brought him back to San Pedro and he went straight to the basement, or dungeon as I like to affectionately call it, and he hasn't left since.

Not even to take a piss or shit.

There's no reason to give him liberties like eating and going to the bathroom.

I should kill him, I really should, but I have a feeling that if I kill him now that will just cause more bad than good. So I guess he can live just little longer.

Grabbing the knife from my waistband, I approach the chair.

Emilio has been completely out of it, so he doesn't lift up his head when he hears me approaching.

Crouching down, I get below eye level and grab him by the hair to make him look up. His eyes are bloodshot and look like they haven't been able to close in days.

Maybe there's some truth to that. Maybe Emilio hasn't slept or closed his eyes much, in fear that I will do something to him.

In my expert opinion, he was right to fear me.

I drag the sharp blade close to his bullet wound. Which, by the way no longer has a bullet stuck in there. Being the nice person that I am, I performed some surgery and pulled it right out. Didn't want the guy to get an infection or anything.

That would be such a horrible way to die.

"Tell me, *pendejo*. Why did you do it?" I apply just a small amount of pressure to the wound, causing him to wince.

"Because Leo is a fucking pussy and deserved to get thrown off his high horse," he spits, trying his hardest to move his thigh away from me.

"Not what I was fucking talking about.," I apply more pressure this time, causing more blood to seep through. "Why did you kill my father?!"

I drag the blade down his leg. His screams fill the room and I get joy in knowing that I'm the one doing this to him.

Once I'm satisfied with my handiwork, I pull away,

finding Emilio staring at me with wide eyes. There's fear in them but there's also surprise.

I smirk. "You thought that you were clever. Avoiding cameras and keeping your head down, but I guess you were just as much a *pendejo* then as what you are now."

I plunge the blade into his thigh, twisting it when it's fully embedded into his leg.

His whole body shakes and he tries to dislodge himself from the chair to pull out the knife.

"You didn't cover all your tracks, Castro. I was able to find you. And now I'm going to fucking make you pay for what you did to my own blood, by taking some of yours."

Stab after stab.

Scream after scream.

I take out all the anger, all the frustration and all the sorrow that I've had boiling in me for four long ass years out on this man.

His thigh will probably not look the same after this, but I don't give a shit.

This man took something from me and it's about time that I get reparation for what he did.

"Santiago!"

The loud male voice sounds through the room, even above the screams that are coming from the bastard in front of me, I was able to hear it.

I don't need to turn to know who it is.

Looks like the king has come down to see my handiwork.

Dropping the knife, I turn to face Ronaldo, who is standing by the entrance of the room, looking as poised as ever. Who knew that a cartel drug lord could look so put together.

I guess when you are the most feared man in all of Mexico and you have two United States federal agencies after your ass, you can look however you want.

"Come to take a stab for yourself?" I wave over to the chair, all puns fucking intended.

"No." He looks around me to Emilio, a look of indifference still on his face. "I came down here to tell you to release him. He's had enough."

Adrenaline must still be pumping through my skull because I'm pretty sure that Ronaldo just told me to stop torturing Emilio. The man that just kidnapped his daughter-in-law and was going to kill her.

Surely that can't be right.

"*¿Quieres que pare?*"

If he wants me to stop, I will but there better be a good fucking excuse behind it.

Ronaldo gives me a curt nod. "*Si*. My daughter deserves a wedding where her husband is able to walk her back down the aisle after the ceremony."

You got to be fucking kidding me.

"He went after Serena," I say through my teeth. I'm about to tell him he also killed my father, but I keep that to myself.

"And from what I heard, Serena is still alive. *Ahora. Dejalo ir.*"

Let him go.

Just like that.

I look at the man before me and try to figure out how

he became this way. How did he become a man so power-hungry that he doesn't care that someone went after a member of his family?

But like the good soldier that I am, I listen when I'm given orders.

I turn back to Emilio and start cutting off his restraints.

"Emilio, when you get situated, I want you in my office." And just as quickly as he came in, Ronaldo leaves.

I'm pissed but I still cut off the last of the restraints. Once he is free, I stand up and start walking out of the room.

I'm about to turn the corner to head back upstairs when I hear him speak.

"Tell me, Reyes. Is she tight? Does her pussy wrap tightly around your cock while you ram into her?"

My blood boils at his words. He's talking about Isabella.

I walk into the room with my hands already in fists.

"I can't wait to have her on her knees and feed her my cock. With that mouth of hers, she must know how to take it all. I bet she will have tears in her eyes while I fuck her throat. I'm dreaming of the day when I can finally fuck every inch of her. I don't even give a shit if she doesn't let me touch her. She'll be my wife after all, I could take whatever I want."

Red.

Red is all I see as I charge at Emilio and punch him in the face. I punch until I hear a solid crunch coming from his nose.

"Talk about Isabella like that again, and I swear to you, that even Ronaldo wouldn't be able to save you."

One more punch and one final kick to the balls, I'm finally done with him.

I walk out of the room, but it's with his laugh ringing through the dark hallway.

The first time I walked through this hallway, I knew that I would never deserve Isabella Morales.

Now ten years later, I still don't deserve her, but I sure as hell will try my hardest to give her everything she fucking deserves.

Starting with not letting her marry Emilio fucking Castro.

24

ISABELLA

Six Months Earlier

"That's such a gorgeous dress!" Serena exclaims, as she walks into my apartment in Austin.

It's been two weeks since Emilio took her and her friend from their apartment. In those two week she has also been spending most of her time with my brother as her shadow.

I had a few things to do at the boutique for the next few days, so I offered to keep her company for a little bit. All the while my brother headed to one of the warehouses that the Muertos own in Austin.

"Thanks. It's just something that I put together." I shrug at her, continuing to pour us our cups of coffee.

"You make it sound like you didn't spend hours making it." She touches the fabric, feeling how soft the material is between her fingers. "It would look absolutely gorgeous on you, Isabella."

I nod, not really knowing what to say. She's right, though that dress would look good on me. I just don't know yet if it's a dress I want to keep for myself or to give to the boutique.

Given that it's the same dress that Santos told me would look beautiful on me all those months ago.

"How's the shoulder?" I ask her as I hand her over her coffee cup, trying to divert the conversation.

Her hand instantly goes to her upper arm. "Better. Still have some more healing to do, but it's getting there."

"I still can't believe that Leo let you go back to work. If it was me or Camila, he would have locked us in our rooms until we got the okay from a doctor."

Leo is a lot more lenient with Serena than he is with me or Camila, that's for sure. But I can see why. We aren't the ones he has to go to bed with every single night. I imagine going to bed with an angry wife is not good.

"What can I say? The man knows what's good for him."

I snort into my coffee. "Jesus."

"Hey, I made you smile a little bit at least," Serena muses.

She's right, she did, and it feels good since my smiles have been very limited in the two weeks since her kidnapping.

"Yeah," I respond, just going back to drinking my coffee. "Do you want to watch a movie?" I change the subject before she can even start it. I head to the couch and grab the remote, with Serena coming over a few seconds later.

I end up putting a random Disney movie on, and we watch it without talking for a good half hour. But of course, the silence has to be broken by my sister-in-law.

"How are you really?" she asks, her voice is low and timid and definitely not a tone that I'm used to hearing when it comes to this woman.

I don't answer right away.

How am I?

That's a question that I don't really know the answer to.

Is 'I've been trying not to cry into a pint of Ben & Jerry's half baked' a good answer?

I'm promised to a man that kidnapped my sister-in-law and her friend and was going to kill them to get at my brother. And said man is also the man that just so happened to kill a man that treated me like his own.

No rational, sane person would be okay after knowing any of that.

In a matter of a few weeks, I went from being optimistic about Santos figuring out a way to stop all this and getting him to break his promise not to touch me to this. Being depressed and lost in my own mind and hating my father for not ending this arrangement the second that Serena was taken.

Which just adds more fuel to the fire of there being more to this arrangement than any of us know.

"I want to be okay," I answer Serena's question as honestly as I can.

Being okay would be a hell of a lot better than everything else that I'm feeling.

"Oh, Bella," Serena scoots over and tries to hug me as best she can with her slinged-up arm. "I'm so sorry."

Everyone is sorry.

I lean into her hug as much as I can without hurting her.

This is a little awkward for me and Serena, we don't hug. Honestly up until two weeks ago, I didn't like her very much. Sure, she was growing on me, but we weren't at the hugging stage just yet.

Not going to lie, this feels nice. Like I have someone else, another shoulder to lean on.

"I told Leo that I wanted to be happy like he is with you, but I think that there's more to that. I want to feel safe too. Do you think that's asking for too much?"

Every woman deserves to be happy, loved and to feel safe, right?

Or is that not in the cards for me?

Because right now as I sit here, I don't feel any of those things, and in a few months, I'm going to be marrying Emilio and there is nothing I can do about it.

Unless he dies, which I'm a little surprised he's still alive and kicking with the shit he pulled with Serena, I have no other way out of this arrangement.

"No, that's not too much," Serena pulls back from me and looks me right in the eyes as she speaks. "You deserve the fucking world and one day you will be getting that. I know that Santos will make sure of it."

I give her smile a questioning look.

"Does everyone know that we were in a relationship for four years?"

"The fuck? Four years? You two were in a relationship for four years?" Her hazel eyes go wide and her exclamation makes me laugh a little. I guess not everyone knew.

I nod. "It was a secret. Something just for me and him. He was going to propose actually, and well, that's when all this mess started."

Serena continues to look at me, dumbfounded by this information.

"Holy shit. I knew that something was going on between you two that night he came to get you, but never thought that it would be a secret relationship. Mind blowing. I can't wait to tell Aria."

"You told your friend?" Does my life really have to be everyone's business?

"She was recovering from a kick to the stomach from Emilio and a kidnapping. I had to tell her something to distract her."

She says it like it's no big deal, and I guess it isn't.

I'm glad she has a friend like that, someone to talk shit to. I wish I had that.

"I'm surprised Leo doesn't know. Since Camila and my dad do." I look down at the coffee cup in my hands.

"Wait. Ronaldo knows?"

I shrug, not taking my eyes off of the cup.

"Wow," Serena says in disbelief, then she all of the sudden, like something just popped into her head, she grabs my arm. "Do you think that there is a bigger reason behind...?" She trails off but I know what she wants to say.

I don't look at my sister-in-law as I answer. "There has to be, but I don't know unless my father says something."

There's no need to tell her that both Santos and I know that something is suspicious about this arrangement.

Serena places a hand over mine and gives me a reassuring squeeze. This time I do look up to face her and I see that she has tears forming in her eyes.

That right there causes my own tears to form. God, why can't I hate this woman?

"I'm sorry, Isabella."

"Yeah, I'm sorry too."

We go back to watching the movie in silence. At the halfway point, she grabs the remote and puts the movie on in Spanish and puts on English subtitles. When I ask her about it, she says she's trying to learn more Spanish. Something about when her and my brother have kids, she wants them to be fluent, so she has to learn.

More power to her then.

I don't know if putting the movie in Spanish worked though, she looked confused the whole time.

As the credits roll on the screen, there's a knock on the door, signaling that my brother's here.

This is a secure building, Leo made sure of that when I moved in almost eight years ago. There is security downstairs, and nobody is allowed up unless they are on the approved list.

Sure enough when I go to open the door, there is my brother with Santos right behind him. Santos, I wasn't expecting.

I open the door for them to come in and they do. Leo giving me a kiss on the cheek before heading over to his wife and leaving me with Santos, who gives me the tight smile that I hate seeing.

Not long after Leo arrives, he and Serena leave, but not before he tells Santos to make sure I make it back to San Pedro. He tells him that he will and off they go.

Now, I'm left in my apartment with a man that I want in my bed more than anything.

We stand there in silence for what feels like hours, just staring at each other.

I break the silence. "I have a few things to do at the boutique in the morning. Would it be possible to head back to San Pedro then?"

I'd much rather stay behind in Austin tha,n go back to Mexico, but with Camila home from school for break, I want to be there just in case anything happens.

Emilio already went after Serena, what if he goes after Camila too?

Santos nods, stuffing his hands in his pants pockets. "Yeah, that's completely fine."

"Okay."

Given the conversation we had a few weeks ago, this interaction should not be feeling as awkward as it does.

"Do you want something to eat? Drink?" Want to stop this awkward situation and stuff our faces with food and alcohol?

"Want to order from that Italian restaurant you like so much?"

I'm nodding right away. That place is amazing but it's the fact that I will be sharing a meal with him that excites me even more.

Even through the feeling of awkwardness, we order our food and within forty minutes we have it delivered and are eating at the kitchen counter.

We eat in silence and when we finish, I give him a smile. "Thank you for the food."

"It's nothing." He shrugs, "You had to eat, and it gave me time to spend with you."

My heart melts a little with that statement.

Then I remember why we haven't spent time together.

"How is everything going on the whole situation front?" I ask, squaring my shoulders, readying myself for any disappointment I might receive.

Santos looks at me and then lets out a sigh. I guess it's not going anywhere.

"Besides Leo shooting Emilio in the leg and me beating the shit out of him, nothing has fucking changed."

He sounds angry and I'm right there with him.

After everything that Emilio did, there is no reason that what I'm going through should still be happening.

There is no reason that my so-called wedding should still be scheduled.

"But we will figure it out, *bella*. We will figure it out and we will put a stop to this, I promise." He reaches over to me and places his hand on mine. I turn my palm over and intertwine our fingers together.

"I know," I squeeze his hand and for a few seconds we just sit there with our hands together.

"How are you? And don't bullshit me, Isabella. How are you really?"

No bullshit.

Not like I did with Serena.

I have to be absolutely open with him, and it's a good thing that he's the only person I can do that with.

"I'm scared." It's two words and they still cause a lump in my throat to form. "I'm scared that you and Leo won't figure a way to end this and I will be stuck marrying Emilio. I'm scared that if I marry him, I will be forced into a life I don't want and I will end up like my mother. I'm scared that I will be dead within a few years, because that is how I see this, as a death sentence."

Everything about this whole thing terrifies me down to my bones and I don't want to feel like this anymore. I want to be strong and be able to keep my head up, and not live this shit life.

I must have been lost in my own thoughts because I didn't notice Santos coming closer to me. I also didn't notice that the tears I was fighting started to flow and he started to wipe them away.

Soon, I'm on my feet and in his arms, sobbing every single fear that I have, out.

"We will figure it out," he says into my hair as I cling to him for dear life.

Santos pulls back slightly, taking my face between his hands, before leaning in and placing a chaste kiss on my lips.

"I promise you, on my fucking life, this will end."

Another kiss lands on my lips, this time with ferocity more than anything that I have experienced in a while.

We kiss until we get lost, and I start to forget the pain, but I need more.

"Make me forget. Break your promise. Touch me, make me forget about every single thing. Remind me that I'm yours, and only yours."

"You're mine and always will be."

25

SANTOS

If I could take away every single ounce of pain that Isabella has ever felt, I would.

The pain from her mother's death.

Every single ounce of pain that I caused.

All the pain that Ronaldo is putting her through currently.

Everything, I would take it away.

I'm not the most perfect man, but when the woman that I love is sobbing in my arms because she is fearful about what could happen to her, I act. I may not act accordingly but I act either way.

And right now, the urge to act is strong.

As I stood there hearing her sobs and hearing the fear that runs deep in her, I wanted to take it all away. She shouldn't be feeling this way and I will be damned if I don't do anything about it.

So, I'm taking the pain away.

"Tell me that I'm yours," Isabella begs once again as my

lips make their way down her neck. I open my mouth over her skin and bite down.

Marking her.

"Every inch of you is mine," I growl into her neck.

We are currently lying on her bed with me on top of her, each of us enjoying how our bodies feel this close together.

Her hand travels from my hair to my neck, and I feel a small piece of metal against my skin.

It may be thin, but I feel it.

Her ring. She's still wearing it.

Pulling back, I leave the glorious way her body feels under me to get situated on my knees.

Isabella looks at me with a confused look and maybe with a tinge of fear that I might leave.

The opposite actually.

I grab her left wrist tightly and look at the piece of jewelry that she's wearing.

I fucking hate it.

She should be wearing the ring that I have for her, not this from a piece of shit man.

"Take it off," I order, as if the thought of even touching it myself makes me want to explode.

Isabella is confused for a second before she realizes what I'm talking about. Within seconds, the offending piece of jewelry is off of her finger and is thrown, landing somewhere on the floor.

"Better?" Isabella asks, her teeth taking her lower lip hostage.

I lean forward again, my chest to hers, my mouth an

inch away from her ear, my hand going straight to her throat.

"The only ring that should be on your finger is the one I give you. You understand me, *bella*? The only ring that will fucking matter is mine."

My hold on her neck tightens just slightly, not cutting off her airway. My girl may like it a little rougher along the edges, but she does have her limits.

"I understand," she says, her body squirming under me as she rubs herself against my leg.

"Good girl, *bella*." I nip her earlobe and instead of a yelp, I get a moan filling my ear. "You're mine and only mine. I don't give a shit what your father says. You will never belong to anyone else."

"I will only belong to you."

I let out a growl at her statement.

As she continues to rub herself against me, I think about our options.

Yes, I want to be inside of her right here, right now, but it's been a while since I've seen her pretty lips wrapped around my cock. If this is the last time I see her, if this is the last time I get to have her, the vision of her on her knees is something I want to engrave into my memory.

I willingly detach myself from Isabella and situate myself at the foot of the bed.

"Take my cock out." I order and instantly Isabella's eyes sparkle with anticipation.

My guess is she's been waiting for this day to come just as long as I have.

My eyes stay on her as she gets on her knees and crawls

over to me. I watch as she licks her lips at what is in front of her and I can't help but look down at her tits as her shirt opens up, giving me a glimpse.

Isabella's face ends up only a few inches from my aching cock. Her eyes travel up to me as she situates herself on her forearms with her ass in the air.

Such a gorgeous sight.

She looks up at me from under her lashes as she reaches for my belt and unbuckles it. As soon as the buckle is free and my dark slacks are opened, she slides the zipper down, coming face-to-face with my cock.

"I fucking love it when you don't wear briefs. Much easier access." My woman doesn't wait for my orders.

No, she slips her small hand into the opening of my pants and gives my cock a few good strokes.

She tugs and pulls on me, and I have to keep myself in check.

It's been some long months without her, having her touching me like this is bringing out the animal in me.

I'm about to tell her to take me in her mouth, but she must be a fucking mind reader because she takes me out and licks the underside before she takes my tip between her lips and sucks.

"Fuck." I groan out when she sucks on my tip, her beautiful brown eyes that are filled with lust, looking up at me.

She takes me in deeper with each pass until I hit the back of her throat and I feel her gag a little. She does it once, twice, more times than I can count.

My hands make their way to her hair, holding her head close to me as I move in and out of her mouth.

"I've missed your mouth so much, *belleza*." I feel like I'm fucking close, but no fucking way am I coming in this pretty mouth before she comes in mine.

Pulling at her hair some more, I notice tears running down her cheeks, so I pull out to let her breathe.

I lean down to her eye level and start wiping away the tears from the mouth fuck while she pants.

"You look absolutely beautiful crying this types of tears." I kiss her with all my might, tasting some of my precum that's still on her tongue.

"Take off all your clothes and get back in this position, but this time turn around, keep that ass of yours up in the air. I'm going to have my dessert."

She lets out a little giggle as she does what I say and gets naked before getting situated with her ass facing me.

"Fuck. Such a sight." I smooth a hand over the cheeks of her bare ass before giving one of them a slap.

"A sight that only you get to see." She wiggles her behind a bit.

"Damn fucking right."

I spread her open and she lets out a moan as soon as my mouth makes contact with her ass.

"Santos!" she yells out but I just smirk again, continuing my attack.

"I've told you baby, I'm no saint when I'm fucking you. That's all the devil side of me coming out to play."

And play, I fucking do.

"You know, whenever you call me in like this, it makes me think I did something bad. That or your father is here."

I walk into the office that Leo and I share at the warehouse that we have here in Austin and take a seat in the chair in front of him.

Ever since all the shit went down with Emilio, we've been conducting all of our work out of Austin. Everything from street-level deals to our business with Sterling Chambers is handled here. We have a few other warehouses in and out of Austin, but this one is like our home base if you will.

"Maybe you did do something bad." he says throwing a pen in my direction.

"I doubt it, I'm a fucking angel. Why else would my mama give me the name that she did?" I give him a wink that earns me an eye-roll.

"It does have to do with my father though."

`Right away, I'm on high alert. Anything involving Ronaldo these days has been grim. Leo knows that Ronaldo stopped me from going further in my torturing of Emilio. And he told me about how he was the one that sent the bastard after Serena.

What Leo doesn't know is that Emilio killed my father and how I think Ronaldo is involved. Given what he's about to tell me, he might be knowing that bit of information soon enough.

"What about him?" I lean back in the chair, acting as indifferent on the subject as possible.

Leo looks at me for a long minute until he finally lets out a heavy sigh.

"I'm going to help Madden take him down."

If that's not a total mindfuck right there, I don't know what is.

"You're serious?" For the last few months, Leo has made it his mission to get rid of anyone that has spoken to the *federales* about cartel business. Shit, we even killed a man that was like a brother to us because he ratted.

Now he's going to be the narc?

Leo gives me a nod. "With all the shit that he has been pulling recently, the arranged marriage, the shit with Serena, it's all becoming too much. He's becoming too obsessed with the notion of power and money. There's no way of telling what else he will do before he's put to a stop. For all we know, he could be planning to put up Camila for auction so that he could continue to have the best coke."

I want to punch Leo for even throwing that thought out into the world. Nothing like that will ever happen.

"So, you becoming a narc is the way to go?" Am I pissed that he's doing this?

Abso-fucking-lutely.

If he talks, he could say the wrong thing and not only bring Ronaldo down, but all of us down with him.

Ronaldo Morales isn't the only one that has committed crimes against the United States.

You want to know how many kilos of drugs I've smuggled through the borders of this country? A shit ton. Past the millions mark for sure.

"I made a deal with Madden. I talk and give him everything he needs, and he leaves us and our men out of it. The Muertos won't be taken down." He sounds so sure.

"And then what? Ronaldo gets put away and you become king?"

This whole fucking conversation is really starting to piss me off. I would rather go back to Isabella's bed and continue my journey of getting lost in her body.

"You know for a fact that if I run the Muertos, it will never be anything like how Ronaldo does business." He stabs his desk with his finger, like it did something to him.

I do know that.

If the cartel ever fell into Leo's lap, he would do whatever was in his power to make the cartel almost nonexistent. His whole life, Leo has wanted to live in a world that didn't have to do with drugs or weapons. He wanted a normal life for him and his sisters. Now with his marriage, that life is just a little closer to grasping and if that means he has to give up the cartel life to get it, he would.

And if I'm being honest with myself, I would probably be right there next to him if I had the opportunity to walk away.

"I know that but being a second-in-command and kingpin are two different things. You can say that you won't do things like your father but when the time comes, things can change."

He can go into a different mindset.

Fuck, he can become more ruthless than Ronaldo.

Leo's facial expression is hard. It's like anger and frustration all tied up all nicely into a bow.

"So, you're not going to help me take him down? You're

just going to call me a narc and be done with it? Not even if it saves Isabella from marrying that asshole?"

It's at the mention of his sister's name that I can feel my facial expression get hard.

Just by looking at my best friend, I can see that he knows what I've been doing with his sister since she was twenty-two.

"You knew?" I raise my eyebrows at him, questioning him.

He looks at me and after about a minute, he gives me a nod.

"How?"

"I've seen the way you've looked at her since we were teenagers. If it makes you feel any better, I didn't put two and two together until this year, before all this shit started. You guys were always together, and whenever she was around you or talked about you, she had this big smile on her face. It was hard to miss. I was just waiting for you to tell me. Some friend you are."

By the smirk he gives me, I know he's joking about that last part.

I still apologize. "Sorry. I should have been man enough to at least open up to you."

"How long has it been going on for?"

"Since the day my dad died. Finally got my head out of my ass until I stuffed it back in a few months ago."

Leo nods, probably trying to do the math in his head.

"How serious did it get?" He's about to be really surprised.

I let out a sigh, getting comfortable in my chair. "I was going to propose."

Leo's eyes go wide.

"Why didn't you?"

"I was going to talk to Ronaldo but instead that day he announced the arrangement with the Castros."

"Well fuck."

I nod in agreement. Fuck, indeed.

We sit in silence for a few minutes, and I take that time to think about what he asked me to do.

Am I not going to consider helping him take down Ronaldo?

I don't even think it's a question.

I know that I will help. If we are able to succeed in doing this, then not only will Ronaldo pay for everything that he has done, but that would mean that Emilio will be taken care of too.

There is nothing to think about. But I do have to do something. Something that might push Leo even harder to do this.

"I'll help you take down Ronaldo." His expression of anger and frustration turns into one of pride and thankfulness. "If we also take down Emilio."

I had to throw it in there. There is no way in hell that asshole is staying alive much longer.

"We'll take care of him. He will never even get a chance to say that he's Ronaldo's son-in-law."

"That's all good and peachy but that's not the only reason that I want to take him down."

There's a change in my tone of voice and I know that

Leo hears it by the way his whole-body stiffens. He just went from a normal man to one of the most feared men in the world.

"You have another reason?"

I nod. Here goes nothing.

"He killed my father and I think that Ronaldo was the one that called the order."

The silence that fills the room is fucking eerie. I'm sure that someone out in the warehouse can drop a pin and we would be able to hear it in here.

I watch as my friend digests what I just told him. It's like watching a cycle of emotions make their appearance, all in a span of a few minutes.

He finally settles on anger when he grabs a glass that is sitting in front of him and throws it against the wall. He even gets up from his chair and starts to pace the room.

"Are you sure?" he asks midstride. All the while, I stay seated.

"Yeah, one hundred percent. I found an image of the shooter a few years ago, the only thing that I could get from it was the fact that he had a tattoo on his hand. The same tattoo that so happens to be on Emilio's pudgy hand."

I tell him as he continues to pace. Even without having the tattoo in front of me, I can describe every single detail.

"And the Ronaldo connection?" Leo is now biting his nails as he paces.

"I haven't figured it out yet. But it's only a matter of time."

Leo finally stops pacing, thank God because I was

about to call Serena to calm him down, and comes to stand in front of me, leaning against the desk.

"There has to be more to this arrangement than we know of." he states, crossing his arms over his chest, looking very much like a man that can run a cartel.

"It has to be something. There's a reason why Ronaldo chose Emilio to marry Isabella, that wasn't just something that he decided on a whim. There also has to be more as to why he asked him to go after Serena and why he stopped me from doing any more damage to him."

I've been wondering why Ronaldo chose the Castro cartel to take under his wing, over all the other small cartels in Mexico. The man had options, but why did he go after this one? But the biggest question of them all is, how did he end up choosing Emilio for his daughter? The man has everyone and anyone in his back pocket, but why this bastard that has nothing to offer him?

"We have to figure it out, and we have to do it before those church bells ring."

Couldn't agree more.

"No way in hell am I going to let Isabella get stuck in a life with him."

If Isabella is going to marry anyone, it is going to be me.

ISABELLA

One Month Earlier

THE SOUND of gunshots ring in my ears even with these stupid earmuffs that are covering them.

The sounds around me, though are the least of my concerns. What I'm most worried about is the fact that Emilio Castro is standing way too close for my liking.

One month.

One more fucking month, until the wedding.

Yeah, you heard that correctly, in one month I will be marrying Emilio Castro. About five months ago, my father came to me and told me that I needed to pick a date for my wedding, that I was taking too long. That I had until June, which is about eleven months after his stupid announcement, to have a wedding. Anything after that, he would be forcing my hand and picking a day himself.

I guess there's something about weddings that make

my father tick. Since the wedding that he had me plan for Serena and Leo fell through.

All that work for nothing.

So naturally, after speaking to Santos and my brother, who somehow also now knows about our secret relationship, they told me what they needed to do, I picked the date. In June, because I was going to prolong this as much as I could.

Now I'm a month away from this fucked-up wedding, which by the way, is all planned out, and I'm in a damn gun range with my future husband. Not even an inch closer to leaving this whole arrangement than I was in November.

A part of me wonders what exactly my brother and Santos are doing, that they haven't been able to put a stop to this yet.

Another part of me wonders if I turn a few inches to the side, if I can kill Emilio myself. I'm holding a Desert Eagle after all.

"I'm impressed. You've hit right on the target every single time," Emilio muses from next to me.

No shit, Sherlock. Do you really think that I would be born into a cartel family, secretly date a cartel soldier for years, and not know how to shoot a gun?

I've been able to hold my own when it comes to weaponry for years.

I shrug. "Something that my father made sure we knew how to do." More like Cristiano, but he doesn't get to know that information.

"Hmmm." Emilio hums before he steps closer to me, his hand landing on the small of my back.

I want to cringe, I want to put as much space between our bodies that I can, but I don't. Why? Because my father ordered me to treat my future husband like he's on a freaking pedestal.

Emilio wishes he was held that high.

"I would have thought that it was your boy toy that had taught you how to properly hold a gun," Emilio speaks into my ear and I try really hard not to shudder.

"Whatever he taught me, is none of your business." I try to square my shoulders a tiny bit to put distance between me and him, but it doesn't work.

Emilio comes closer to me. I can feel his fingers digging into my waist and even though I'm wearing high waisted jeans, it feels like he's touching skin.

The gun that I have in my hand has one bullet left in the chamber.

I can just turn and add to the scar that he has from when Leo shot him all those months ago.

"That's where you are wrong, *bebé*. If that bastard taught you something, I have to know. Have to protect myself if you end up using it against me."

The second that his teeth meet my earlobe, I pull the trigger, letting the sound of the shot ring out through the room.

I throw my elbow back, hitting Emilio in the stomach as I lower the gun to the small shelf in front of me. I do all the safety measures and take off my earmuffs before I turn to face him.

He has a smirk on his face that if I still had a loaded weapon in my hand, I would shoot off.

"Don't ever call me *bebé* again," I say through gritted teeth, stepping closer to him so that his men don't hear what I'm about to say next. "I'm nothing to you and it's going to stay that way. I don't give a rat's ass what kind of deal you have with my father, but you will never own me. Get that through your fucking head right now." I shove him out of the way and surprisingly he steps back. With a snarl on his face but he steps back either way.

I grab my gun, yes, the Deagle I was just shooting is mine, one of the many perks of having a residence in the state of Texas, and walk out of the shooting range.

My guess is that Emilio brought me here to scare me, so that I could go running to my brother and Santos and tell him what a good shot he has.

A scare tactic that didn't work.

As I walk back to the black SUV, courtesy of my father, I'm aware of the footsteps following me. Emilio's security, or should I say my father's.

Emilio wants to think that he is the one that is running this, but he's in for a rude awakening when he sees that I'm the one that has all the power outside of my father's estate. I'm the cartel princess, after all, and I have to be protected.

He has to be fuming inside of the building because his men followed me out and didn't stay with him.

"*Todo está bien, Señorita Isabella?*" Arturo, my brother's loyal security detail and driver, asks when I open the door to the SUV.

Arturo has been with me these last few months, something that I asked my brother for. If I was going to be spending more time with Emilio, then I needed someone there with me that I trusted and Arturo is that.

I give him a nod. "I want to go home."

Arturo gives me a nod back, waving me to slide into the back of the vehicle before he closes the door behind me.

I watch as Emilio walks out of the shooting range and just stands there as Arturo drives away. He looks angry, but I don't give a shit. I don't want anything to do with him.

"Should I call Señor Reyes or Señor Morales?" Arturo offers, looking through the rearview mirror at me.

I shake my head. "*No, todo está bien.*"

There's no need to involve my brother or Santos in this. I'm just acting like a petulant child because I don't want to spend time with Emilio.

Arturo and I make it back to the estate in no time. It's not surprising though that Emilio and the security team arrive only a few seconds after us.

Ignoring the glare that I'm getting from Emilio as soon as I get out of the car, I go into the house without a care in the world.

If we do end up going through with this marriage, he should get used to the silent treatment, because no way in fucking hell will I be treating him like a real husband.

Again, I hear footsteps behind me, but I don't think anything of it, just putting it down as Arturo making sure I make it to my living quarters.

I should have double-checked though, because as I turn the corner to head to my wing in the estate, I get grabbed by my elbow and get pulled back.

Everything happens so fast that I don't even realize that I'm getting pushed up against the wall until my back is slammed against it. Right away, a pain radiates all through my spine.

I let out a small scream, but a hand covers my mouth before any sound can escape further.

My eyes open and right away I'm met with Emilio's murderous stare. One of his hands is on my mouth, while the other is holding both my hands, keeping me from shoving him off me.

I let out a muffled yelp, but he just pushes his hand harder down on my mouth.

"Shut the fuck up, bitch." His fingers dig into my skin. I wish I was stronger so that I could push him off.

I try to move but he just pushes his body more into mine holding me in place.

"You better learn where you fucking stand, because once we get married, that shit that you just pulled won't work. I will fucking own you and you will stand by my side like the perfect wife that I know you can be."

His face is only inches away from mine. Being this close to him makes me want to puke.

When I don't try to fight him, he lets go of my arms, which fall limp at my sides, just waiting for whatever he's about to do next.

"You will be the perfect wife," he coos, his hand that is covering my mouth, somehow caressing my cheek. "The perfect wife that does what I say, when ordered to."

I feel his other hand back on me, feel it as it travels to my hip. I can feel his fingers gliding against my clothing.

"You will cook, clean, be the perfect housewife. Which, by the way, also means that I get to fuck you whenever I want."

A scream escapes my covered mouth when he grabs me between my legs. He is doing it so tightly that it feels like his fingers are ripping through my jeans.

"I can't wait to claim this cunt as mine and show you how a real man fucks. I will have you screaming."

Emilio rubs me between my legs and tears start to well in my eyes.

This is a day that I'm grateful that I decided not to wear a dress.

He leans forward and takes my earlobe between his teeth as he continues to rub me. As close as he's standing, I can feel the hardness that is being pushed into me from his groin.

He's hard.

My head is spinning, trying to find a way to get out of this before he decides to do something. Like rape me.

I'm about to start hitting the wall, possibly to get someone's attention, when Emilio pulls away and lets me go completely.

Tears are running down my face as I watch him readjust himself.

I just stand there not knowing what to do.

I should run. Run as far away from this man as I can, but I can't seem to make my legs work.

"I can't wait to put you in your place on our wedding night. The day can't come soon enough." With one last snarl, he walks away, his hand still on his dick.

As soon as he turns the corner and is out of sight, I run straight to my safe space and lock every possible door that I can.

When I make it to my room and look at the door behind me, I sink to the ground and cry.

I cry and pray that Santos and Leo can figure out a way to stop this wedding.

Because I don't know how much longer I can survive this.

27

SANTOS

One Week Before

"THIS IS FUCKING BULLSHIT!" A tequila bottle flies through the room, hitting the wall before falling to the ground in a million pieces.

The frustration of all of this has finally caught up to me. It's been over six months and the wedding is next week, and we have nothing, and I mean absolutely nothing ,to stop this fucked-up holy matrimony bullshit.

Throwing the bottle wasn't enough, if only I could throw the desk we are currently occupying, I would.

"We'll figure it out." I hear Leo's voice coming from the other side of the room, and just hearing it makes me want to stalk over to him and punch him.

"It's been almost seven months and we haven't figured out a thing! At this point, you and I will be standing in that church watching Isabella sign her life away, like *pendejos*, because we couldn't figure it out!"

We should have been able to find a way to take down Emilio by now. There are so many things that we can take him down for. We could just put a bullet through his head and be done with it.

But the asshole is protected by Ronaldo and his men. Everywhere he goes, he has five to six men acting like security right behind him. Leo and I can't even head to San Pedro and step foot on the estate without being followed constantly.

According to Isabella, they've been doing it with her too. She says that both Emilio and Ronaldo are on high alert, thinking that we are going to do something to Emilio, so they don't even let her leave the house by herself.

Thankfully, she has one man among the team of security that she can trust and that's Arturo. When Isabella told Leo what was happening, he sent him right over to her.

She's scared and all me and Leo are doing right now is playing sitting ducks.

Such fucking bullshit.

"We should have handed him over to Madden when we had the chance," Leo lets out.

When the whole ordeal was happening with Serena and Aria, and Agent Madden helped us, we told him that Emilio was ours but that he could have any other man in the house.

Well, we got Emilio, but every other man ended up dead, so Madden didn't get anything.

Maybe if we had handed him over, Emilio would be in prison right about now being someone's bitch. If they were able to hold him at least.

"The only thing that they'd be able to pin him with is kidnapping and attempted murder of Serena and Aria." I sigh, throwing myself on the leather couch that Leo has here in his office.

"We also have him on Cristiano's death. Which will lead the DEA back to Ronaldo."

I'm shaking my head before he even finishes the sentence. "All speculation. You and I both know it's true, but the DEA needs more than just a photo of a tattoo to put someone there."

I'm sure if we went to Madden with all the information we had, he would tell us that he still needs more and not to go back to him until we had it.

"This shit has to go deeper than Ronaldo paying the Castros for a favor for killing Cristiano."

For weeks, we've been throwing idea after idea around. One of them is the idea that Ronaldo hired the Castro family to do him the favor of getting rid of my father. We haven't figured why Ronaldo wanted Cristiano dead, but he did, and he couldn't do it himself, so he got outside help.

"Emilio was in debt and had to pay money to Belize. He probably reached out to Ronaldo, offered to do a job for him, which was to kill Cristiano. And after all was said and done, Ronaldo would give him the money to pay for his stupidity."

It's the most logical theory. Especially since, per the information Elliot Lane was able to get for me, his debt was paid off within weeks of my father's death.

"Where does Isabella come in, though?"

That's the question of the fucking century, isn't it?

I look up at my ceiling and give him my answer.

"Ronaldo said so himself, it's all about money and power. He probably noticed that the Castros were growing and expanding quickly, and that he needed to put a stop to it. So he most likely told them that he would take over all their businesses in exchange for something. Emilio probably knew about your sister and so he took the shot and he got it. Now here we are."

In a black hole of hell, that feels like we are repeating the same day over and over again.

"There has to be more to it," Leo says, not dropping it.

There isn't any more, is what I want to scream at him. If there was more, we would have found it by now, but we haven't.

This is all just about money and power and we have to fucking take our heads out of our asses and accept it.

"Unless…" Leo starts but trails off.

Unless? Unless what? We've gone through so many "Unless" scenarios, there shouldn't be more.

I don't move from my place on the couch, but I turn to see Leo take out a storage box from the small closet he has in the office.

He places it on the desk and starts to rummage through it like a madman. Papers are flying everywhere and every few seconds he asks himself where it is.

Whatever 'it' is, I have no idea.

"What the fuck are you looking for?" I finally ask, sitting up and making my way over to him.

Leo continues to flip through the files and the papers

inside the box until he finds what he's looking for I'm guessing.

"This." He grabs a red file and lays it on the wooden surface, all of its content spreading out. "A few months ago, I had Elliot's brother, Drake, look into something for me. Mostly it was to find anything on who was after Serena, and to see what the FBI and DEA had on the cartel. While I was looking through the file, I found this."

Leo holds up a picture of his parents posing with some strange man.

"What am I looking at?" The picture just looks like any other picture of the elder Morales'.

"Look at the man. Who does he look like?" I take the picture in my hands and inspect it, looking at the man's face very closely.

He looks familiar. Like I've seen him before, but where?

I look at the face for a few more seconds, until it finally clicks.

"Well, shit. He looks just like Madden." Same eyes, same facial structure, just change the mouth and take away the small bump and you have the special agent.

"I asked Ronaldo about it for weeks, but he never gave me an answer. That picture tells me that Ronaldo and Madden Sr. were friends and close ones at that. Given what's on the table, they also had to be working together."

My eyes travel to the edge of the picture and see what Leo's referring to. There are wads of cash just sitting there like they just got paid.

"You talk to Madden about this?" I hand the picture back to Leo, who shakes his head.

"No. Our conversations have been strictly about Ronaldo's everyday life and some of the stuff he's done in the past, nothing about the picture or why he has a vendetta against the Muertos."

Leo has been giving information to Madden for a few months now. You would think that the DEA would move faster in arresting Ronaldo, but that's just me.

"Were you able to get any information on Madden Sr. and what he did for a living?" If Drake was able to find the picture, he must have been able to find out where the man works.

And also, who in the actual fuck names a kid Drake? Were his parents thinking that he was going to become a famous rapper or something?

"He worked for the FBI until his death."

Well color me surprised.

"I guess like father, like son." Leo doesn't realizes just how much he and Madden are alike.

"I guess so." Leo looks down at the picture in his hands and inspects it as if something new is going to jump out.

My mind is still on the fact that Madden Sr. was FBI until his death.

"Does that pretty file of yours say how exactly the man died?"

Leo puts down the photo and grabs the file and shuffles through the papers until he finds the one that he is looking for.

"Car accident about thirty-two years ago." He hands me the sheet to look at.

"How old is Madden?" I ask as I look over the paper that just so happens to be a police report.

"Thirty-four."

My eyes scan the police report, and right away I notice two things.

The French wording, and the fact that the car accident took place in Quebec, Canada.

Where my father met my mother. Where he lived for months before moving her down to San Pedro.

There's no way.

I scan the document again, this time looking for a date. In the right-hand corner the date is written in pencil.

The date is right around the time that my father was sent to Canada to cross over some cocaine.

Fuck.

"Leo, why did you show me that picture?"

I look up at him and his dark brows bunch up in confusion.

"For you to see if maybe you saw something that I didn't."

I nod, not saying anything, just going back to reading the police report.

Madden Sr. was in a car accident caused by a faulty brake line. Not only was the brake line faulty, but the gas line was also punctured.

When we entered the cartel, Ronaldo made sure that Leo and I were taught everything about cars, and how to cause an accident when needed.

This right here would have been a great example.

"What are you thinking?"

"I'm thinking that maybe Madden Sr. was working both sides. Was working on making money with the cartel but at the same time being an informant for the FBI."

I look at my friend and a look of realization crosses his face.

"Ronaldo found out and had him killed," he theorizes and I nod.

"And I think that my dad became an informant while he was in Canada when he and my mom first met. The dates line up with when Madden died."

Fuck. That has to be it.

The only reason that I could think of for my dad talking was because he wanted to get out, he wanted out and to live his life with his new woman.

He probably had plans but all that went to shit when he was ordered to off Madden, so he went back to San Pedro and continued with the cartel until Ronaldo ordered his hit.

"Ronaldo starts the cartel," Leo muses, starting to pace the length of his office. "Starts to make a name for himself in the drug world, gets the attention of the FBI. Madden decides to infiltrate and become buddies with Ronaldo to get as much information about the cartel as possible. Possibly make some money along the way. Goes back to the FBI to report. Madden probably found out that a member of the Muertos was in Canada, so he made contact."

Everything is right on the fucking money.

"My dad probably wanted to get out, so he talked," I start, finishing up his thought process. "Ronaldo possibly found out about Madden's day job and ordered Cristiano to cut the line and make it look like an accident. Which he did, and once Madden was dead, he came back to Mexico to be loyal to the Muertos. Ronaldo found out somehow that my father was talking to Madden and when Emilio came to him for money, he figured it was the perfect way to take him out. Even if it was decades later. And when Ronaldo saw that Castros were growing and offered to take over, Emilio probably cashed in his favor and asked to marry Isabella."

We just figured it out. After months of trying to put all this shit together, of trying to find out anything that will help put an end to Ronaldo, we finally did it.

"Fuck."

Fuck indeed.

We stand there in silence, marveling at just how well orchestrated all of this was. It spanned decades, and people are still paying for it to this day.

"Figuring out that connection doesn't help us to get Isabella out of the marriage," I muse.

Sure, we finally put the puzzle together, but we still haven't fully figured it out.

"Then we kill him," Leo says as if it were that simple.

"Just like that?"

"Just like that. We kill the bastard. We have information that ties Ronaldo to two murders. One of them being the murder of an FBI agent. Ronaldo will be behind bars; he won't be able to protect Emilio anymore."

I've been wanting to kill Emilio since the day I met him, and now I'm about to get my chance.

The bastard is about to meet his untimely demise.

About time.

"We take care of Emilio first. If you talk to Madden right now and he takes in Ronaldo, it will all look suspicious. We have to make him think that we are after Emilio and only Emilio."

We both know how Ronaldo works, his suspicions will be raised. We have to be methodical with this. It may take some time, but it will happen.

Leo slaps me on my shoulder. "I like how you think, *hermano*."

I give him a shoulder slap back.

"Let's get to work on how to finally take down Emilio."

Once and for fucking all.

28

ISABELLA

Night Before

THE MUSIC IS PLAYING LOUDLY, people are interacting, and I want no part of it.

It's like a sense of déjà vu. Actually no, it's like reliving the past, because I've been here before. When I graduated from high school.

Except now it's a rehearsal dinner for the big wedding tomorrow.

After months of not wanting this day to come, it's finally here, and it looks like tomorrow at noon I will become Mrs. Emilio Castro.

Fucking perfect.

The one bright side of tonight is that Camila and Serena haven't left my side. If they weren't here next to me, I would probably be on the floor curled up in a ball, crying my eyes out, sobbing for my father to put a stop to this.

"Do you think that if I take a bottle of tequila from the

bartender and we head inside to watch a movie that anyone would notice?"

Camila asks, looking at the bar that is at the edge of the courtyard, a few people deep.

I can't help but laugh a little. She knows that I'm miserable right now and she is trying everything in her power to make me feel better.

"She's the bride. I'm sure if she left, someone would notice. Maybe not the fucker, but possibly your dad or brother for sure," Serena answers her with a sigh. I'm sure she wants to leave this party as much as we do.

"Did you just say 'fucker'?" Camila looks at our sister-in-law, a giggle escaping from her as she asks the question.

Serena looks at her, a little confused. "Yeah?"

"You're a second-grade teacher. I didn't know you had it in you." Camila gives her a smile.

"I may be a second-grade teacher but I can curse, I can be fun. Hell, I married a cartel drug lord in Vegas after a weekend of drinking," Serena defends herself and that only causes Camila to laugh.

"I think it's badass," she says, giving Serena another smile.

Camila leaves me and Serena as she goes and hunts down a waiter that is going around with champagne flutes.

"She called me badass." Serena muses when it's just the two of us.

"She's nineteen, she thinks that everyone that is older than her is badass," it's true. I think I heard her say the same thing to Arturo last week.

The expression he gave her, though, was priceless.

I look around the courtyard again, and this time as I do my visual sweep, I realize even more that I really don't want to be here.

But Serena's right, I'm the stupid bride. Not a lot of people would notice me being gone, but the key people would. I can't go anywhere.

Just because I can't go hide in my room though, doesn't mean that I can't escape to the restroom for a few minutes.

"I'll be right back." I say to Serena, and walk away before she can even give a response.

The second I step foot inside of the house and away from all the music and the people, I feel like I'm able to breathe again.

I don't even know half the people that are currently congregating in the courtyard. They are mostly people that the Castro family knows or acquaintances of my father. The only people that I know by name are my siblings and Serena.

You could have known someone else.

Santos.

He was supposed to be here tonight, you know, since he's my brother's best friend and a member of the cartel, but Emilio banned him from the party.

I found out when I talked to Leo earlier and asked him where his friend was.

Learning about the ban made me want to throat punch Emilio during pictures. And if I wasn't terrified that he would do something to me, I would have.

My fear of Emilio keeps growing with each passing day and starting tomorrow it's going to get much worse.

For right now, I shake my head and get those dark thoughts of the future out of my mind. That is something I will deal with tomorrow.

I make it to the restroom and I'm about to close the door behind me when a hand lands on the door, holding it open.

I feel my stomach drop to the floor for a quick second, then the door opens wider, and the hand's owner walks in.

"Santiago." I let out a sigh of relief.

"*Hola, mi bella*." He gives me a smile that I missed so much and closes the few feet separating us before he wraps me up in his arms.

For the first time in weeks, I feel safe. I feel like whatever is waiting for me tomorrow doesn't matter and I could get lost, even for a few minutes, in this man's arms and I will be okay.

In the six months since our night together, we have been at a distance but still close at the same time. We've been together a few times since but we both had our roles to play and that didn't leave much time for us to figure out where we stood but, in a way, we were still able to show our love to each other.

"What are you doing here?" I ask pulling away from him so I can collect myself.

He cups my cheek and helps me wipe away the tears.

"I knew tonight was going to be hard, and I wanted to come check on you. Also gave me the opportunity to stick it in Emilio's ass by showing up."

I receive one of his smirks, and I can't help but laugh a little through the tears flowing out.

"I'm glad that you did." I didn't know how much I needed to see him tonight until this very moment.

"How are you holding up?" He caresses my cheek, which causes me to lean into his touch even more.

"I want this to be over. I want to be done with this. I don't want tomorrow to come and I sure as hell don't want to marry Emilio Castro."

More tears are brewing but I keep them inside. I don't want to continue crying over this. One, because it dries my skin and two, if I continue to cry, I'm letting this define who I am and it doesn't.

Santos takes my face fully in his hands and leans his forehead against mine.

"Me and Leo are working on something. It has taken us longer than we thought it would to get all the loose ends tied but we are working on it. We will figure this out and we will get you out of this."

I want to believe his words, I do, but given the time constraints with the wedding tomorrow, it's a little hard to do so.

"But the wedding is tomorrow." Whatever they are planning is cutting it a little too close.

Santos moves his head against mine. "I know. I know," he says through gritted teeth, anger starting to radiate off him. "But just trust us. Please. We will get you out of this."

I look into this man's eyes and I see that he is just as broken about this as I am. I know it breaks him to not only see me as an emotional wreck, but also seeing me marrying another man, can't be easy.

Trust him.

I do, that's why I give a nod and silently tell him that I will continue to wait.

But I have to tell him one thing that might make this whole thing go faster.

"Something happened between me and Emilio." Santos pulls back from me instantly, his eyes changing to whatever he was just feeling to anger. Everything about him is on high alert.

"What?" he asks through his clenched teeth.

"About a month ago, he took me to the shooting range and we kind of bit each other's ass off while we were there. Some words were said. When we got back to the estate, he cornered me, and —" I stop, not knowing if I can say the words.

"And what?" Santos growls out.

"He grabbed me between my legs and started to rub at me."

Santos just stands there, fuming in anger. I try to put my hand on his face, but he steps back before I make contact.

I think he's going to storm out of the restroom and go find Emilio, but no, he turns toward the mirror and punches it straight on, shattering it.

All the glass falls to the counter, and I jump back at the sound of the glass shattering and at the primal growl that comes out of Santos.

"Motherfucker! That motherfucker is dead. Fucking dead. I don't give a shit if he's playing teacher's pet with your father, I'm going to kill him with my bare hands."

He continues to punch at the mirror until it's nonexistent. His fist is covered in cuts and blood.

Finally, Santos stops, and hunches his head down, his chin meeting his chest.

"Are you okay?" he asks, a raspiness to his voice.

"I should be asking you that." I go up to him and take his hand in mine, carefully brushing the small shards of glass off his skin.

"I mean, are you okay after what Emilio did?" I concentrate on his hand a little more than necessary while I answer his question.

"Made me more fearful of marrying him," I say honestly.

Here I am a woman he doesn't know, that is set to marry him, and he still did what he did. What would he have done if I was a strange woman?

I was scared that he was going to rape me in that moment. If that fear was strong then, imagine if we do end up married. Fear will be a constant thing.

"I'm going to fucking kill him," Santos growls again as I continue to pull out the pieces of glass.

I just nod. I want him to kill Emilio too.

We stay silent as I continue to clean his hand and once I'm done, I wrap it up in a bandage that I find under the sink.

Once everything is cleaned up, Santos takes my face between his hands again and kisses me.

There is nothing slow or sweet about this kiss. No, this kiss is everything that we are feeling, letting everything out.

Our tongues dance together, fighting to get everything that the other can give.

We lose ourselves in the action, in the moment. It's not until we hear a sound from outside flow through the walls of the restroom, that we remember where we're at.

"Don't come to the wedding tomorrow," I say when we pull apart and stand there, catching our breaths.

"Isabella." He starts to fight me on this but I'm already shaking my head.

"Tomorrow is going to be hard as it is. It will be harder if I see you at the church. Besides, if Emilio sees that you are there, it might cause problems. So please, don't go." I beg.

What I don't say is that if Emilio sees him there, he might want to kill him for ruining his big day. I can't have that happening.

"Is that what you really want?" he asks, sadness swimming in his eyes.

No.

That's not what I want at all.

"Yes. That's what I want."

He looks down at me, his mouth opening and closing a few times, but he doesn't say anything. Finally, he nods.

"I will do anything for you, *bella*. Even this." He places a chaste kiss on my lips. Nothing like the hot kiss from a minute ago.

"Thank you."

A part of me is telling me I'm going to regret this decision.

29

SANTOS

Present Day

THE CHURCH BELLS ring throughout the small town of San Pedro.

People are congregating all over the square to be able to witness the newlyweds come out once their vows have been said and the rings are in place.

If it even gets that far.

Isabella asked me not to come today, that seeing me would make this day a lot more difficult than what it already will be.

I wanted to obey her orders, I wanted to listen and keep my promise to her that I wouldn't be here today, but I couldn't do that.

Leo and I had come up with a plan, a plan to finally end all this, and that plan consisted of me being in that church.

If she hates me for being here, I'll accept it, but I'm here to keep her safe and that's all I care about.

So, this morning, I got dressed in my best slacks, put on my boots and made my way to the town center. Nobody is going to think that me attending this wedding is anything out of the ordinary. Most of the people will think that I was invited to this, given my relationship with the Morales family. Nobody will know that I'm actually here with an ulterior motive.

I walk through the laughing people that are getting together for picnics and enjoying their time with their kids on this hot June day.

Smiles and greetings are thrown in my direction as I make my way to the church, and I return each and every single one of them.

Before I make it to the church, I catch sight of Leo and Serena a few yards away, having a moment for themselves.

They look happy given the circumstances, and hopefully they continue to find happiness in their unconventional marriage.

Leo catches a glimpse of me somehow and gives me a nod.

I send one back to him as I step into the church.

Like the good Catholic boy that my mother raised me to be, I wet my fingertips with some holy water and say a prayer while making a cross gesture.

Given all the sins that I have commited, it's a wonder I didn't burst into flames as I walked through the doors.

Walking through the church corridor, I try to stay as hidden as possible. No way do I want to alert a member of the Castro family or Ronaldo that I'm here. Isabella was right on that end, if Emilio sees that I'm here, it could cause problems. Some deadly ones, and if everything goes to plan, only one person will die today, and it sure as hell isn't going to be me.

The church bells ring again, this time signaling that it's almost time for the ceremony to start.

I should get into place. I should stick to the plan, but I need to see her.

I need to see her and make sure she's okay.

So instead of taking my seat in the last row, I head down the hallway where the bridal suites are.

I'm able to find a small corner that keeps me somewhat hidden. As soon as I see her, I will head for my seat and continue with the plan, but to give my mind some peace, I need to see with my own eyes that she's okay.

A few good minutes pass by, and I'm thinking that I'm out of view when Camila comes to stand in front of me.

"Why are you hiding?" she whisper-yells at me and is looking at me like a crazy person.

I sigh. "Because I'm not supposed to be here."

Camila continues to look at me with confusion until she finally nods.

"Whatever it is that you are planning, do it fast," she tells me, before she walks away.

I should give Camila more credit. She knows a lot more about what happens in this world than what I want to believe.

A few seconds after Camila leaves, Serena walks right past me without noticing me.

That's when I step out of hiding, because I know her husband is not far behind.

"Everything all set?" he asks, not even questioning me about not being inside already.

I nod. "Yup, just waiting for this stupid ceremony to begin," I say looking around making sure I don't catch anyone's attention.

Leo nods. "She'll probably be pissed, but it's the only way," he says as I hear a door open down the hall.

The white skirt catches my attention first, and as more and more of the dress comes out of the room, my eyes travel up.

Isabella is standing at the end of the hall, looking like an angel. She looks absolutely stunning. She's literally taking my breath away.

Leo abandons me and walks over to his sister, where she's surrounded by Camila and Serena.

It takes everything in me not to walk over to her and take her in my arms before placing my lips on hers, all while I tell her how beautiful she looks.

Today she's not my bride, she's someone else's. I was able to see that she was okay, now it's time for me to do the job I came here to do.

Yet my feet stay rooted in place and I continue to watch her as she walks down the long hallway. She doesn't notice me until she's only a few feet away.

Her eyes tell me that she wants to be angry with me because I didn't listen to her orders, but after a few seconds I can see that the anger is replaced with relief.

I give her a small smile and for a few seconds, we're lost in our own little bubble.

That is until I hear Ronaldo's voice.

Both of our gazes fall to her father, who is just looking at his daughter with indifference.

So much for being happy on your little girl's big day.

Isabella tells him yes and they start lining up in formation. I take that as my cue to take my place within the chapel, but before I do that, I give one last look over to Isabella, but she doesn't notice that I'm looking at her.

Forgive me, *bella*.

Please forgive me.

Before I turn away, I notice the murderous stare on Ronaldo's face aimed in my direction.

He might have seemed indifferent a few minutes ago, but that indifference is now gone. I can tell by how tightly he is holding his jaw that he knows I'm up to something and he's mad that he won't be able to stop me.

I give him a curt nod and make my way into the chapel and take my seat.

The music starts to play and slowly the progression of the small wedding party starts to file in, but I don't look at them.

No, my eyes are focused straight ahead. To the bastard that is standing in front of the altar with a smug look on his face like he won the lottery.

Sorry, motherfucker. Luck will be on your side but not in the way that you think.

The music changes and everyone stands up to watch the bride enter the room on her father's arm.

That's the signal.

Instead of watching Isabella walk down the aisle, I make my way out of the pew and with every single person in this church standing up, I'm able to make my way to the front.

I make it to the front of the chapel and through the door that leads to a small balcony that is on top of the altar.

My timing is impeccable as I make it to the balcony, which is covered in artificial vines, a good twenty seconds before Ronaldo and Isabella step in front of Emilio.

Moving a few vines out of the way to get a clear shot, I put on gloves, and I grab my automatic reloader from my waistband and screw on the silencer. The only people that will hear the shot will be the people in the front.

Could I have done this any other time besides a wedding?

Yes, yes, I could.

But we needed to make a statement. To both the Castro family and Ronaldo that not everything is about being powerful and money hungry. Not even in the cartel world.

I could have also done this point blank, but I'd rather Emilio keep all the attention for himself.

I situate myself on the floor of the balcony, the gun in the opening and I wait.

My eyes find Isabella right away and I watch as she makes the last final steps to Emilio. I switch my gaze to Leo quickly and he gives me a nod.

It's time to kill this fucker.

Ronaldo places Isabella's hand in Emilio's and the music stops.

One beat.

Two.

My finger lands on the trigger and I shoot.

Forgive me, Father, for I have sinned in the house of God.

30

ISABELLA

When in sight, blood will always be the main focal point. It's bright and when you're wearing something light colored, it stands out even more.

After I heard the shot ring out, the blood was the only thing I was able to concentrate on.

It wasn't the screams or mass chaos that ensued right after. No, it was the blood splatters that had landed on my hand and on my dress.

I knew it wasn't mine, since nothing in me hurt. Nothing felt like it was out of place.

So, whose was it?

The blood splatter on my arms was no longer what grabbed my attention. I frantically looked over to my father and he looked more in shock than anything else and he also only had blood splatter on him.

The blood had to come from in front of us.

My next line of sight was the man in front of me. The man whose hand my father just placed mine in.

Unlike my father and me, he wasn't covered in just blood splatter, no, the blood that was on him was different.

The spots were bigger and darker and seemed to be getting bigger as the seconds continued to tick by. He was the one that got hurt, it's his blood that's covering my hands and arms and coating my dress.

For a quick second, our eyes meet.

I've heard before that when a person gets shot or is near death, if they had done something bad in their life, their eyes would be filled with remorse and regret.

But as I looked into Emilio's eyes, that's not what I saw.

There was no remorse and no regret swimming in his dark eyes. All I saw was evil and corruption floating around.

I kept my eyes on him as I watched him spit out the blood and fall to his knees.

That's when the chaos started.

People were screaming and yelling for a doctor. Invitees were running out of the church, not wanting to have anything to do with what just happened.

Someone had yelled that the police had arrived and that they were the ones that shot Emilio. That caused even more panic.

Even as I was getting pulled away from someone, my eyes stayed on Emilio as his family carried him off to possibly save him.

The vision of him bloody, and evil eyes is the only thing that I see even minutes later while I'm tucked away safely in the bridal suite.

I hear my brother talking, saying words to reassure

both my sister and Serena, but I can't pinpoint the actual words that he is saying. All I know is that they are both crying, not because Emilio was shot but because of how close to death they were.

At some point, I must have zoned out because I didn't hear the door open or notice that we had a new person in the room. I don't realize it until he is crouched down in front of me, taking my blood-stained hand in his.

"Bella," he says my name in the softest tone, that you wouldn't even expect coming from a man of his stature.

He called me Bella, not *bella*. I hate it when he doesn't call me *bella*.

All other noise in the room goes silent. They are probably waiting for me to say something.

"Isabella. You're okay." He raises the hand that isn't holding mine and caresses my cheek. "You're okay. You're safe."

Am I though?

I look down at my hands again and remember the blood.

"My hands are all bloody." The red stains are large and look like it's going to take a lot of soap for it to come off.

"They are, but the blood isn't yours," he gives my hands a squeeze. "Did you hear me, Isabella? The blood isn't yours."

"It's Emilio's," I state, looking up from my hands and staring at the door. "It's his blood."

"Yes, it is."

I look back at the man in front of me and look into his

eyes. The remorse that wasn't in Emilio's eyes is in his. It's not very strong, but it's there.

This is what he meant when he told me to trust him.

He said that he and Leo were working on something, and he told me to trust him.

This is what they were going to do.

This is why I needed to trust him.

Before I can say anything or even ask if he was the one that shot Emilio, Camila speaks.

"What the hell happened out there?" her voice is shaky and she sounds terrified.

Before anyone could answer her, the door to the suite busts open and my father comes barreling in.

He's angry and he's looking right at me.

No, it's not me his eyes are focused on. It's on the man that is crouched down in front of me. The man that shot down my future husband to stop the wedding and protect me.

"*Hijo de tu puta madre.*" My father charges over to where Santos and I are, his face going red and anger radiating off every single inch of his body.

Serena and Camila both let out a yelp when Santos stands up and my father grabs him by the collar of his shirt before slamming him into the wall.

"*Pendejo.* Do you have any idea what you just did? Do you have any idea how much money you just cost me?" My father slams Santos into the wall a few more times.

My father isn't as big or as strong as Leo and Santos, but even with a few inches in height difference, my father is able to hold his own. Which scares me.

"You have no idea what you just cost this cartel and this family," my father spits in his face, but Santos just takes it. He could fight off my father, but he just continues to stand there and take whatever my father gives.

"I did what I needed to do to protect your daughter. You know the same daughter that you've been using as a pawn to get more power."

The face-off between the two men is intense. Leo even has to step forward to stop anything if it gets out of hand.

"You don't know jack shit about anything." Ronaldo shifts himself so now his forearm is pressing against Santos's neck.

That's when I get up, causing Serena and Camila to come over to me.

Even with an arm pressed to his airway, Santos still finds a way to smirk.

"Like I don't know that Emilio came to you years ago so that you could take care of some debt for him? That all he had to do was complete a job for you and you would take care of it? That job being him killing my father for you?"

I feel a hand slip into mine and grasp it tightly.

Camila.

A growl escapes from my father's throat as Santos finishes up speaking.

"I didn't kill your asshole father."

"No, you just hired someone to do it for you. Just like you told my father to kill the FBI agent that was once your friend. Because you're a coward and let other people take the fall for your actions."

Being called a coward is what breaks my father. One

second he is holding Santos by the neck, the next his arm is swinging back and he is hitting his face repeatedly.

Screams fill the room and Leo is scrambling to get my father off Santos, who is now on the ground, taking every hit that my father has to offer.

"I'm fucking Ronaldo Morales! There is nothing cowardly about me."

Leo is able to get a hold of my father and starts to pull him away but that is not before he is able to get a good kick to Santos's chest.

"*¡Basta!*" I yell when Santos spits out blood from the countless hits he received.

The room goes silent as I run to Santos and check his face. It's swollen and there are multiple cuts all over that must have come from my father's rings.

"You are a bastard for betraying me, just like your father. Be warned right now Santiago, you won't live as long as Cristiano did."

I think if Leo wasn't holding my father back, he would kill Santos right here and now.

"Like what you say means anything to me." Santos spits out more blood, this time he aims it toward my father's feet.

"Tell me, Santos. When did you turn against me?"

Santos looks at me quickly before looking back to my father.

Before he answers, he starts to push himself up off the floor, wiping off the blood that is pooling at the corner of his mouth.

"When you decided to use your own daughter for

personal gain. That's when all the pieces started to fall into place."

Santos moves so that he is toe to toe with him, and my stomach starts to churn at the thought that fist will start swinging again.

"You are done. You are no longer a part of the Muertos Cartel."

"Yes, he is."

It's the first time that my brother speaks. We all turn to him, even my father, to see what he means. My brother is second-in-command of the cartel, but I have never heard him go against my father's word like this.

"I told you that this was going to happen, *Papà*." Leo lets my father go and goes to stand next to his best friend, his brother.

"If I remember correctly, we had a conversation in your office when you sent Emilio after my wife. And I told you that I would do everything in my power to stop this marriage, and I didn't give a shit what you lost. Looks like I was able to keep my promise and guess what, I still don't give a shit."

Leo and Santos stand as a united front against my father.

"You two must have forgotten who still runs this cartel, and I will run it until I'm in my grave. Try to take me down, but you will fail." My father spits before readjusting his suit. "You are a disgrace. Both of you."

"Disgrace or not, this cartel will be mine. My previous statement still stands. You're dead to me, and we both will only deal with you when absolutely necessary." Leo squares his shoulders and looks our father straight in the eye.

I don't know how long this lasts, but it does until my father gives one final growl and turns to leave the room.

"*Vamonos, Isabella y Camila.*"

What?

He wants us to go with him.

"No. I'm not going," I stand my ground, finally standing up to my father. Something that I should have had the courage to do a very long time ago.

His nostrils flare at my statement but he doesn't say anything, instead he looks at my sister.

"*Vamonos Camila,*" he orders her, but Camila stays in her place. not moving an inch closer to him. She looks at him with fearful eyes and arms wrapped around herself, shaking her head.

"No. I don't want to." The fear is clear in her voice as she cowers deeper into herself.

"I don't have time for your bullshit, Camila! You will come with me. I can't have your siblings corrupt you anymore than they already have."

He stalks over to her and grabs her arm and starts to drag her out of the room.

"*Papí*, no. I don't want to go. Let me stay," Camila begs and everything in me is breaking.

"Let her go." Leo growls and stalks over to them and tries to pry my father's arm off our sister.

"You don't get to tell me what to do. She's my daughter and she will listen to me when I tell her to do."

Our father yanks Camila closer to him. Tears are running down her cheeks.

"Okay," I say to him. We've been through enough today, and we don't need to continue to add to it.

"Bella," my sister cries out.

Swallowing down my own lump, I go to my sister and wrap her in a tight hug.

"I will get you out of his house. I promise," I whisper in her ear before I lean back and give her a kiss on the cheek.

She gives me a tearful nod and soon she is getting dragged out of the room by our father.

This is definitely not how I thought this day would go.

Emilio was shot by Santos.

And then Camila was dragged away by our father.

It all makes my head spin. Spin to the point that I'm seeing black spots.

"I think I need to go home," I say.

That is before my eyes close, and everything goes dark.

31

SANTOS

I watch her as she sleeps, all curled up in her seat as we fly to Austin.

After she announced that she wanted to go home, she ended up fainting. My guess is all the events from the day were finally catching up with her.

I can't fault her for it either. It was one thing after another after another, her body was most likely tired of everything.

The wedding.

Emilio being shot

The fight between me and Ronaldo.

Ronaldo dragging Camila out with him.

It was all too much. I would have fainted with her, especially with all the blows to the face that I received.

We were able to wake her up after the priest gave us some smelling salts to run under her nose. It worked. She woke up, and as soon as she was stable enough to stand, Serena helped her out of the dress, and we left the church.

The atmosphere outside of the church was not like it was before the ceremony started. The families that were out in the town square enjoying their day, were no longer there. There was no children's laughter filling the air or any music playing in the background. It was as if the enjoyment that was going on only an hour or so before, never happened.

The one thing that surprised me even more than the townspeople nowhere to be seen, was the fact that the Castro Family was nowhere to be seen as well. You would think that when their son was shot during his wedding there would be hell to pay.

Which reminds me that we have yet to learn if Emilio is even still alive or not.

When I pulled the trigger, I aimed it directly at his chest. If I was going to shoot the fucker, might as well go all out, since shooting him in the head would have been too messy.

I felt the shot as it left the gun and I saw the second that it hit his body. There was silence before there was chaos and all I could concentrate on was Isabella.

I watched her as she looked at what was happening around her and tried to put everything together. She didn't freak out. No, she was lost in her own mind before Leo whisked her away when people started to rush the altar.

Now here we are flying in a private plane owned by the Morales family heading to Austin, where we will wait for any sign of retaliation.

The curtain separating the two sections of the plane opens up and Leo's head pops through.

"She still sleeping?" he asks, coming over, brushing her hair back slightly before coming to sit next to me.

I shift the ice packs that I'm currently holding to my face. Thankfully nothing is broken.

"Yeah, it's been a long day." I check my watch. We've only been up in the air for about fifteen minutes, but Isabella has been asleep from since the second we got in the car to drive to the hangar. With me carrying her onto the plane.

Leo nods. "I just talked to Camila. She's crying and doesn't want to be at the estate by herself the rest of the summer. She doesn't even want to be within a hundred miles of Ronaldo. She wants out."

Camila has always been like a little sister to me. So, when I saw Ronaldo grab her arm and yank her out of the room, I wanted to go after him and beat him like he did to me.

It was clear in her face that she was terrified of her father and now she's there alone with him.

"We'll figure something out. We'll get her out of Ronaldo's grasp." Hopefully I can keep that promise.

"I sure fucking hope so." All I could do is nod.

We are silent for a few seconds before Leo clears his throat. "I'm calling a meeting with him. We need to get our lines straight if we want to continue having a successful business. We also need to show him where we stand and tell him that we aren't going to be taking his shit any longer."

Again, I nod.

He has every single right to call a meeting with his

father, and we need to figure everything out. But I can't help but wonder, if the last meeting Leo called with his father didn't work, what makes him think that this one will?

"While you're at it, you should call that other meeting too. I know that I said to take some time, but I think we need to get the ball rolling before it's too late.

I can see from my peripheral that Leo turns to look at me, but I keep my eyes straight ahead on his sister.

Maybe this whole day has made me go crazy.

Maybe the blows I received from Ronaldo gave me brain damage.

Whatever it is, it's time to talk to Madden and get Ronaldo behind bars sooner rather than later.

"I'll make the call." Leo stands up from his seat and starts to go back to the other side of the plane.

He's at the curtain when he turns around and looks at Isabella.

"Take care of her, would ya?" he says, with concern in his voice.

I nod, even though if his back is to me.

"Always."

He gives me a nod and goes back to the other side of the curtain.

For the rest of the flight, I watch Isabella sleep. She looks so peaceful the whole time that it kills me that I have to wake her when we land in Austin and disembark.

"Want to come back to my place?" I offer when we are in a car, while Serena and Leo are in another.

All Isabella does is nod and lean her head on my shoulder as we make the drive over to my place.

The place that she spent almost every single night in for years.

When we get to the townhome, Isabella jumps straight into the shower, and I make some canned soup for her to eat.

Yes, it's June, but soup is comforting, and canned shit is all I have.

I warm up the soup and when I head to the bedroom, I find Isabella already in the bed all curled up under the sheets.

Seeing her in my bed like this does something to me and I have to take a quick second to refocus.

The last time she was in my bed at all was right before she headed to San Pedro to stay at her father's estate before the engagement was announced.

It's been almost a whole year since.

Crazy to think where we were last year at this time and how things changed so rapidly.

"I made you soup," I announce into the room and instantly her eyes pop open.

I make my way over to her while she sits up. She takes the soup from me and starts to eat it right away, while I settle on the edge of the bed watching her.

"Bella, we need to talk about things."

She looks up at me from under her lashes all the while her spoon is in the air.

I see my word going through her head and finally she nods, putting her spoon down.

"Is he dead?" Her eyes are on the bowl in her lap and not on me.

"I have no idea. I sent a message to a few of our men while I was in the kitchen but as of right now, I don't know." I hope he is.

No way in fucking hell do I want to deal with a pissed-off Emilio. The fucker is a moron on his best day but who knows how miserable he could make our lives.

Isabella nods, accepting my answer, still not looking up from her bowl.

"Why did you do it at the wedding?"

Why in-fucking-deed.

Out of all the places that we could have shot Emilio we chose the most impractical place. If our plan hadn't gone how we wanted it to, a lot of people could have gotten hurt. Isabella was already too close for my own comfort with how I did it, I can't imagine if something had gone wrong.

"It was a power move. Show whoever was in that room what could happen if you cross us. What it could really be like when you get involved with our cartel."

It's a shitty reason nonetheless.

"You couldn't do it any other way?" She finally looks up at me. There is a tinge of anger in her expression.

"We could have, but we were running out of time. It had to be done and I'm sorry I did it that way."

I should tell her that it was Leo's idea to do it at the wedding. If it was me, I would have done it last night, but Leo wanted theatrics.

I scoot closer to her, place the soup bowl on the nightstand and take her hand in mine.

"I'm sorry, Bella. I really am. But I did what I had to do to get you out of that situation. No way in hell was I going to let the wedding progress further than it did and have you legally tied to that fucker."

I have no idea what I would have done had I waited until after she married him to execute the plan. Seeing her marry another man right in front of me is not something I want to experience ever again.

Isabella looks at me, not saying a single word. For a second, I think that she's going to dump the soup over my head.

Finally, she speaks.

"I hate it when you call me Bella."

I smile a little. Definitely not what I expected her to say.

"Noted." I give her a curt nod to drive the point.

She takes her bottom lip between her teeth and looks down at our joined hands.

"What are you thinking?" I ask when she's silent for a few minutes.

"You've hurt me a lot. You hurt me when you threw me to the side when I was sixteen. You hurt me when I gave you a big part of myself and walked away when I was eighteen. Then you hurt me again last year when you said that you wouldn't fight to get me out of the arrangement. I know the last one doesn't really count because you were trying to do things yourself, but it still hurt. It hurts that you kept something so big from me and I had to basically force it out of you. There's been a lot of hurt throughout the years and I don't know how much more I can handle. I don't know if I could handle more of the back and forth that has taken place throughout the last year anymore."

If she ends what is happening between us once and for all, I will accept it.

Because she's right.

I did hurt her.

I hurt her because I was trying to mold our situation into my own agenda. Before our relationship started, I was trying to have Isabella when it was convenient for me. And when it wasn't, I walked away because I thought that was what she needed. I did the same thing last year when all this fucked-up shit with Emilio started.

"A simple act of conversation would have saved me a lot of heartache. You could have told me to wait for you and I would have. I would have waited for you as long as you needed me to, even if I had to go through with the wedding, I would have done it. Because that's how much I loved you, how much I believed in us."

Believed.

Loved.

All past tense.

Does she not feel those things anymore?

"You said you believed and loved," I state, not moving my hand from hers. "Are those two things something that you no longer feel?"

Isabella takes a second before she lets out a sigh. "I love you, with all my heart, you know that. I just think that maybe, if we continue this relationship, that we take some time and find ourselves individually before we can find who we are together. Neither of us is the person we were a year ago. I feel like I lost a big part of me this last year. That I lost a lot of my strength due to fear and I need to gain it back. I need to build myself back up and be someone that I absolutely love. If I don't do that, I will never be happy."

I give her hand a reassuring squeeze.

"What do you want us to do, Isabella?"

"I want to be with you, that much I know, but maybe we don't jump into the way things were. We could go slow and find who we are again while we spend time together and get to know each other again. We both have changed, and it might be nice to finally figure out a way to navigate this relationship in public where everyone could see."

I shift on the bed scooting closer to her, placing my hands on either side of her face.

"Whatever you want. Whatever you need, I will give it to you. Because you deserve the world, Isabella Morales, and I will fight to give it to you." I lean forward and place a chaste kiss on her lips.

I mean every single word. If this is the route she wants to take, then let's do it. I'm not going anywhere. I'm in no way going to walk away from this woman ever again.

"There's one more thing that I want," she places her hands on mine, holding me to her.

"What is it?"

"I want to be in that meeting you and Leo arrange with my father."

32

ISABELLA

W‍ant to know what I thought the response was going to be when I asked to join the meeting between Leo, Santos and my father?

Fuck no.

No way in fucking hell.

Are you out of your fucking mind?

Granted, I did receive a variation of all three responses from my brother when Santos informed him of what I wanted to do, but after some very heavy convincing, I was able to get him to agree.

Now the three of us, freshly off the family plane, are on our way to the estate.

Even the thought of seeing my father makes me nervous. Which is causing my leg to bounce up and down the whole drive there.

Santos must have noticed my nerves, because halfway to the estate, he places a hand on my thigh.

"Everything is going to be okay," he tells me before he leans in and places a kiss on my temple.

All I can do is continue to shake my leg and nod.

I do turn to him and give him a small smile. And he gives me one in return, and my eyes go to the bruising covering his face.

They're still dark, not as bad as they were last week, but they are still there and will possibly still take a few weeks to disappear.

"So, I'm being forced to ask this, but what is going on with you two? Are you together?"

I turn to watch Leo shift uncomfortably. I guess he really would do anything for his wife, including getting information like this, no doubt, to tell her friend Aria.

"I'll answer your question if you answer mine, why is your wife so invested in our relationship status?" I raise an eyebrow at him, challenging him.

He shrugs. "She says that your relationship is better than the *novelas* on TV."

"Serena watches *telenovelas*?" Santos leans around me to look at my brother.

Leo rolls his eyes. "She started a few weeks ago. She wants to learn Spanish and apparently the only way to do that is to watch overdramatic women on Netflix."

"Aw, someone sounds bitter," I pat his thigh.

"I mean, I'm right there. I could teach her. But no, the second she gets home a *telenovela* gets put on. She even called me a *pendejo estúpido* the other day because I didn't clean the kitchen."

I try to hold in my laugh. "And what did you say when she called you a *pendejo estúpido*?"

"I tried not to laugh, which made her angry that I wasn't supporting her in 'her endeavor to learn Spanish.'"

I think Serena has officially won a bigger place in my heart.

"Did you sleep on the couch that night?" Santos teases my brother, and I can't help laughing a little at his big ass body on the couch.

"No asshole. I spent the whole night in our bed worshipping her body, whispering sweet nothings in her ear all in Spanish."

Okay, definitely not a visual I wanted to picture.

I even gag a little at his description. I probably would have puked if he had said the word pound or fuck.

Leo notices my expression. "What? Don't like to hear about my sexual adventures with my wife?"

"You want to hear mine?" Right away, his face changes from one of teasing to pure anger and discomfort. "That's what I thought."

"*Ya llegamos*," Arturo announces as we pull up to the estate.

Already?

Leo distracted you.

That was the whole point of that conversation, to distract me from my nerves and get me to calm down.

I turn to Leo and lean in to give him a kiss on the cheek. "Thank you."

He nods. "You still didn't give me an answer to report back to the wife."

"Tell her that we're together but taking things slow. We have to build up to where we left off when all of this started."

Leo nods again, this time taking my hand and giving it a squeeze. "It will work out."

I sure hope so.

"As for our father." He opens his door and slides out, holding out a hand to me. "You'll be able to handle him."

I hope that is true too.

Placing my hand in my brother's, I slide out of the car and make sure there is not a wrinkle in place.

Was it necessary to dress nicely for a meeting with my father? No.

But I wanted to. I wanted to wear a dress that I designed to show my strength. I wanted to come off as a boss ass bitch and I feel like that with the dress, the black heels and my hair nicely pulled back.

I look like a real cartel princess.

The three of us walk into the house and head straight to my father's office.

A part of me wants to divert and head straight to Camila's side of the house.

In the week since the wedding, I've been talking to her every single day.

She sounds scared every single time I speak to her, and I want to be able to make her feel safe.

My sister is one of the main reasons why I wanted this meeting with my father. I overheard the conversation between Leo and Santos on the plane ride to Austin on my wedding day. I heard Leo say that Camila wants out, and I may know a way to make that happen. I just need her to agree to it. It will be hard since it will mean she will be away from us, but this will be a good thing for her. She just has to do it.

Like every other time, the door to my father's office is closed. This time though, Leo approaches the door and doesn't knock. He just waltzes in like he doesn't give a shit.

And possibly, at this point, he doesn't.

As we walk in, my father looks up at us like we are bothering him and taking him away from important business.

"Leonardo. Santiago. Is there a reason why the two of you are here? I was under the impression that you two only wanted to come and talk to me when it involved business. And given that one of my daughters is here, I'm guessing it's not."

Has my father always been this smug? Or is it something that I always overlooked because of who he was to me?

"This is business," Leo takes a seat in front of his desk and leaning back, crossing his legs and showing that he doesn't have a care in the world.

Santos waves for me to take the second chair, which catches my father's attention. I keep his stare as I make my way around and take a seat, trying to convey as much confidence like my brother.

"Then, if it's business, you should know that the little stunt you pulled cost me millions because you decided to murder Emilio."

The second I hear the words, cold rushes through my body.

Emilio is dead.

Santos killed him.

Holy crap.

I don't know how to handle this piece of information. Should I be happy that the asshole is dead? I think so. Am I though? I don't know.

"You don't look very happy about the news, Isabella. I thought that you would be jumping for joy that the man that you were set to marry is dead."

I look at my father in disbelief.

Does he really think I'm coldhearted?

I square my shoulders and hold my head up high. It's time to confront my father.

"The man that I was supposed to marry saw me as a transaction and only that. I was a prize to him; he didn't care about me or my life. If you would have been a good father, you would have seen that before you arranged anything. I wouldn't have survived that marriage. Apparently, everyone in this room knows that. Except you of course."

"He would have made a good husband." My father's response, not even affected by my words.

"Like hell he would," Leo spits out but I hold up a hand for him to stop talking.

"Leo's right. He wouldn't have been. Had we gotten married, he would have made my life miserable. A month before the wedding, he said that he couldn't wait to put me in my place on our wedding night. That's not something a future husband should say to his bride. If that wedding was successful, I would have ended up like my mother."

That's what changes my father's facial expression, the mention of my mother. I can see him get angrier by the second.

"Leave your mother out of this," he growls through his teeth.

"Why? It's true. It may have taken a few years but given the personality that Emilio had, he was bound to piss someone off and make me pay for his mistakes. Just like my mother paid for yours. Or did you also have her killed like you did Cristiano?"

The last part was supposed to be a sarcastic comment. Something that wasn't meant to be true but the way he is looking at me, it has to be.

I always suspected that my father had something to do with my mother's death, more than just being her husband.

Now I know there is more to her death, I just don't know what.

"You did, didn't you? There is more to her death, than just someone that was after you, isn't there?" I feel anger boiling inside of me, and it's just getting worse as he sits there in his chair looking pissed off.

Like I have no right to ask about my mother's death.

I'm done.

"You can't even be honest with your own daughter." I shake my head and push all emotions down.

"I don't know what you want me to say, Isabella." He gives me a shrug.

A shrug.

I never thought I would hate my father so much.

"I want you to be honest with me. I want you to tell me that you are sorry for trying to marry me off to a despicable man. I want you to apologize for failing me as a father."

I feel my whole body shake.

Like all the anger I've been holding inside from years ago is finally coming to the surface.

"I won't be doing that, Isabella."

Of course not.

"Then like Leo, you're dead to me," I grab the small purse that I came in with and stand. "I'll leave you men to do business." I start to walk away, but before I walk over the threshold, I turn back to look at my father. "I'll be taking Camila with me. She deserves a lot more than whatever you will ever offer her. Congratulations Ronaldo, you have failed your children. Rosa Maria would be so proud of you."

With my head held high and not a single tear shed, I leave my father's office without a second thought and head straight to my sister.

The second I step into her room, she sees me and rushes over to me, holding on to me for dear life.

I hug her back as tightly as I can.

"You're here," she cries out. Seeing her tear up just from seeing me, breaks my heart.

"I'm here and you're coming with me."

Camila pulls away from me and looks at me with her big brown doe eyes.

"I am?"

I nod. "All week, all I could think about is you and how you needed to get out of this house and this life. So, I'm here to take you with me. To Austin. For now."

"For now?" A small crease forms between her eyebrows, and I reach forward to smooth it out.

"I talked to my boss. Told her I had a very talented sister and she deserved to get the best education. She said that she had connections to the art department at NYU, that she could make a few calls and possibly get you a spot."

It was a hard ask but if it got Camila as far away from our father as possible, I was going to do it. I would do anything for my sister.

I even mentioned it to Leo, and he agreed. He said to me that if it was something Camila wanted, he would front all the expenses she'll have.

"NYU doesn't just hand out spots." She's right, they don't.

"They don't, but they do look at portfolios. And it so happens that the deadline is in two weeks. You're good Camila, great even. I showed my boss some of your pieces and she agreed. She was able to talk to her connection and get you an appointment. And it's yours if you want it."

I watch as Camila goes through the motions. Her mouth opens but then closes again when she can't find the words to say.

She's like that for a few minutes until more tears escape from her eyes and she nods.

"I'll take it," she says, before coming back to me and

hugging me as tightly as she can. "Thank you."

"*Todo por ti, hermanita.*"

Anything for you little sister. Anything for you.

"You should pack a bag, so you can come with me now," I say to her when we pull apart.

"I kind of already did," she says sheepishly, putting a few strands of her grayish-white hair behind her ear.

I can feel my eyebrows coming together in a confused look and she just waves around her room.

I must have been so invested in seeing my sister that I didn't notice that most of her stuff is all packed up.

"There was no way I was going to be staying here. So, when I heard that Leo and Santos were going to be here today, I thought I would hitch a ride with them or something."

"Hitch a ride?"

Was she going to climb in the back of the SUV and just pop out at the airport and yell out surprise?

Camila nods. "Yeah."

"I guess you wouldn't be you, if you didn't try something like that." I give her a smile and go to grab one of her bags.

My sister is coming home with me.

She will no longer be under our father's thumb and have her life dictated like mine and Leo's.

She will be able to live the life that she wants to live and be able to succeed.

And I'm going to do everything possible to make that happened.

And I know Leo will too.

33

SANTOS

I SOMETIMES WONDER how my life got to where it is.

Yes, I was born into this life, but I could have chosen to walk away before I was ever in too deep. I could have walked away the second I stepped out of the basement that first time with my father.

But I didn't.

Did my life become what it is because I was destined to have it go like this? Or was I too hardheaded as a teenager and just decided to take this path?

Whatever the case may be, it led me to a coffee shop in Austin waiting for a damn federal agent to arrive.

"Are you sure he's coming?" I readjust my baseball cap.

I have no idea why the fucker asked us to dress conspicuously, it's not like there is an active warrant out for our arrest or anything.

Leo nods before cutting into his omelet. "He said he would be here. Maybe he's running late or something."

Or something.

I swear, if this is some sort of ploy against us, I'm going to strangle Special Agent Madden.

"How is it going with Camila and Isabella under the same roof?" Leo asks, taking another bite of his omelet. The way he's eating that thing is disgusting.

It's been three weeks since Leo, Isabella and I went to the estate and Camila left with us. For the first week and a half, she and Isabella stayed at her apartment. I would occasionally pop in to feed them but then leave them again to continue their sister time.

When Camila went to New York last week for her interview, me and Isabella got together and talked. It wasn't about anything serious, but we needed to figure out a few things. One of them being if she wanted to move in with me at some point.

She was practically already living with me when all this shit with Emilio started up, and I sure didn't have the balls to touch her stuff when she basically lived in San Pedro for the past year. So most of her stuff is still there.

I didn't want to pressure her into anything that she wasn't ready for just yet, but now that Camila was living with her for the rest of the summer, they needed more space.

Space that I have.

So, I offered it to her. Even suggested that we could swap homes if it made her feel better.

She told me she would think about it.

It took about an hour of thinking before she told me that she was ready to move in.

Not going to lie, it took me a little by surprise, but I

jumped at the opportunity and moved all of her and Camila's stuff to my place. They were both moved in by the time Camila got back from her interview.

Here's the kicker though, I've spent most of my life around these two. How didn't I know how much of a hassle it was to live with both of them?

I appreciate Leo a little more now but he's still an asshole for not warning me.

"A pain in my ass," I mutter into my coffee.

Leo laughs and shakes his head. "Welcome to the club, *hermano*."

He looks like he's about to say something else, but something must have caught his attention because he stops when he looks up.

"You're late." Leo wipes his mouth, greeting our guest.

The special agent has arrived.

Sure enough, he slides in next to me like we are long-time friends and takes a menu from the center of the table.

The bastard doesn't say anything, just waves over the waitress and places his order.

As soon as the girl is done, he turns to us.

"How are you, boys?"

I hate him.

"Oh, you know, just waiting for your ass to show up," Leo answers, sounding slightly more annoyed than he was a few minutes ago.

Madden sighs. "Yeah, sorry about that. Had something to take care of and it took a little longer than I thought it would."

The waitress comes back and sets Madden's coffee on the table.

Of course, he drinks it black with nothing in it. It's just like his soul probably.

"So," he says once he takes a drink from the black liquid. "What brings you to this lovely breakfast? Not that you two aren't my favorite people, but I got shit to do."

Leo nods to me.

I reach for the backpack that I walked in with and pull out the first file.

"This is all the information you need to close a cold case from five years ago." I place the file on the table.

"What cold case?" Madden says, tentatively opening the file.

"The murder of Cristiano Reyes," I state and instantly he recognizes the name.

I don't know if it's because he knows the case or if he knows him as his father's killer.

"Who did it?" he asks, opening the file and scanning it.

"Emilio Castro."

Madden looks me right in the eye when I say the name. There is definitely recognition with that name.

"He still alive?" He looks between me and Leo looking for an answer. He probably thinks he died last year when he went after Serena.

"Died three weeks ago," Leo states, taking another bite of his omelet.

How is he not done with that thing yet?

"How?" Madden asks, closing the file to my father's

case, just in time too because the waitress comes back with his food.

"Shot in the chest at his wedding." Leo shrugs like he just said the most casual sentence in the world.

"He got killed at his wedding?" Madden asks, his voice low and only heard by us.

Leo nods, while I take the file on Emilio's death out.

"He was shot with an automatic reloader, which is owned by Ronaldo Morales."

It was Leo's idea to kill Emilio at his wedding, and it was mine to pin it on Ronaldo.

That was part of the reason why I was at the estate the night before the wedding. Yes, Isabella was my priority, but with Ronaldo occupied with his guests, it gave me an opportunity to sneak into his office.

I knew exactly what gun I was looking for, so as soon as I found it, I put gloves on and took it. When Ronaldo would come back to his office, he would notice nothing.

Now we are just waiting for the Castro family to come after us. It's only a matter of time.

"I'm not even going to ask how in the hell you are able to prove that the gun belongs to him."

I riffle through the papers until I find what I'm looking for.

"He did all the work for us. The one and only weaponed registered to Ronaldo Morales in the state of Texas."

Madden takes the registration from me and scans it over.

"This registration is from the late eighties."

"When Ronaldo wasn't very well known as a cartel kingpin." Leo finishes the thought.

The reason why we chose this gun to shoot down Emilio. It's the only one that ties Ronaldo to the crime.

Because even in Texas, known members of the cartel, mafia or gangs aren't lawfully able to carry.

"Fuck," Madden scrubbing his hand over his face.

"Now you can add murder to his rap sheet." Leo says, leaning back and placing an arm on the back of his booth.

Madden continues to look at all the evidence that we have handed over to him. All so that he could take Ronaldo down.

"I'm not one to ask if anyone has a moral compass, I've done my fair share of heinous things, but I do have to ask this. What happens to the cartel once Ronaldo is taken down?"

He looks straight at Leo when he asks the question since that decision is going to fall on him.

"I can't very well tell you that the cartel is going to continue, can I? Whatever is decided that's between me and my brother-in-law here. Not you. But I can promise you this, you won't find another file on the Muertos on your desk after this."

If Madden isn't shitting his pants right about now, he should be.

Surprisingly he nods. "I can get behind that."

He collects all the paperwork that we just handed over and folds them so that the files fit inside his jacket pocket.

Madden throws a few bills on the table and stands up. "I'll reach out if there's a development."

And with that he leaves the café.

"Hate the guy," Leo mumbles and I can't help but agree.

Whoever ends up with the bastard is going to have their work cut out for them.

Within minutes of Madden leaving, we follow suit.

It's when we are in the car driving to my place when I finally broach the subject.

"You don't know what you're going to do with the cartel once Ronaldo is behind bars, do you?"

Leo shrugs. "I have some ideas, but nothing concrete. Don't know if I want to be running drugs my whole life and end up like Ronaldo. Serena is thinking about kids, and I don't know if I can give them the same life we got."

"Some difficult shit," I say as I turn onto my street.

"Abso-fucking-lutely."

I pull into the driveway of the townhouse in the nice gated community and as soon as I'm in park, Leo starts to get out.

"Hold up," I say before he is able to step out fully.

Leo raises his eyebrow, questioning me.

"You told Madden that I was your brother-in-law." It's not a question. When he said it, it threw me off a bit.

"Well, I can't very well say that my brother married my sister, that right there raises enough eyebrows as it is."

This cheeky fucker.

"So does me getting the label mean I have your blessing?" I can't go to Ronaldo to ask for his permission anymore and Leo practically raised Isabella next to my parents. His blessing would mean everything.

A hand lands on my shoulder. "You've had my blessing since we were in high school."

"You told me to stay away from her in high school," I narrow my eyes at him. Sure, I may not remember those years very clearly, but I would have remembered if Leo had told me he was okay with me being with his sister.

"That wasn't the right time for you, I think you know that. You two just needed to find a place where you worked, and you've found that. So yeah, you have my blessing."

"That easy?" There has to be more to this.

"That easy."

I nod and place my hand on his shoulder, copying his stance.

"Thanks, *hermano*."

"Always."

With one final pat on each other's shoulders, we finally make our way out of the car.

We walk into the house and instantly we hear the laughter of the women enjoying their morning.

Leo walks right in and heads straight to Serena, taking her attention away from Isabella and Camila and planting a kiss on her lips.

It's quick but you can see by the smile on Serena's face when he pulls away, that she loves every single minute of it.

I stand back, leaning against the wall leading to the living room, and watch the interaction of the four of them.

Every single one of them looks happy.

Isabella turns to face me and gives me a small smile

when she sees that I'm already looking at her. I send a small smile back at her.

A smile is what it takes for her to get up from the spot on the couch and come over to me.

"What are you thinking about over here?" she asks as she comes to stand in front of me, a hand landing on my chest.

"I was thinking about how happy you all look," I say, placing my hand over hers and holding her hand to me.

Isabella smiles at me and turns to look back to her family and watches for a few seconds as Leo and Camila bicker.

"I guess we are happy," she says, turning back to me, her fingers playing with my shirt. "Are you happy Santiago?"

That question takes me by surprise.

I don't think anyone has asked me that in a very long time. I don't even remember what my answer was when it was asked.

Am I happy?

I don't think I've been happy in a very long time.

The only times that I have ever felt happy, content, were when I was around Isabella. Those four years when it was just the two of us were some of the best years of my life.

Now that I know I'm not going to lose her, the years to come will most likely not compare to those four.

Does that make me happy?

Anything that consists of Isabella by my side, with a

smile on her face and her trust to take care of her heart, makes me happy.

"Yeah, I'm happy. As long as you are here with me. I will always be happy."

Isabella stands up on her tiptoes and places a kiss on my lips.

"Good. Because you deserve every ounce of happiness."

I lean down and place a kiss of my own on her lips.

"I love you, you know that?"

She nods. "I know and I love you too."

Isabella Morales is mine and I will love her until my death and beyond.

34

ISABELLA

I will forever be surprised when someone buys one of my designs.

I'm a low-level designer that sells out of a small boutique in Austin, so I don't sell many, but when I do I want to jump up in happiness.

Right now though, I want to have a firework show, jump up and down and scream at every single person that I encounter because I just sold every single one of my designs that is currently in the boutique.

Every. Single. One.

Twenty-six of my dresses are on the floor right now and I sold every single design.

I'm trying really hard to keep my excitement at a bare minimum.

"Okay, your total comes out to eight thousand, four hundred and fifty dollars," I tell the girl that just bought my dresses.

And I say girl because she must be a few years younger

than me. And can I ask how someone has that much money? Is that being too nosy?

She pulls out a black American Express card from her black YSL bag and hands it to me.

She definitely comes from money, that purse alone cost eleven hundred dollars. I should know, I own the same one.

"Can you add another two thousand dollars to that please?"

"I'm sorry?" I must have heard that wrong.

"Another two thousand to the card. I can't carry all the dresses out of here, but if you can ship them to me that would be great. The two thousand should cover all the shipping and whatever is left over you can keep for yourself."

Okay, who is this girl and how can I make her my friend?

"Is that okay?" she asks when I don't even try to say a word.

I nod and do what she says and charge her card over ten thousand dollars.

And of course, it went through.

I hand her the card back and she gives me a bright smile.

Still a little dumbfounded, I go and wrap two dresses up before coming back to the counter and handing her the garment bags.

"Thank you." She takes the bags and then snaps her fingers. "Before I forget."

I watch as she takes a piece of paper out of her bag

with a pen and starts to write on it.

"Here is the address to send the dresses to. I'm also including my number, just in case you ever want to branch out and do your own thing. You can call me whenever you want if that's something you're interested in."

She holds out the piece of paper to me when she's done writing her information.

"This is going to sound completely stupid, but branch out?"

The strange girl nods. "Yeah, your designs are amazing. You're the only reason that I came here. I've been seeing your dresses all over social media and I had to get some for myself. You should really think about it and if you do it, I'll be your number one client."

I look down at the piece of paper in my hand and give her a bright smile.

"I will. Thank you so much."

"You're welcome, Isabella." A smile and she is out the door.

That just happened, right? I didn't imagine that happening, did I?

I look down at the piece of paper and see all her information.

"Thank you, Samantha Lane."

I scream and skip all the way to the back of the store.

I can't wait to tell Santos!

―――

I TOLD him as soon as I got home from work. Within seconds of the news spilling from my mouth, I was in his arms and he was telling me how proud of me he was of me before taking me to celebrate

And no, our celebration wasn't a fancy dinner. Our celebration consisted of him eating me for dinner, you know since we are back to it being just us with my sister in New York and all, and what a great dinner it was.

So great, I'm just now deciding that I want seconds.

"And here I thought that you were tired," he gives me a smirk as I sit up and straddle his stomach.

"Nope. I'm still hungry, I think I'm ready for round two." My hands land on his chest, as I rub myself along his abs, already spreading my wetness on his skin.

"And what does round two consist of?"

Santos leans forward and takes one of my bare breast in his mouth, sucking hard enough that I know will leave a mark. All while his hands travel to my ass and push me farther up his body.

I throw my head back, marveling at the feel of his mouth on me. My hands traveling to the back of his head to hold him there.

"What does round two consist of?" he asks again this time with his fingers digging into my ass cheek, closer to my hole than they were a few seconds ago.

"Riding your face." I let out a moan at how good everything feels. "And you fucking me."

I know what I want, but at the rate that this is going my round two might turn into a round three.

"Whatever my *bella* wants."

He pulls back from my chest and leans back down until his head hits the pillow. I get that sexy grin of his thrown my way and if I had a little bit more friction, I would be coming right about now.

Biting my lip, I finish my climb up his body until his mouth is only a few inches away from my pussy.

"Tell me when I become too heavy," I say as I position myself and grab hold of the headboard.

"Never," he says before his lips attach to my pussy.

"Oh my." I let out as he licks every single inch of me.

Santos hums against me and the vibration of his hum travels all through my body and it feels fucking amazing.

I hold on to the headboard to keep myself from grinding on his face.

Santos's hands land on the back of my thighs and push me forward.

"Grind, baby. Grind on my face." He continues to lick at me and it's when his tongue teases my entrance that I listen to him and grind.

I get so lost in everything that is happening that I didn't realize that an orgasm was so close.

"So fucking wet. So sweet." His hands make their way back to my ass and he holds me to him.

My legs start to shake uncontrollably and when he takes my clit between his teeth, I lose it. Covering his face with my release.

"Fucking perfect," Santos groans out as I try to get off him, but he continues to hold me to him. Licking every single ounce of my release.

I'm barely catching my breath, when he grabs me and maneuvers me so that I'm now lying on my back, with him on top of me.

"As much as I want to feed you my cock, I need to fuck you. Right now."

I give him an enthusiastic nod, because that is all I can muster at the moment.

Santos leans forward and kisses me, giving me a taste of myself on his tongue. I let out a moan when I taste myself and another when I feel the whole weight of his body on mine.

Everything about this man is perfection and I can't believe that I get to call him mine.

I shift slightly only to be able to move my arms to his back and grab him by the ass, pushing him down toward my needy pussy.

My nails dig into the skin of his ass as he continues to grind his cock against my mound not giving me what I want.

"Santiago." I let out a frustrated moan, as my tongue dances along his.

"You need more, baby?" he whispers against my lips before he travels down farther and starts playing with my tits.

His fingers wrap around my right breast, so tightly it's going to leave bruises, and as long as they are from him, I'm okay with it.

"So much more."

"I'll give you every single thing you want, *bella*." With that, he pulls from my chest and opens my legs wide so that he can get situated right where I need him to be.

His eyes stay on mine as he gives himself a few good tugs and strokes right before he slides his thick and heavy cock into me.

"Yes," I moan out, absolutely loving how he feels inside of me.

"Such a beautiful sight," he growls out before he starts to move.

And move he does. This man is a fucking sex god and knows how to work my body perfectly.

I guess that's what happens when you've had a partner for so long. They come to learn exactly what you like.

He pounds into me, fucks me to the point that sweat is rolling down both our bodies. Over and over again, he hits the right spots.

"Oh. Fuck. Don't stop. Please," I beg him. I need him to give me every single thing he has, because I'm at the edge ready to fall.

"Come, *bella*. Tighten around me. Let me feel this pretty pussy of yours hold my cock like a vise. Fucking come."

I pant his name over and over again as he continues to pound into me, my legs about to give out, but finally I'm able to listen to orders and let go of my release.

"Santos! Fuck!" I see fucking stars and black spots and I feel like I'm about to pass out. It was that good.

Santos continues to move and within seconds he is grunting and shaking as he releases inside of me.

"Fucking hell," he pants out when he throws himself on the bed next to me and I cuddle into his arms.

We should really clean up, but I think both of us are too spent.

A few minutes pass by as we continue to lie there wrapped up in each other's arms. Eventually though, he does get up to head to the bathroom and comes back with a washcloth to help clean me up.

This man.

We go back to cuddling and just living off the high that we just experienced.

As the TV gets turned on and I'm cuddled up in Santo's arms, I realize only a few weeks ago, my life could have gone a completely different path. Had Santos and Leo not come up with a plan to put an end to Emilio and done what they did, I would be living in fear.

I would be terrified of what Emilio would do to me and wondering if I would live to see my next birthday.

But because Santos shot him, that life is something that I would never experience. And for that I'm grateful.

I'm grateful for this man, and I'm grateful for the possibilities that he brings with him

Yes, this relationship is far from perfect, and we have a lot to figure out, but I know in my heart and soul that this man is it for me.

Fourteen-year-old me was brilliant for seeing that this boy, this man, meant something more to her than just her brother's best friend.

He helped save me.

He supports me in my work.

He loves me with all his heart.

And he is giving me the world that I deserve.

"Hey," I say, patting his stomach, getting his attention.

"*¿Si?*"

"I think you should ask me to marry you, right now." That catches him by surprise.

He untangles himself from me and sits up, looking down at me.

"You want me to do what?"

"You should propose tonight." I sit up too and give him a smile to show him that I really mean it.

Santos looks at me with his mouth wide open. He looks like fifty levels of confusion.

"Not that I don't love the spontaneity of this, but what brought this on?"

I hold out my hand for him to take and he does.

"I've known since I was a teenager that I wanted to be with you. Then everything between us became this hurricane, and I never knew if it was going to stop, but then it did and it was the most amazing feeling in the world. Then, of course, another hurricane came flying through and I thought that that one would be a lot more powerful than the last. It was violent and deadly, but somehow, we were able to escape it. Not unharmed, of course, but enough to be able to still be there for each other. You're my everything Santiago Reyes, and I want to spend the rest of my life with you. I don't care about the number of bodies that you bring down, or the number of drugs that you move. You're it for me. So, you should propose tonight."

The light-brown eyes that I love so much look back at

me with so much love and admiration that I know he is going to say yes to my crazy idea.

Santos starts to shake his head and gets off the bed, buck naked of course, and I start to think that he is going to say no when he walks into the closet.

"You know I had this whole elaborate plan," he says when he steps out of the closet with a box in his hand.

The same one he showed me over a year ago.

A huge smile grows on my face. I feel like I have to place my hands on my cheeks so that my face doesn't break.

"This big ass plan and you had to ruin it with your crazy idea."

He opens the box and takes out the beautiful ring. It is absolutely the most beautiful piece of jewelry that I have ever seen.

I watch as he grabs my hand and slides the ring onto my finger. Once it's in place, it looks even more perfect than it did in the box.

"It's so pretty," I say, marveling at it.

"It should be. It cost me a fucking fortune." I slap him across the stomach, not taking my eyes off the ring.

The more I continue to look at it, the more I feel the urge to cry.

I'm happy.

I'm really fucking happy.

My most wanted dream was to be happy and here I am. Wearing a ring from a man that I absolutely love, I'm out of a life that was poison, and I'm happy.

I turn to Santos, tears rolling down my face and of course the man reaches forward and wipes them away.

"We're engaged?"

He nods. "We're engaged. It's me and you forever, *bella*."

Me and him forever.

I absolutely love that.

EPILOGUE

ISABELLA

Flowers.

White ones, pink ones, the dark red ones that look almost black in some light. Every single color you can think of for a flower to come in, I'm surrounded by them.

There are beautiful bouquets everywhere around me and a smile comes across my face when I remember why they are here.

The smile grows even bigger when I remind myself even more that in two short hours, I will be standing right in the middle of all of this, in the dress that I designed. In the dress that I've been working on for almost two years, waiting to be worn and waiting to be out in the sunlight,.

I was fourteen when I first thought that maybe, just maybe, the boy that I had grown up with would one day see me in the same light that I saw him. That he would see something special in me and that special thing would turn into something more. That one day, far in the future, he would be the man that I would walk down the aisle to.

That day is finally here. Fourteen-year-old me was right.

"Shouldn't you be getting ready?" My brother's voice echoes through the garden that I'm currently standing in.

A garden much like the one my mother built in San Pedro, but not nearly as sentimental.

I turn to face the man that is going to walk me down the aisle and give him a smile.

"My makeup artist isn't here yet."

Leo nods. "Just got word from Arturo. He has Camila and they're on their way. They should be here in about twenty minutes."

Camila has been in New York working tirelessly on her art degree for the last six months. She even got a job to keep her busy, so her coming here for this, means the world to me.

"You think that she brought that boyfriend of hers?" I just ask the question to see his jaw lock at the comment.

I know for a fact that she didn't, but it's nice to tease my brother.

"Arturo said it was just her," Leo says through his teeth and I can't help but laugh.

You would figure he would be okay with a twenty-year-old having a boyfriend.

It's because he cares.

I'm just glad I didn't have to experience this overprotective side of him too much when my relationship with his friend started.

I drop the subject and go back to just taking in the flowers.

Today's celebration is going to be just a small affair. Just me and the love of my life with a few extra people. My brother and Serena, Camila and Serena's friend Aria, a few men that work for Leo and a few of the women that I met while working at the boutique.

And of course, Mrs. Reyes came down from Canada for the special occasion.

The one person that won't be here is my father.

When I asked him to be here, he told me no. I think his exact words were that he won't support any of my endeavors with a man that isn't loyal to him.

In other words, he didn't approve of my marriage because it's not one he arranged.

Was I mad about it?

Absolutely.

Was I going to fight him on it?

No. If my father didn't want to be a part of one of the most important days in my life, so be it.

"Are you ready for this?" Leo asks, taking me out of the thoughts of my father.

I give him a smile. "I've been ready for this for years, and it's finally happening."

"Now you don't have to hide it."

"Now I don't have to hide it." I'm going to officially be Isabella Reyes and I could scream it from the rooftops if I wanted to.

"I know it's stupid for me to say this, especially on your wedding day, but Mom would be proud of you. She's probably looking down right now, thinking about how happy she is with how you turned out. Proud of the woman that you've become and how you made a name for yourself. She would have been proud to see that you don't need a man to define you, and how you can hold your head up and get through anything. She would have been happy that you found someone that will give you the world and treat you in the way that you deserve. If she were still here, she would probably be telling you that you need to get dressed because she wants to see your wedding now. She would have been so lucky to meet the woman that you are, I know I am. I'm lucky to call myself your brother."

It's a good thing that I'm not wearing any makeup right now, because the tears that are currently rolling down my cheeks would have ruined it.

"You're not supposed to be making me cry so early in the day." I wipe my tears away through a laugh.

"If not me, then who?" He gives me a smile and holds up his arms for me.

I walk into his embrace and hug him as tightly as I can.

"She would have been proud of you too, you know. She would have loved Serena and would have been so excited that you were making her an *abuela*."

Serena and Leo announced almost six months ago that they were having a baby. They wanted everything that happened with Emilio to die down before they said anything. And when they did, me and Camila freaked out and started spoiling the baby right away. Now he's due to arrive in the world any day now, and I can't wait to meet him.

"Yeah, I just hope that I don't mess him up, like

Ronaldo did to me," he grumbles as his hold on me loosens.

"You won't. You will be a great father. Just look at me and Camila, we turned out okay and you helped raise us."

He did teach us how to properly shoot someone between the eyes, but hey, that could be valuable information someday.

"I guess you're right." He knows that I'm right. "You think that you can handle him twenty-four seven? I can show you a few things you can do when he gets annoying. Because he might be a broody motherfucker but he's like a parrot that doesn't shut up."

I laugh, because that's absolutely true. Santos can be very talkative when he is not carrying anything over in his head.

"I think I got it covered. I've been handling his mood swings since I was sixteen, after all."

My phone beeps, keeping me from saying anything else.

I pull it out and see that It's Camila.

CAMILA: *Um, excuse me! Why aren't you in the room, getting dressed? Don't make me spring the pregnant woman on you!*

I LAUGH. Serena's been a bitch these last couple of days, and it's definitely a little scary. No need to make her angrier than what she already is.

"Looks like my makeup artist has arrived and is looking for me."

Leo nods and he walks me back to my room.

We are having the wedding at the compound that Leo bought for Serena a few months back. He said that they needed more space than their loft, so he decided it was time for them to upgrade.

The house is just outside of Austin and is surrounded by security. With everything that is going on with my father, there has to be.

Leo and Santos are still very much involved in everything Muertos, but Santos told me that things might be changing soon. Whatever that means is beyond me. I don't want to know until it's absolutely necessary.

My brother walks me to my room and greets Camila quickly before he is off, and we get to work on getting ready.

Soon my makeup is ready and so is my hair and I'm stepping into my dress.

The same dress that Santos saw when he came to my studio that one night many months ago.

The same dress that I've been working on since he told me he wanted to propose.

With my makeup done, no hair out of place and Santiago's ring on my finger, I'm ready to walk down the aisle.

It's not long before everyone is ready, and we are only seconds away from starting the ceremony.

As everyone lines up and Leo takes the space next to me, my mind wanders to my last wedding ceremony.

That was one of the most dreadful days of my life. I

hated everything about that day. What I hated most was the man that I was walking toward.

I'm finally getting the wedding I have always wanted and walking toward a man that I absolutely love.

Not a stranger I know nothing about.

Not someone that I'm being forced to wed.

I'm ready for this.

The music starts and once every single person in the wedding party walks down the aisle, Leo nods to me and I give him one back.

It's time to get my happiness.

There's a smile on my face the whole time I walk, and it grows even more when I see Santos wipe at his eyes.

I made the big broody man cry.

The second my hand is placed in his by my brother, I want to burst into tears.

After all the trials and tribulations that we have been through, we are finally here. We were finally able to get to this place and I couldn't be any happier.

Before turning to my future husband fully, I close my eyes and look up at the sky, taking a deep breath.

Voy a estar bien, Mami.

Voy a estar bien.

Te quiero con todo mi corazón.

I open my eyes and right away I'm met with light brown eyes staring back at me, a loving smile on his lips.

He knows that I was talking to my mother. He knows that I was telling her that I love her, and how much I wish she was here.

Santos grips my hand with all his might and I can't help but smile at him.

This is really happening.

"You ready for this, *bella*?"

"For you, always."

And I will forever be.

SANTOS

I WILL PROTECT this woman until I die.

I will love her until my last breath and beyond.

I will try my hardest to be every single thing that she deserves.

I will kill for her.

Everything that I do from this day forward is to keep this woman safe and alive.

Even with every single obstacle that we face and that includes her father.

But soon we will be free. We will be able to live normal lives and be able to love each other with all our might.

Today, as I said my vows and slid the ring on her finger, I did the one thing that I wanted to do since I was eighteen-years-old.

I made Isabella Morales mine.

And she will forever be.

Everyone and everything that is against us, can fuck off.

This woman is mine and I am hers.

EXTENDED EPILOGUE

Camila

"Camila."

I hear my mother's voice calling my name. Her voice rings through the room, bouncing off the walls and making it seem as if she is here with me.

Is she?

I look around but I don't see her.

My mind must be playing tricks on me.

The painting in front of me takes my attention away from waiting for my dead mother to appear.

It's dark, the painting. Nothing like what I usually draw or paint.

There are reds and blacks everywhere and in a way it looks like...

"Muerte."

I turn and there she is in all her glory. Dark chocolate brown hair swaying down her back. Eyes, like my brother's, so dark that you can feel them sucking you into the abyss. Her face is painted the same as I paint mine every single year for the Día de los Muertos celebration.

She's just as beautiful as when I saw her last.

Turning from her, back to the painting, I see that she is right.

It's death.

"La muerte no es algo qué se debe pintar."

Death is never something that should be painted.

And she's right.

Death is a bad omen and never should be touched.

So why is it that I painted it?

"Tal vez algo va a pasar."

The words leave her mouth in the most nonchalant way, it makes me wonder if I should worry, but I don't. I just keep looking at the painting in front of me.

Something is going to happen.

But what?

"Te quiero muchísimo, mi niña preciosa."

I look up at her, giving her a smile. The smile is still in place even as I watch the makeup melt away.

"Te quiero también, Mamí"

"La muerte está cerca."

She then melts away completely.

My eyes snap open, the darkness of the room and the night enveloping me and making me realize that it was just a dream.

One of the strangest dreams that I've had in a while.

Groaning, I feel the bed next to me, hoping that I feel his body next to mine. Hoping that maybe he came home to me sometime during the night and will help me go back to sleep and make the bad dreams stay away.

But when I feel the cold sheets, I feel a tinge of disappointment when I realize that he hasn't come home to me just yet.

Only a few more days.

A few more days and I will be back in his arms, feeling safe, and putting all the dreams about my mother and death behind me.

Because he's the calm to my disaster. The light to this dark life that I was born into.

Rolling over, I grab his pillow and bring it to me, taking in his scent, and I try my hardest to go back to sleep.

But the second my eyes are closed, they fly back open when a phone starts to ring.

It takes me a second to realize that it's the phone that I have hidden in my dresser. The phone that only four people have the number to.

Looking at the time on the alarm clock on the bedside table, I see that it's three in the morning here in Brooklyn.

It's late.

The only reason that phone is ringing is because something is wrong.

Tal vez algo va a pasar.

Was she right?

I never dream about my mother like that, but what if she was trying to tell me something?

Throwing the blankets off my body, I try to walk over to the dresser at a slow pace, so that I don't have a panic attack over the phone ringing so late.

I really wish he was home right about now.

I open the drawer as slowly as possible, as if a bomb was about to be detonated.

As soon as I have the phone in hand, the ringing stops.

Flipping the screen over, I see that it was an unknown number calling.

I wait, staring at the screen, for the unknown caller to start calling once more.

Within seconds, the ringing starts up again.

As if my brain knows that whoever is on the other side of this call has something bad to say, my hand moves to press the answer button as slow as possible.

I take a deep breath and try to center myself as best as I possibly can before bringing the phone to my ear.

"Hello?"

"Camila." My sister's voice comes through. It's shaky and something about the way she says my name that has me on high alert.

It takes me back to the time I told her about Cristiano Reyes's death.

Is this what is happening?

"Wh-why are you calling me so late? Did something happen?"

Is it Leo?

Or what if it's Santos?

Worse yet, what if it's my nephew? He's just a baby, but what if something happened to him?

"There was a raid at the estate. Leo and Santos were there, and..."

"And what, Isabella?"

"Men were killed." Her voice hitches, telling me that what she has to say is a lot worse than what she wants to let on.

La muerte está cerca.

Dreaming about my mother was a warning that this was going to happen.

A ball forms in my throat and I feel wetness in the corner of my eyes.

"Leo? Santos?"

"They are both alive." That reassures me but it's not enough. There's more to this. I know there is.

"Then who, Isabella? Who was killed? Whose death is so important that you had to call me in the middle of the night?"

Ya sabes quien. La muerte está cerca.

My mother's voice rings through my mind.

I may know, but I need my sister to confirm it.

"Camila." Her voice breaks again, and I know what she's going to say.

"Who, Isabella? Who?"

She is silent for a long minute.

I stand there waiting for her to speak, counting the tears that are running down my cheeks.

Say it. *Please* just say it.

"*Apá*. Our father is dead. They killed him."

A sob escapes my throat when the words come through the earpiece.

La muerte está cerca.

That's why I dreamed of her. Why I dreamed of painting death. It was a warning. A sign.

Death was near.

The kingpin of the Muertos Cartel is dead.

My father is dead.

Want to read Camila's story?
Get a copy of Vindictive Blood today!

PLAYLIST

One Mississippi - Zara Larsson
Feel it - Michele Morrone
I'll Make You Love Me - Kat Leon
She Thinks Of Me - Landon Tewers
Play With Fire - Sam Tinnesz
Expectations - Lauren Jauregui
You Don't Own Me - SAYGRACE, G-Eazy
Imposible Amor - Natti Natasha, Maluma
Do It For Me - Rosenfeld
I Want To - Rosenfeld
Drink Me - Michele Morrone
Walls Could Talk - Halsey

ACKNOWLEDGMENTS

Isabellas and Santos story is finally out in the world!

These two were hard. At the beginning, when I first had the idea for this story, I thought that Isabella was going to be the easiest one to write. Her story was the only one that I actually knew how it would play out, so I went into writing this book with a smile on my face.

I wanted Isabella to be strong and someone that people feared more than they did Leo. I had a vision for her and I tried my hardest to make sure that she became that person.

But as I wrote the first couple of chapters, I started to doubt how I was portraying her. Was she too soft? Was there not enough cartel? All these questions started to pop into my head and I started to doubt the story that I was writing left and right.

I reworked the first six chapter about four different times until I finally told myself that I needed to move on and write the rest of the story. So I wrote and and wrote and when I like the way the story was going, I started to rework the story.

As I was reworking it, I hit an emotional mountain that wouldn't move. I tried to fight it for almost a month and I just couldn't. Everything that I was writing, I was hating and there was a point where I wanted to throw Isabella and Santo's story out the window.

I missed my deadlines and I even told my editor that she could fire me as a client.

Somehow, I was able to get through with it and finish writing the story that Isabella and Santos deserved.

Was it the story that I though I would write back in February when I though of this series? No, but I love how their story played out and how it all came together. It seems fitting that there was a hardship in getting this story out, since there was countless obstacles for these two.

They never broke, so neither did I.

Now to my thank yous-

Ellie at My Brother's Editor - Thank you. From the bottom of my heart, thank you. Thank you for not firing me when I put it out there and thank you for working for me and this story.

Shauna and Wildfire Marketing - Thank you so much for helping me spread the word for Violent Attraction and for everything that you and your team has done. Tens of thank yous!

Yesi - Thank you for telling me when the story sucked and reading this story and loving it.

Readers - I hope I made you proud with this one! I hope you loved this story just as much as I love it. Thank you for your support. Thank you for the cover reveal shares, the teasers, the currently readings, thank you for everything that you have done. You make an author's heart grow a little bit more.

Now onto Camila!

I hope you are ready for a bumpy ride!

BOOKS BY JOCELYNE SOTO

One Series

One Life

One Love

One Day

One Chance

One for Me

One Marriage

Flor De Muertos Series

Vicious Union

Violent Attraction

Vindictive Blood

Standalones

Beautifully Broken

Worth Every Second

ABOUT THE AUTHOR

Jocelyne Soto is a writer born and raised in California. She started her writing journey in 2015 and in 2019 she published her first book. She is an independent author who loves discovering new authors on Goodreads and Amazon. She comes from a big Mexican family, and with it comes a love for all things family and food.

Jocelyne has a love for her mom's coffee and writing. In her free time, she can be found reading a romance novel off her iPad or somewhere in the black hole of YouTube.

Follow her website and on social media!
www.jocelynesoto.com

- facebook.com/authorjocelynesoto
- twitter.com/authorjocelynes
- instagram.com/authorjocelynesoto
- bookbub.com/authors/jocelyne-soto
- goodreads.com/jocelynesotobooks
- pinterest.com/authorjocelynesoto

JOIN MY READER GROUP

Join my ever-growing Facebook Group.

https://www.facebook.com/groups/jocelynesotobooks

NEWSLETTER

Sign up for my Newsletter!
You will get notified when there are new releases to look out for, giveaways and more!

https://www.subscribepage.com/authorjocelynesotonewsletter

Made in the USA
Columbia, SC
25 October 2021